Praise for the Base Branch Series

“Megan Mitcham's books are well-paced, well-plotted suspense novels edged with stunning sensual intensity. Her lovers are cold and deadly--except when they are skin-to-skin. I can't wait for the next book in the series!”

- **DELILAH DEVLIN**
New York Times and USA Today bestselling author

"Nail-biter all the way to the end."

- **Michelle**, MsRomanticReads
Adult Romance & Erotic Book Reviews

"This is a fresh and exciting story with lots of great characters."

- **5 Star Amazon Review**, Enemy Mine

“Megan now joins my elite team of must read authors. I fell in love with her work in *Enemy Mine*, and it just gets better the more I read."

- **TNT Reviews**

BOOKS BY MEGAN MITCHAM

BASE BRANCH NOVELS
ENEMY MINE
JUSTICE MINE
STRANGER MINE
WARRIOR MINE
DANGER MINE
PRISONER MINE
SURVIVOR MINE - 2017

BASE BRANCH SUBSERIES
VERSIONS - updated 2016
VIRTUES - 2016
VARIATIONS - 2016

BUREAU NOVELS
FOR ALL TO SEE
PAINTED WALLS

ANTHOLOGIES
ANTICIPATION
CONQUESTS
ROGUES
COWBOY HEAT
HIGH OCTANE HEROES
SEX OBJECTS - 2016
WILD AT HEART VOLUME II
benefiting Turpentine Creek Wildlife Refuge

BOX SET
HEARTS IN DANGER - July 2015
benefiting The American Heart Association

Prisoner Mine

Base Branch Novel #6

Megan Mitcham

Copyright Warning

The unauthorized reproduction or distribution of this copyrighted work is a crime punishable by law. No part of this book may be scanned, uploaded to or downloaded from file sharing sites, or distributed in any other way via the Internet or any other means, electronic or print, without the publisher's permission. Criminal copyright infringement, including infringement without monetary gain, is investigated by the FBI and is punishable by up to 5 years in federal prison and a fine of $250,000 (http://www.fbi.gov/ipr/).

This book is a work of fiction. The names, characters, places, and incidents are fictitious or have been used fictitiously, and are not to be construed as real in any way. Any resemblance to persons, living or dead, actual events, locales, or organizations is entirely coincidental.

Published by MM Publishing LLC

Edited by Lacey Thacker

Proofread by Tina Rucci & Lynn Mullan

Cover Design by Deranged Doctor Designs

Prisoner Mine
All Rights Are Reserved. Copyright 2016 by Megan Mitcham

First electronic publication: January 2016
First print publication: January 2016

Digital ISBN: 978-1-941899-17-5

Print ISBN: 978-1-941899-18-2

To Kimberly Gale and Tina Marie. Pain may hold you prisoner, but you both refuse to be its captive. Thank you for the joy and beauty you've created in spite of your daily battles. I admire your courage and determination in the face of overwhelming odds. Hugs for the hard days. Cheers for the good ones.

Chapter One

"About time we're getting on with it." The man sitting to Zeke Slaughter's right hiked a gaudy gold belt buckle over his paunch. His gruff Russian burr cut through the cold air. On his left, another man shoved his ring-stacked sausage fingers into the pocket of his shiny suit coat. Surreptitiously, or not, from Zeke's point of view, the guy stroked the front of his pants.

A heavy velvet curtain no more than ten feet in front of them spread open. Heavy tassels at the bottom swung back and forth with each yank of the cord. He couldn't see the man working, but Zeke knew he stood in the shadows of the small stage hefting open the gateway to heaven...and hell. Light boxes ricocheted brilliant white light up, whilc above, three red lights rained down the color of seduction. The color of sin.

From stage-left the clack of stilettos drew the men's hot gazes, and Zeke's eager one. Four girls, maybe nineteen to twenty-three years old, walked toward center stage. One sashayed, trying a little too hard to look sumptuous with bags under her eyes. The two in the middle shuffled, seeming past the point of caring.

"*Shag*," a male voice hawked from behind the thick fabric.

Bringing up the rear, the youngest of the group hurried her discordant steps at the order.

Zeke's Russian was about as rusty as his dick. He guessed the unfamiliar word meant *hurry the hell up.* Thank goodness it had only taken a wad of green to get him inside. That, and the word of a high-ranking member of the old country's mob.

"Yes," sausage-fingers breathed. He'd given up subtlety and pumped his hips into his palm.

Scum of the earth.

And here he was mashed between them. A shit sandwich.

At stage-right a man in a classier-cut suit than the other men stepped into the light. He rushed to the front of the line and lifted his hand toward the commodities, for that's what the women were. They'd been stripped of humanity long ago. Their ashen complexions and dull eyes showed it all too clearly, if a person cared to look.

"Smile, ladies," the dirty, male version of Vanna White ordered with a coo. As commanded they flashed teeth, some yellowed from drugs, some not. "Good. My name is Mr. Anosov, and I'll be your auctioneer this evening." He half-turned toward the girls. "Now, let's show these gentlemen what you have to offer."

There wasn't a gentleman in a five-block radius of this back-alley club just off 278 in Queens, including the traffic that buzzed past on the interstate. Zeke propped one ankle on his knee and relaxed back into the plush chair. The other men pushed forward, the one...a little too literally. Zeke's fist ached, wanting nothing more than to sink deep into the crude fuck's gut and end the overt display. He curled his palms over the end of the chair.

The two more world-worn girls yanked down corset tops. They revealed pretty, natural hanging breasts as though they were no longer private parts of their bodies, but tools of a trade they'd tired of. Too quickly they righted their shirts and turned away. While the saucy bird plumped fake breasts in her hands and tweaked her nipples, the other two bent at the waist, reached between their garters, and stretched back their thongs. Not to be outdone, the temptress squatted—boobs jostling from the sudden descent—parted her knees, and flashed a tiny landing strip and an engorged pair of slick lips.

On the other end, the youngest of the bunch hadn't budged. Her slender fingers trembled at her sides.

Anosov's gaze shot from the row of seats to the girl farthest from him, and then back. He smiled, flaunting crooked teeth and a fresh batch of irritation. His dress shoes tapped across the floor until he stood directly in front of her. He spat something in Russian too fast for Zeke to understand, but he got the gist.

Long lashes shut tight over brown eyes. The girl inhaled. Her chest shook with the effort. She reached up and worked the top down over sweetly-rounded breasts. The host snaked out his hand, pinching one of her flaccid buds.

Her cry echoed in the room. Dark eyes shot wide.

"Nice," Paunch said, patting his large belly with easy strikes. "Nice."

Everyone watched the girl's brown nipple flush red, and then grow to a point. Not everyone saw the tiny tear that slipped down her cheek.

Once again Anosov took it upon himself to move things along. He yanked the panties off her hips and left them around her thighs. When the girl covered her thick patch of pubic hair a crack erupted in the room. Five fingers, outlined in red, stained the girl's cheek.

Despite his best efforts to remain aloof, Zeke heaved a breath. Inside him every nerve ending crackled to life.

The men must have taken the huff for impatience. Paunch raised his hand and whirled it. “Can we get on with the bidding?”

“Of course. We’ll start here.” The classily-dressed man with zero class did a show of exhibiting the damn-near child who clutched her cheek, while simultaneously managing to cover her breasts. “Bidding starts at two thousand.”

“How long do we get to keep them?” Jack-off asked, managing to hold his hips still long enough to get the question out.

“Tonight only. They can be leased for longer, but it will cost quite a bit more.” Again he showed off the girl’s responsive breasts. “So, renting or leasing, gentlemen?”

“Renting,” Jack-off replied.

“I’ll let you know after tonight,” Paunch said.

Zeke just glared.

“Two thousand it is.” The host plucked her breast again. “Do I hear two thousand?”

Jack-off lifted his free hand.

“Three,” Paunch countered.

“Do I hear thirty-five hundred for this fresh beauty? She needs one of you to break her in. She’s not a virgin, mind you, but she’s new to this scene. She could be yours. You could teach her, show her how we do things.” The host’s eyes scanned the bidders. “Three thousand, going once. Going twice.”

Zeke reached into his jacket, retrieved a stack of cash, tossed it at the host’s feet, and relaxed back.

The sack of crap picked it up and flipped through the hundreds. “Ten thousand?”

Zeke nodded.

"Ten thousand, going once. Going twice. Sold for one night to Mr. Basov." Paunch smacked his belly hard. "Not to worry," Anosov continued, "we have three sirens left."

Sirens? Not one came close to the term or what he was looking for tonight. But first things first.

Bidding continued. When it was all said and done Paunch had the money for the eager beaver and one of the others, while Jack-off had the drive and only enough money for the leftovers. Zeke kept the rest of the cash in his pockets.

"Gentlemen, please proceed to your rooms and the ladies will join you shortly," Anosov said.

It took the big guy three tries to stand from the low slung chair. Jack-off paused his pumping, stood, and practically ran out into the maze of hallways. The girls shuffled from the room much the way they'd come in.

Zeke kept his seat.

Anosov hesitated at the back of the stage. "Is there something I can do for you?"

He'd yet to speak. Hiding his British accent was hard enough. Layering a Russian one on top of that, well, he'd snap this guy's neck if he so much as blinked at his attempt. "I wanted two women."

"You didn't bid on two." The scrawny guy shrugged.

"You didn't offer any women. You offered girls, mostly used-up girls at that." Anosov opened his mouth to speak. Zeke lifted his hand. Anosov's lips closed. "I'll take the girl I bid on, but I want another. I want her blonde and blue eyed." He tossed another sheaf of hundreds onto the stage.

"I'll be right back." The host scooped up the money and rushed off stage.

On his way in Zeke had counted seven cameras. There were more, surely. He let his foot fall off his knee, but he didn't indulge the need to find a more defensive position. Live the lie. Be the lie. Until you can't be it any longer.

Four minutes passed before the click of dress shoes and stilettos sounded on the stage. Anosov thrust a woman toward the front of the stage. Stringy blonde hair was matted to the side of her face. Dirt clung to the creases of her hands. Her murky green-blue eyes told Zeke all he needed to know.

"She's used up. I want a fresh woman. Blonde haired and blue eyed. Those aren't blue."

The man nodded, but cursed under his breath as he dragged the woman off the stage with him. Ten minutes passed in relative silence. The hairs on Zeke's arms stood on end.

About time.

It was the first bit of nerves to torment him since the first day he'd been taken captive in that shit-shack in the middle of the Alaskan wilderness. The wary jangle felt as familiar as an old T-shirt.

Two minutes later and the thud of boots brought his gaze to the stage. Four beefy men hauled a woman between them. She wore a long, silky-white gown that thrashed about supple hips. Her round breasts shook with her effort to escape the men holding each of her limbs separately. Hair, wet from sweat or water, he couldn't be sure, clung to her face.

Anosov skidded onto the stage from the other side. He barked Russian at the men. Something about *still an animal* and *teaching her a lesson*. He whipped a syringe from his pocket and ordered the men to hold her still.

"Wait," Zeke barked. "I like my women conscious."

"You think you can handle her all on your own? She put one of my men in the hospital already. The drugs are the only thing that keep her pliable. It's just been awhile since her last hit."

Zeke's guts twisted. These weren't just sedatives. They were narcotics. Addictive-as-fuck narcotics.

"If she suits me, I'll risk it. Let me see her face." He stayed back in the chair and tried not to double his grip on its arms.

The guy with his arm hooked around her right shoulder released the grip with his left hand, grabbed a handful of hair, and yanked the woman's head back. Harsh light sliced over the high cheek bones and wild eyes.

Greer Britton's full pink lips curled into a sneer. Straight white teeth gritted and gnashed at the men. Her blue gaze slashed through the air in fear and rage. Pert nipples stabbed the silk of the gown.

Zeke's cock stirred. He hated himself for it. "I'll take her."

"I'm afraid she's not like the others." The host shoved the syringe into his coat pocket and clasped his hands together in front of him.

"Well?" he prodded.

"You wanted a fresh woman. She's as fresh as they come. Virginally so, and quite more expensive, I'm afraid."

"How much?"

Greer bucked and kicked at his question. The men's arms bunched under too-tight T-shirts. One whipped his gun out of the way just in time to keep her from snatching it from the holster.

"Thirty."

He let a boisterous laugh shake his chest. “That’s for lease, right?”

“The night, I’m afraid.”

I’m afraid I’m going to kill every last one of you.

Zeke brushed a hand over his beard, not because he was thinking, but because the damn thing itched him like a mother. Plus, he couldn’t give in too easily. “Twenty.”

“The price is firm. Pure ones are nearly as rare as a Valkyrie these days.”

“She is a virgin?” It was a good thing she didn’t recognize him with a beard and shaggy hair in her altered state. She’d shoot him for the question and honest curiosity that came with it.

“Of course.”

“How do you know?”

“All our women are given physicals when they come in. It’s part of what separates our girls from the hookers on the street corner.”

He nodded, retrieved three more heaps of cash from his emptying pockets, and tossed them over.

“She’ll be in your room shortly.” Anosov gestured to the back door.

Zeke hated to take his eyes off her. It had taken him nine long days to find those haunting blue eyes. There wasn’t anything scary about the usually-crystalline orbs, except their ability to see through his carefully fortified walls. Fact was, he’d be better off leaving her here, in the devil’s mouth. But, the conscience he’d often thought forfeit wouldn’t allow it. He turned away and headed for the door. These guys weren’t loyal, but they were business men and he had plenty more money, if that’s what was required to get to Greer. He had other things, if money didn’t work.

The more time Zeke spent in this upscale whore house the more he hoped the money didn't work.

Dimmed fixtures hung on the wall, shadowing the desperation inherent in a place like this. At the T of the next hallway he paused, reached into his pants pocket, and extracted the key he'd been given when the valet took his rented Rolls. A stamped H indented the silver key ring. The label above the door directly across from him read *Security*. He'd seen it on the way in. Before he'd stepped foot inside the building he'd pegged it on the blueprints for the most probable location. He'd been led into the auction room from the door to the right at the end of the hallway, a banal reception area, save for the busty broad atop the counter. On the left next to security the dens of iniquity started with A.

His feet propelled him farther into the club. With each room he passed an invisible assailant stalked him. The sensation of being closed-in cloaked his shoulders more than it had in the hospital. There he'd had his sister's irritating and comforting support. Here only the memories of being cramped in a shed too small to straighten his legs kept him company. Of all the violence and abuse he'd endured over those eleven days the inability to stretch had been the worst.

Frayed edges of a scream from inside D redirected his attention. *Not completely sound proof.* Zeke arrived at H, slid his key in the lock, and turned the knob. Quiet sobs seeped through the small crack. Instantly he knew Greer wasn't waiting for him.

Surprisingly high ceilings accommodated a four-post bed. Gauzy red linen hung from the tops, a paradoxical halo. Along the right wall a wet bar stood stocked and ready, but the rows of alcohol couldn't compare to the shelves of all manner of sexual paraphernalia across from it. Caught in the middle of the debauchery stood the girl he'd bought. Her arms wrapped protectively around herself.

Zeke stepped into the room and closed the door behind him. He set the key on a small end table and walked to the bar. He outwardly ignored her. In his periphery he watched every shaky intake and exhale, every glance at his back, at the key, and at the door. Only a key could open it. Glasses clinked together under his less than attentive hands. When he reached forward to grab the bottle of Russian Standard she stepped toward the only exit in the fifteen-by-fifteen room.

She wanted out.

Good.

"Take your heels off and get on the bed," Zeke barked without turning around.

Her subsided cries renewed with more verve than before. Defiantly, she held her ground.

Zeke grabbed the two shots off the bar and stalked toward the young woman, who'd already endured more humiliation than anyone should. Her fingers clutched her arms so hard her skin whitened under her touch.

Maybe it wasn't defiance, but a lack of understanding. Though she wanted out, she didn't have the guts to even look him in the eyes, much less defy an order.

"Do you speak English?" he asked.

She didn't budge.

"English?" he asked again.

Her head, small enough to crush between his palms, shook.

Great.

"Kahk ti-byeh zau-vóot?" Her name would be a start.

"Raisa," she whispered, seemingly to the floor.

He thrust the shot of vodka at her and nodded.

It took several beats, but her quaking hand pushed the hair from her forehead. Her wary gaze found his. He held still. The whimpering slowly dried. When he stretched the drink toward her one quaking hand eased out to grab it.

"Bóo-deem zda-ró-vye." Zeke lifted his drink and hoped she understood the double meaning of the phrase, "to our health."

She shrieked Russian words he knew all too well and tossed the liquid at him. Vodka hit his lids and slid down his chin.

Nope, she hadn't gotten it, but security watching through the camera mounted in the light fixture above the bar would if he didn't do something about her outburst.

Zeke tossed the shot down his throat and slammed the small glass against the concrete floor. It shattered and scattered to the corners of the room.

"Shoes off. Get on the bed," he said, jabbing his pointed forefinger in union with his words.

She stumbled backward, turned, and ran to the bed. The pointed shoes he'd rather not have impaled in his flesh fell to the floor with dual thuds. Raisa climbed up the hip-level—for men of average height—bed and scrambled to the headboard. Her legs folded up to her knees. Her arms banded around her shins.

Shit. He didn't want to scare her, but if it saved her life, so be it. He stepped toward the bed.

Her weeping echoed in the room, almost drowning out the clack of metal on metal from the door knob.

The brass lever turned. Raisa stifled her wailing. One man stepped into the room, holding the door open. Another followed, with Greer draped over his arms like a wet towel.

"I paid thirty-thousand dollars for a blonde haired, blue eyed, conscious, virgin," Zeke pointed out.

"She's conscious." The man holding her pivoted her head toward Zeke.

Black pupils ate the pristine blue of her eyes. Red veins veered every which way against the white around the bloated pupils. Her lips parted with sluggish breaths.

"Hardly," Zeke countered.

The guy at the door stepped out and let the door close behind him, while the one holding Greer stood her between them. She stumbled forward and then fell to the floor like a wet noodle. The brute placed his boot onto her side and shoved her forward. "Get up, bitch."

Every muscle in Zeke's body tensed, ready to pounce, ready to strike the man dead with a single blow to the temple. But he couldn't. Greer couldn't defend herself. Fuck, she couldn't even stand. If she couldn't stand, she couldn't walk. If she couldn't walk, she couldn't run. If she couldn't run, she damn sure couldn't fight. If she couldn't fight, she couldn't help them escape. Instead of killing the wanker like he wanted, he stepped forward. "She's mine. I will discipline her, if necessary."

"She's ours. She's yours for the next few hours." The lucky son of a whore puffed out his thick chest.

Zeke used a few of the Russian curse words he knew, bent down, and hoisted Greer off the floor.

She was almost dead weight. He pulled her hair back. His gaze danced over her pretty face, despite the drugged out haze in her eyes. “What do you expect me to do with her for a few hours, watch her coma?”

“I expect you to fuck her.”

“I don’t fuck the dead. Not my fetish. I like for my women to fight.” Zeke shook Greer, stressing the operative word, trying to get his message across. “Why’d you drug her? I told Anosov not to hit her with another dose.”

“She fights too much without the drugs, more than any cunt who’s come through here. And we see lots of those.” The man looked at Greer and snarled. “Bitch knocked out Ivor’s front teeth on the way to the room.”

“I want her detoxed. I want her to struggle, to try to escape, to make me dominate her.” Greer’s head fell forward onto Zeke’s shoulder, throwing her weight against the front of his body. When his body responded he knew without a doubt he was no better than the men he was trying to rescue her from.

Greer breathed into his ear. The word wasn’t clear. It wasn’t even a word, but the breath in his lungs cemented. Once more she wheezed, “Saulter.”

He liked and hated the name on her lips in equal measure. Its presence meant she recognized him or, more accurately, a version of him. It also put them both in a world of danger. If anyone else heard her call him by another name they wouldn’t make it out of this room.

Zeke tossed her onto the bed and climbed on behind her. Raisa flattened her body against the headboard and averted her gaze. He yanked Greer’s ass to his hips and pressed his full erection into the crack of her firm cheeks. A groan rumbled from his throat. He tried to make it sound like disgust, which shouldn't have been hard since he was beyond pissed by his reaction to her body in this helpless state.

"See. No fight," Zeke yelled and shoved her away. "I can't even get her to cry."

"She doesn't cry. Hasn't since we got her in." The guy pointed to Raisa. "She cries."

"Too much, but I'll take care of that." Zeke pointed to Greer. "She has strength. All the better when I break it." He pulled the last of the cash from his jacket and tossed the three stacks onto the bed. "I'm leaving. Stop drugging her. Lock her in here. When I get back I want her fierce."

"The boss won't like it."

"But he'll love my money." Zeke leaned over Greer. He turned her face to the glorified bouncer, and then pointed to Raisa's. "You see these faces? I don't want them bruised. I've paid for the privilege." His gaze found Greer's hazy one. Her cheek rested heavily in his palm. He injected the proper amount of threat into his voice for his audience, but hoped Greer wasn't too far gone to decipher his message. "When I get back you better be ready."

"Don't," she croaked in the stale air between them. Her throat worked, struggling to swallow. "Go."

Zeke stood. Her dilated eyes followed. He turned and stalked from the room.

Chapter Two

One hour. Zeke had closed the laptop for one hour and now the video feed he'd had into the Stas' "gentlemen's" club was a diagram of twelve small black windows on his screen. He'd showered and dressed with an eye locked on the unfolding scene. The scuzzy bastards prepared for another night of depravity, while Raisa cared for Greer with nibbles of bread, drinks of water, and a cool rag through the night and long day.

Now…nothing.

"Bloody fuck." He tossed the laptop into the passenger seat and beat his fists on the expensive steering wheel. The impact rattled the leather and plastic dashboard.

Were the Stas onto him?

Zeke slammed the laptop lid closed and turned up the volume on the walkie talkie. Scratchy air waves filled the interior, clawing up his already prickled nerves. Three security guards argued over who would tell the boss.

"Tell the boss what?"

Xavier Grisha Filipov ran the New York faction of the Russian Mob known as the Stas. He'd ordered Zeke's capture. His son had tried to blow up Zeke's sister, Khani.

Despite his mounting irritation a smile pulled at Zeke's lips. Grisha Filipov, Xavier's son, nor his sycophants had succeeded in extracting information from Zeke. Neither had they succeeded in exploding his sister. They'd succeeded in becoming popsicles for the next few centuries. His sister's team erased every scrap of evidence that a cabin, the small shed that had been his hell, and the men ever existed.

He was about to do the same thing to this gentleman's club...obliterate it, which was the only reason he'd left his round-the-clock retina fry. Explosives didn't place themselves. Due to the club's extensive security set-up Zeke had parked blocks away, scaled the building at the end of the club's block, and run the rooftops to the large facility's tar-topped one. The night before he'd taken the same route to clip into their mainframe. When he'd left the rigs of different size balls of C-4, the wire and transmitter he'd secured to their hard wiring hadn't been compromised.

So why could he no longer see inside?

The plan had been to blow security, the front and back exits, breech the building, and then clear it of all Stas and Stas supporters one room at a time. Not knowing for certain that Greer and Raisa were still locked in their room slashed that strategy's throat.

Security's argument crackled over the airwaves, but no one reverted back to the actual incident that prompted their discord. The clock read 9:45 pm.

Time for plan B.

Zeke removed his thigh and chest holsters and then stuffed them into the large bag in his backseat along with a string of cheeky expletives. It had been hard enough going in last night without a weapon. Disarming tonight shot fresh pain into his ribs and the wounds on his neck and chest.

He yanked off his black shirt with little regard for the marks of his captivity. The boots and trousers came next, plopping into a heap on the floorboard. Zeke stuffed them into the smaller bag. Approaching footsteps jerked his attention around. His hand found the grip of one of his Glock 17s on the seat.

At the mouth of the adjacent alley three teens shuffled along. When the leader passed back a joint his gaze alighted on the two-toned Rolls Royce Wraith. Six feet stopped. Three jaws dropped. The feet changed direction into the alley. One yanked a jimmy stick from his baggy drawers.

Fucking great. Some limp-dick slackers wanted to steal nearly half-a-million dollars' worth of car, while Zeke was next to naked inside it. He didn't have time for this shit.

Zeke turned on the car, hit them with high beams, and revved the engine. Too bad it barely purred. A throaty growl would've had more effect.

Two of them stopped. The leader pulled a gun from the front of his trousers and waved it in the air. The kid's head bobbed with the motion of the pistol.

Zeke's laugh rumbled against the car's supple leather.

With a slight of hand, Zeke shifted the car into gear and put all 12 cylinders to the test. Loose gravel flew from under the tires. The machine accelerated from zero to sixty in a little over five seconds. It took three seconds for the sordid gang to turn and run. He depressed the brakes with enough leisure that the Spirit of Ecstasy, mounted to the hood, threatened to jam right up the mastermind's keister.

After corralling them round the block and up the street Zeke wheeled to the nearest quiet alley and dressed in Alexi Basov's suit. The man didn't exist, but if someone looked—and the Stas had—they'd find him a wealthy, ruthless son of a bastard.

He stuffed the computer into the large duffle, opened the coach doors, and placed all evidence of his duplicity in the trunk. Instead of pulling around front to the valet as he had the previous night, he parked the car at the back exit and knocked on the door.

"Mr. Basov?" A member of the security team opened the door and extended his hand into the dimly lit space. The man held his gaze, but a dimple plagued his brow. "Why don't you come in? Your key should be ready at the front momentarily. I'll take the car around to the valet. It will be—"

"I parked it where I want it." Zeke dropped the statement like a gauntlet at the threshold and continued toward the receptionist's desk.

Behind him the door closed with a hefty smack. Boot treads thumped close enough that Zeke exhaled long and slowly, ready to defend an attack.

"As you wish, sir." The guard beat him to the security door, blocked the keypad with his bulk, and entered a seven-digit code.

9584629.

Thanks to the camera, he'd seen four different codes used by various Stas employees, their use delineated by organizational rank.

Anosov stood next to the front door, wringing his hands. Beside him, in a single row of red leather wingback chairs, a handful of bidders stared in rapture at the receptionist's desk. The manager of the fine establishment wiped sweat from his brow and watched the front door with a wide gaze.

Before the security guard could speak, Zeke used the principle of surprise to throw the man further off his game. “Anosov Sadovsky.” He smacked his palms together in a deafening blow, and then spread them wide. “I know you have a treasure awaiting me.”

Every hint of eyelid Anosov possessed disappeared in stark reaction to the use of his full name. The man’s gaze shot to Zeke, and then to the row of men. They couldn’t give a shit less about the man’s name. After rounding the wall he could plainly see their minds were enthralled with the fervent coupling of the receptionist and what looked to be her identical twin.

As Anosov crossed the room the soles of his shoes scuffed the ground. “Mr. Basov, good evening.” The lanky man bent imperceptibly at the waist. “Protocol dictates that I be referred to as Anosov in all our dealings. No one knows my full name.”

“That’s not true, is it?” Zeke plucked a handkerchief from his breast pocket with a snap of his wrist and offered it to the dripping man.

The manager flinched.

“Come now, Anosov. It’s just a hankie.” Zeke’s gaze lifted to the man’s beaded forehead.

“No, thank you.” A flick of his long fingers and shake of his head further denied the offer.

“Suit yourself.” Zeke stuffed the fabric back into the pocket.

“How do you know my name?” The man nearly gagged on the question.

“I wouldn’t be who I am or where I am in our business without knowing a thing or two to which others are not privy.” Zekc fished a stack of hundreds from his inside pockets and extended it to Anosov. "I am thorough because I like the luxuries it affords me. Now, I have more than sufficiently paid for my pleasure and am more than ready to indulge."

Anosov stepped back and entered the crowded parlor without grabbing the bills. "Please, have a seat and enjoy the show." He smiled at the two women mauling each other.

"I didn't pay for a preview." Zeke allowed the rasp of agitation to escape his throat. He leaned forward and allowed his height to intimidate further.

The security guard stepped forward, but Anosov waved him off. The man straightened his shoulders and squared to Zeke. "I won't take any more of your money, right now, Mr. Basov."

"Why the fuck not?" His voice raised for the first time. It drew the attention of some of the bidders.

Lines creased Anosov's mouth. His nose crinkled. "Please, step back here with me."

He dipped around Zeke, slipped a key off the desk where one twin's ass cheeks pressed against the glass while the other girl's face disappeared between her legs. Anosov rushed to the back door and opened it. When Zeke stood his ground the manager shooed away the security guard. "Just keep an eye on them. We're fine, are we not, Mr. Basov?"

"That depends." Reluctantly, but without much choice, Zeke stuffed the money into his jacket, followed the man through the door, and to the left into the narrow corridor with its low lantern light and labeled doors.

Anosov stopped outside of room H, but didn't move to insert the key. A tingle of unease skated up Zeke's spine.

"When you left yesterday," he said accusatorially, "you demanded the unstable virgin be left to detox."

Zeke pursed his lips.

"We did as you asked, as you paid for, contrary to our better judgment."

"Get to it, Anosov. My patience is thin."

"I'm afraid it's going to cost you a bit more than we agreed upon for you to enjoy these women."

"You think so?" Zeke challenged.

"Yes. That demon woman..." The smaller man's jaw clenched and then jutted. "Well, I'll just let you see for yourself." Anosov slipped the key into the knob and opened the door.

Glass shards covered the floor. Fuzzy bits and large chunks of cotton joined it like freshly fallen snow. Hunks of sheet rock collected in heaps around the wall. Insulation protruded from each hole. Light fixtures slouched at odd angles around the room.

The women looked much like they had the previous night. Raisa quaked in a ball clutching the headboard with a white knuckled grip. Greer lay in the middle of the bed, her arms splayed wide. Her legs dangled over the side with the shredded covers.

"You see," Anosov interrupted, "we had to sedate her or risk complete ruin."

Zeke stepped into the room, at a loss for Greer's spastic behavior. Glass and grit crunched under his hard soles. She'd recognized him. She'd known he'd come for her last night. So, why had she freaked and destroyed the room? Had they incited her? He'd given them enough money to ensure they wouldn't. She'd known he was coming back.

But then...

When he'd been locked in the shed he'd clawed his fingertips to nubs, working every unforgiving surface for escape. Judging by the damage, her prison was more merciful.

Anosov stayed back while Zeke walked to the bed. Upon closer inspection, small cuts and dried blood covered Greer's dainty hands. Her lids lulled at half mast, but the visible part was more pupil than iris, telling him all he needed to know. She couldn't run or fight her way out of this. He'd have to do it on his own.

Nothing new there.

Raisa whispered, drawing Zeke's scrutiny. Though he was here to help, she would only make escape more difficult. They didn't speak the same language and she couldn't stand being in the same room with him. What would she do when he tossed her over his other shoulder and bolted? She'd probably scratch his eyes out.

Their gazes caught. Raisa leaned ever so slightly to the right. Her gaze jumped high and to the far right before snapping back. She did it once more. This time his gaze followed. In the far corner the wall camera, which had been mounted in a fixture, dangled from the drywall. From a one inch hole behind it yellow, red, green, and black wire drooped to the floor like day old party streamers. Judging by the heap she'd yanked them from the server...dismantling the club's security system.

Genius. Make the destruction so complete that no one notices your actual motive.

It seemed Raisa had a greater understanding of his role in this scheme. Greer had to have instilled the knowledge in this girl during the long night and day. Maybe they *could* get out of here in one piece.

"Leave," Zeke snarled.

"But, sir, payment?"

Zeke turned on him. "You'll get yours. Don't worry. But first, she'll get hers." He nodded toward Greer's prone form. "It may take all night for her to realize it, but she'll get it all right."

"At the front desk when you're done then." The man began to retreat.

"Anosov," Zeke said, stopping him short. "Leave the key."

"Oh." His gaze dropped to the key enfolded in his hand and then lifted to Zeke. "My apologies, Mr. Basov." He moved to drop the large skeleton-style metal piece on the end table, but stalled. It had been tipped on its side and the legs broken off. One of the four legs protruded from a stallion sized dildo, another from a deflated doll, and the remaining two from the flat screen, installed exclusively for porn.

Blinding.

Respect welled for the woman who'd given him nothing but grief during their mission for US Elite.

Anosov's pale skin darkened at his white collar. He dropped the key into the blanket of rubbish on the floor, and then exited with an abrupt slam of the door. With the snick of the mechanism into place Zeke leaned over Greer, hoping she'd acted most of her non-responsiveness. When she didn't flinch at his proximity hope dove off the edge of the rooftop.

Zeke lowered his head to her mouth. A hint of blue lined her pale pink lips. Greer drew shallow breaths too far apart from one another. He placed two fingers at the side of her neck. The reassuring beat knocked against them in a steady rhythm.

"Greer? Can you hear me?" When she didn't respond he pinched her jaw in his hand and turned her to face him. Her lids flagged. Zeke smacked her cheek with three sturdy pats. "Greer, make a noise or something."

He released her face. It sank to the side like a boat caught in the unrelenting sea. "Damn it." He grunted and stood. The hands on the Rolex pressed him for a decision. More than almost anything, he wanted to release these women from the club and level the damn thing. But in that almost...he needed to save Greer more.

At the scratch of bed linen Zeke jerked. Raisa covered the lace of her corseted top with the drape of one arm and eased from the headboard to Greer's side. Her shaky hand stabilized on the crown of blonde hair. Seeming to summon strength from the unconscious woman, Raisa's dark gaze met his. "Zach?"

His head bobbed. To Greer and US Elite, and this lost girl, he was Zach Saulter.

"Friend?"

Again he nodded.

Raisa slipped her legs to the floor and stood on the obscene shoes she'd been made to wear. Her arm still draped her breasts, but her shoulders straightened. "I will help us leave." She pronounced each word carefully, a hint of a question at the end of the statement.

"Good."

Her eyes widened at his British lilt.

Zeke slipped the suit jacket from his shoulders and held it open for Raisa, high enough that he blocked the line of sight to her bosom. When she hesitated, he shook the coat, feeling the weight of the fifty-thousand dollars he'd stuffed into the pockets.

She stepped into the cavernous cocoon and slipped her arms into the sleeves. "Danke."

"You're welcome." Zeke dropped the fabric.

Raisa turned faster than he anticipated. She reached for his watch. He held perfectly still to keep from scaring her. Intelligent eyes studied the face and ticking hands. Thin fingers clasped the band, careful not to touch his skin. She turned the timepiece toward him. Her index finger circled the numbers, completing one hour. Next she pointed to Greer, and then to her own forearm. She mimicked a syringe and injection with her other hand.

They'd drugged Greer with another dose one hour ago. She wouldn't be any help for a while.

Zeke scooped Greer off the bed and tossed her unceremoniously over his left shoulder. He pointed to Raisa, to his side, and then to the door. "You stay close. We're leaving."

The young woman nodded and fortified herself with a breath before stepping to the littered bit of ground where he'd pointed.

At the door Zeke squatted for the key. When he slipped the key into the lock, Raisa wrapped the coat tight around her chest and sidled closer. He strode from the room with his head high like he had every right to be there. The clack of stilettos may as well have been a never-ending series of shrieks in the stifling space. Then again, this place had its fair share of stiletto clad feet...and shrieks. Zeke covered his lips with his index finger, and then pointed to her shoes, just to be safe.

No one occupied the long corridor, but with security, the receptionist, and ten playroom doors between them and the rear exit that could change in an instant.

Whispers of moans and grunts trickled from the thresholds, haunting Zeke with his shortcomings. Each door was a prisoner, or two, he left behind. He hadn't bought a trailer to drag his failings along behind him. Somehow, though, they never managed to lose him for long.

Greer weighed less than the dying soldier he'd carried over the Anti-Lebanon mountain range nearly ten years ago, but damn, every shift of his hips jostled her limp form and tweaked his mending ribs. Zeke quickened his pace. Each advancing step brought them closer to freedom, and consequently, danger.

Raisa fisted a clump of his shirt and tugged in short, panicked jerks. When he spared her a glance her gaze honed on the *Security* label as though the letters themselves might leap off the door and tackle them.

"It's okay." Zeke reached behind, grimacing at the pain that knifed through his middle. His finger encircled her wrist and tugged her in front of him. He kept his hand on her in a gesture anyone watching would think of as possessive-though, compared to Greer over his shoulder, a little wrist-holding wouldn't even register.

He rushed her past the ominous black door. Raisa's panted breaths ceased until they cleared the door to reception. No gun wielding 'roid-rats poured out into the hallway. Anosov didn't pop out from the front demanding an explanation.

Two doors left at the end of the hall and they were home free. Zeke doubled his grip on both women.

Raisa sighed. A smile cracked her terrified facade.

The unmistakable whoosh of the loo blocked their path as surely as a cement wall. Twenty yards stood between them and the exit...the exit that required a security code to open.

Zeke propelled Raisa forward. He pushed his own legs against the floor, driving himself and Greer on.

Too soon the paint-chipped door on the right opened. Raisa faltered. Her feet slowed to a near stop.

His grip urged her ahead several more feet before he released his hold. He hoped she'd stay with him. But...

A muscle-fluffed guard stepped into the corridor. One of his hands shoved the end of a black T-shirt into his trousers. The other worked on fastening his belt buckle. Zeke's thundering steps pulled the man's gaze from his crotch.

For a full second the man stared with drawn brows. In that wasted fragment of time Zeke cleared several more feet.

The guard stumbled back a step. Zeke advanced another stride.

Five meaty fingers reached across his torso. The guard palmed his pistol.

Zeke dropped his right shoulder and pushed harder.

His 235 pounds, combined with Greer's 135 —give or take a couple—plowed into the man's sternum. Zeke used him as padding against the metal door frame. A deep thud and nasty crack broke the relative quiet.

Zeke gripped Greer's thighs with his right hand, planted his feet, and righted them. The guard slid down the wall and collapsed into a clump on the stained concrete floor.

A strangled scream left Raisa's throat. It pierced his ear like a fucking gold loop. If she wanted freedom, it came at a cost. One unconscious man was an easy price to pay, especially since she didn't have to do the knocking out. But if she kept up the screech, there would be significantly more bloodletting, and it just might be theirs.

He wheeled around ready to cement his hand over her mouth. She wasn't where she was supposed to be. Raisa stood ten feet back, next to the other door they'd passed. Her cry became strangled. More accurately, someone strangled her cry.

Three men clogged the hall. One clamped a hand around Raisa's throat and lifted. The ugly points of her plastic shoes dangled an inch from the floor, seeking it with frenzied kicks. Fear distorted her pretty face. The other two men crouched with their hands up, ready to smash in his skull, while the man with Raisa on the far right of the hall faded back a step.

No talking his way out of this one.

Their guns and walkie talkies remained fixed in their belts. The receptionist's door remained closed.

One corner of Zeke's mouth quirked.

The two straightened ever so slightly.

Zeke hurled Greer at the one on the left. Instinctively the man's arms opened wide to receive her. Zeke launched himself at the one in the middle, whose gaze followed Greer's impact. Her dead weight toppled Leftie about the time Middle-man realized that the devil knocked on his door.

The bloke's fists drew high and tight in defense. Zeke packed all his momentum into a punch. It connected with the man's ribs. One cracked under his fist. The slack of bone giving way smarted pain in his own side. The guard's elbows dropped, covering his middle too late, leaving his jaw exposed.

Zeke's left hook covered it. Middle joined the growing pile on the floor. He wouldn't get up for a while either.

Leftie wiggled under Greer, stuck by the wall on the left and his unconscious comrade on the right. Zeke stepped toward the asshole who'd retreated a few more steps with Raisa.

The bastard groped for his gun, or maybe walkie talkie. Both hung on his right side. Poor Rightie was a rightie and had grabbed Raisa with his dominant hand. No way could he reach the comms clipped to his back pocket.

Zeke wouldn't give him the opportunity to get to his gun. His fist clenched, ready to center the arse's temple.

A blow rang Zeke's bell. The point of impact radiated from the back of his skull to the front. It snapped his head forward. The dim hallway tunneled to a small circular window.

Raisa's red face knitted in rage. Her knee shot forward. It sank into Rightie's crotch.

Zeke closed his eyes. He dropped to a knee.

He pivoted and punched.

A groan wheezed from Leftie's lungs. When his eyes opened the man's cheeks had paled several shades. The bloke clutched his stomach. Zeke sailed an upper-cut into his jaw. He didn't watch the man fall.

Zeke whirled to Raisa, ignoring the stars that shot past his widening field of vision. She needed his help...only...she didn't.

Raisa cradled her throat with one hand. The other braced the wall while she rammed the scuffed points of her stilettos into the bastard's lower torso again and again. The man hunched into the fetal position like the pussy he was, cupping his balls.

They had no time to revel in the quick beating they'd given the four men. Nor was there time to wait until the stars stopped shimmying in his periphery. The longer they stayed the more chance they had of getting shot.

Zeke scooped Greer off the floor and then tugged Raisa's wrist. He urged her toward the door, squatted, retrieved the pussy's gun and walkie, and then ran for freedom.

Stark panic paled Raisa's cheeks. She stabbed a finger toward the security pad on the door. Zeke foisted the weapons and radio into her hands, and then grabbed the edge of the suit coat still wrapped around Raisa. She gasped, but didn't budge while he fished forty thousand from the jacket pockets and tossed it onto the unconscious guard next to the door.

Raisa canted her head to the side.

"They won't look for us as hard with the money," he whispered as he punched in the security code. He didn't expect her to understand, but maybe his tone would communicate something.

When the light turned green Raisa shoved the door open with her hip, then held it wide for him and Greer. Zeke hustled out the door and to the car. The clack of Raisa's shoes stayed on his heels.

He wrenched the back door wide and eased Greer into the seat. Sweat-damp hair clung to her face. It stayed there. Her seatbelt was more important. He reclined the seat slightly to keep her from slumping and pulled the strap across her chest.

Zeke stood and motioned Raisa into the car. When she didn't leap inside he found her gaze... right above the barrel of the guard's gun.

Her chest rose and fell on choppy breaths. The hunk of black metal shimmied with every gasp. Wide brown eyes danced left and right, searching for...escape? She'd trusted him enough to get her out of the whore house, but apparently not much further.

Hands at his side, Zeke softened his gaze, but held his ground.

Raisa's gaze danced from him to Greer to the back door of the night club several times, and finally landed on him.

"Friend." He held out his hand for the gun.

Her gaze narrowed.

Zeke pushed back the need to take control of the situation. He let her decide how they'd proceed.

After several stilted seconds Raisa's breathing slowed. The quiver of her hands tapered. She eased the barrel to the ground and stepped to Zeke. Chagrin quirked her mouth as she released the gun. The cool barrel and heated grip weighted his palm. She set the radio next to the gun and dove into the backseat.

Thank fuck for the unracked slide.

Without it he wouldn't have been so gentle. Shot on accident was still shot.

Zeke jumped in behind the wheel, stowed the guard's stuff in the center console, and drove. He drove through Queens, dodged traffic in Manhattan, and crossed into Jersey. In Newark he dropped off the interstate, weaved through city streets to a garage in a sketchy part of town.

He depressed a button and the bay door receded. They rolled into the dark. Another tap of the button closed the door behind them.

"Just a minute." Zeke opened the door, retrieved the gun from the center console, stuffed it into his waist band, and then walked five paces. His hand roved the rough brick wall until he found the lever.

When he slid the metal rod to the upright position, lights blinded him for a fraction of a second. At the far parking spot slick black paint gleamed off the 1970 Barracuda he'd rebuilt from the ground up. A notch loosened on his nerves. Not a good thing when relaxed usually meant dead.

"Come on." Zeke clipped any hint of ease from his demeanor. He had a hell of way to go to clear his teammates and fix his mistakes.

Raisa crawled from the car like a mouse at the mouth of its flooding burrow with a hawk circling overhead. While she examined her options Zeke moved the bags from the Royce's trunk into his. He waffled at the trunk, but only for a second before pulling a pair of gym shorts with a draw string, a T-shirt, and a white business card with a single phone number in blunt black print at its center from his bag.

The young woman clutched the top of the open car door. Her gaze shifted from a tour of the garage to Greer. When he closed the trunk she jumped. Those plastic shoes scuffed against the oil stained concrete. That scared, yet brave, dark brown gaze met his.

Zeke walked to the back end of the Rolls and set the clothes—along with the key fob for the ridiculous car—on the Royce's trunk. He patted his pockets and then pointed to the jacket.

Raisa's head tilted in question.

"On the inside pocket there is money." Again he repeated the gesture, trying to compensate for the language barrier.

She tugged the top of the jacket together, covering a hint of exposed cleavage before slipping her other hand beneath the fabric. When she pulled it out a single stack of hundreds lay in her palm. Raisa's throat worked on a swallow. Her hand trembled ever so slightly. The shoes danced from one sole to the other. After a ragged breath she extended the cash toward him.

"No. It's for you." Zeke raised his hands. "Just for you."

That soulful brown gaze skittered to Greer.

"I'm taking her."

The space between Raisa's brows furrowed.

Zeke held the business card between his first two fingers and waited for Raisa to look at it. "You stay. Hide from Stas. In two weeks. Today is Friday. After Friday and another Friday, after two weeks hiding, call this number for help."

Shit, he hoped it would be over by then.

Raisa looked at him as though he spoke a Martian language with his tongue hanging out his mouth to one side. He may as well have been, but damned if he could remember the days of the week in Russian.

"Hide from Stas for two weeks. Two weeks, then phone this number." He placed the card on top of the pile of clothes, and then grabbed the key fob. "Use the car, if you have to, but be careful. People will want to take it from you."

Again with the crinkled brow.

Zeke added gestures. Who the hell knew if she'd gotten any of it. But right now it was the best he could do.

He bowed his head.

The young girl hugged her arms around herself and inclined her head.

His gaze traveled from Raisa to Greer.

"Friend?" Raisa pointed from him to Greer.

Would the unconscious woman consider him a friend? Hell no. She would just as soon douse him with gasoline and strike the match, but right now, he was all she had. So, Zeke nodded.

Raisa stepped back several paces.

Zeke hefted Greer from the Rolls and strapped her into his car. He opened the garage, started the engine, and pulled out into the night. When he closed the large bay door Raisa still stood, squeezing her arms around herself.

Chapter Three

Greer surfaced to inordinately loud thumps. Each thump jarred the hundred-billion nerve cells inside her body like she stood too close to a pulsating concert speaker. If only she were in the front row at the Verizon Center with her girlfriends, listening to Ed Sheeran's smooth voice and his magical guitar. Somewhere deep inside her subconscious she giggled through the pain. No, magical guitar wasn't a euphemism. And this wasn't the throes of a musical orgasm. This ached. The throbbing grew more zealous with each passing second. Who turned up the damn volume?

Her lids opened, looking for the culprit. She instantly regretted it. Tears pooled, distorting her already-fuzzy vision to the equivalent of a fun-house mirror reflection.

"Drink this." The deep, familiar voice rumbled in her ear. Hot breath soothed a path across her cheek.

A sharp inhale stabbed Greer's throat. To her utter horror the tears spilled over her lids. They ran down her cheeks, cooling her already chilled, wet skin. Why was she soaked? Why was she so cold? Better yet, why was she crying?

Greer clamped her eyes shut. She hadn't allowed herself to cry before, but now...

He'd come back. Now she was safe.

A shiver wracked her frame. Her bones rattled like a baby's toy. Safe, yes, but not okay. Not yet, anyway. Something cold hit her lips. It triggered a shock wave that stung her raw nerves anew. She cringed from the pain.

"Drink." The barked order leapt head first off the high dive straight into her ear. Its impact rippled across her brain.

Greer tried to cover her ears, to still her quaking head from the vibrations. Her right arm flailed high and wide until she hit something immovable. The impact added to the tilt of her formerly-ordered world. Her hands splayed, searching for an anchor in the tumult of her agony. The tips of her fingers hooked the edge of something hard and cold.

"Mother fu..." His curse turned to a growl. The crack of shattering glass splintered the air. "It was just water. All you had to do was open and swallow."

His harsh words shattered Greer along with the glass. A sob seeped from her lips. Greer buried her face against her arm.

Why was she so oversensitive to noise and light...and him?

Through the pain, the emotions that—seconds ago—threatened to dent Greer's pride, evaporated in the heat of her anger.

Zach Saulter had saved her, but it didn't mean he gave a shit about her. The man she called Captain Saulter for six long months of training with the private securities firm, US Elite, the man she'd taken orders from before dawn until after dusk, the man whose unreachable stare she'd suffered hadn't changed a bit. This had nothing to do with her and everything to do with completing the mission they'd been tasked with a month ago.

She and her partner, Derrick Coen, had been given a top-level exit-training mission: Infiltrate the Stas, the US faction of the Russian mob, learn as much as you can about their facilities and inner workings, then report back. Captain Saulter—though mercenaries didn't really have rank—hadn't given them orders on the mission, but he'd been sent to assimilate into the Stas pecking order and make certain they didn't screw up.

After so many days fighting the drugs, she'd given up hope of rescue and let them take her to oblivion. Too soon the bliss of the void faded. His voice penetrated the haze and his heat drove it back. She'd opened her bleary eyes and his piercing gray eyes stared back. He'd looked different. A beard covered his chiseled jaw. The arsenal he usually strapped across his wide chest had been replaced by a tailored suit. But the complete focus with which he assessed his target remained. And she'd been his mark.

Greer took to mentally chanting *Zach... Zach...Zach.* His unreachable, unfeeling, sexy-as-sin features had filled her head. The hope of him returning had been the only thing to shake her from the fog long enough to tell Raisa what she needed to know to help save them. In all that hope she'd made him out to be more than he was. She'd made him out to be the fantasy that had instantly supplanted her intelligence and seeded itself in her subconscious the moment he'd stalked onto the training field.

Where was Raisa? Where was she for that matter?

"You have to drink," Zeke demanded.

She would have told him to go screw himself, but the void pulled her back. Now that she was safe she didn't fight the rapture of ignorance.

Greer didn't know how long it lasted, but it could have lasted longer. Agony checked her like a 200 pound defenseman. Greer pumped her legs in a desperate attempt to find the blankness. Her feet slipped on the ice. Her lids popped open to the darkness of night, not nullity. This time the pain stayed with her. Nothingness slipped away. Pain ground her into the glass...only it wasn't glass. Her palms pressed against cool wood, smooth from use, not the work of a sander. The planks dipped and rose in uneven waves. They dug into her hands.

Greer tightened her muscles. Try as she might she couldn't get her cheek off the dirty floor.

"Stop fighting it." Zach rose from a misshapen bed. No, not a bed, but a small mountain of hay covered with a blanket. He crossed the room without a sound, though he wore scuffed leather work boots, jeans, and the weaponry she'd learned to expect on his work-horse body. The brown-rounded tips of his large shoes stopped inches from her face. He loomed above her. "I told you, no."

No? Like she'd asked him for something or permission to do something. They'd failed their mission, and as far as she was concerned US Elite could shove it up their ass. They'd sent them in with backward, if not all together bogus, intel, plus no support. Greer wouldn't take another order off him and she'd tell him so, just as soon as she swallowed past the dust bunnies in her throat.

Two weeks ago Zach had disappeared. She'd thought he'd completed his part of the task and dropped from sight like they'd been ordered to do, just without giving her the signal like he was supposed to. When she'd been taken she'd known he must have been too...though she couldn't imagine anyone getting the goods over on Zach

Saulter. The man never looked relaxed, not even when reclined in an easy chair watching the football games on which he and the other trainers at US Elite used to gamble.

Greer's body jerked of its own accord. She huddled into the fetal position. Her fists clamped together. The points of her knuckles dug into her chest.

"Please...give me a hit?" She would have been surprised at the grit and desperation in her voice, but she hurt too damn much.

"Even in American English no means no. How many times do I have to tell you no before you get me?"

How many times had she asked? She didn't want drugs. She wasn't a druggie. Sure enough though, she'd asked for them. This was bad.

One of Zach's steely arms jostled her shoulder, and then she flew. The ceiling dropped high and fast. Her stomach constricted. Helpless to stop it, Greer retched into her T-shirt and black boxer briefs. Luckily, or not, nothing escaped her mouth. His arms tightened around her until the never-ending fit subsided. The ceiling receded more slowly.

A thousand tiny points stuck into Greer's skin, agitating her further. She rolled onto her side, found she also had a hay bed, and realized that comfort wouldn't find her tonight...not even if she slept on a cloud.

"Everything hurts," she croaked.

"I'm not here to make you feel good. I'm here to help you."

Zach snatched a blanket off the floor. The bulge of thigh-sized biceps eased her attention from the discomfort for a brief, if euphoric, moment. Bits of hay clung to the worn comforter. She only noticed because he tried picking them off one by one. When that proved too time-consuming Zach lifted the fabric high into the air. The fitted T-shirt clung to the distinctive flare of his lats. His arms sliced toward the ground. Partially frayed ends snapped like whips. Tiny fragments of hay rained in an unusually beautiful spectacle.

He leaned forward and draped the comforter over her shivering body. He stooped low. His clean shaven face threw her. Well, in all honesty it was his face—shaven or not—that did stupid things to her insides. The fine lines around his impenetrable eyes crinkled.

"Now start helping me." Zach jabbed her with those simple words and then stood and walked away.

Greer didn't hear or see him again during the unrelenting night. His makeshift bed remained empty. She twisted and tossed herself around, tangling the covers about her legs in the vain effort of finding relief from her physical irritation and the hollowness his absence stirred. No, it wasn't his absence. It was the loss she endured only when ill. She yearned for the unconditional love and care only a mother could give, even the maternal nagging she'd never experienced.

Yeah, that had to be it.

Pain distorted the sunrise through the gap in the chained barn door. By the time the sun lit the interior from all directions the worst seemed to have finally abated. Her lungs filled without the hitch. The tensions in her neck relented. She no longer shivered or dripped sweat. Best of all the pulsing of her heartbeat receded from her eardrums and back into her chest.

"Raisa?" She whispered the girl's name. Greer doubted she could scream if she tried. Three more times she put her scratchy voice to use with no results.

Shortly after she found that lying on her back with her arms out to her side no longer hurt, the scent of bacon hit the air. Greer rolled to her side and clutched her stomach in preparation for tremors that never came. The rich salty smell sailed up her nostrils and over her tongue, seducing her to the first hint of hunger she'd had in...she didn't know how long. How long had the Stas had her? How long had she been here? Where was here?

A dull ache in her frontal lobe stopped the line of inquiry. Right now it didn't matter. She needed a bathroom, asap. The stench she'd thought to be hay during the night was more than likely her. First, she needed to sit up, which seemed a feat at the moment.

Greer extended her feet over the edge of the dried grass. Gravity did the rest. The tips of her toes tingled as though she'd suddenly regained circulation. She wiggled them until they steadied. Hay crackled and dipped under the weight of her braced forearm. She pressed against the surface. Her shoulder felt more like gelatin than muscle, but inch by labored inch her world shifted back toward normal, though it remained quite out of reach.

It took several minutes for Greer to catch her breath. Each one zapped strength she needed to stand. Her head hung between her shoulders without permission. She saw it then, the evidence that her body hadn't asked her for permission for anything over the last day or days. Greer let her horrified gaze drift back to the white cover on which she'd lain. Three significant yellow rings marked her disgrace.

"Oh God."

Bolstered by humiliation and resentment for the sons of whores who had drugged her, Greer gathered the covers into her arms with clawed hands and sharp, angry swipes. Panting and at a loss as to what to do with the soiled bedding, she dropped them into a heap and turned her back with a huff that threatened to loosen the tears she'd kept at bay for the last few hours.

Greer firmed her lips and sucked in a breath so deep her lungs burned. Determination and rage drove her. She settled her palms on either side of her thighs and pushed. Her bottom cleared the prickly bed, but adrenaline and anger proved insufficient fuel.

Her legs buckled under her weight. Momentum pitched her forward. Greer's hand shot out to cushion the fall, but again she lacked the strength to follow through. Her palms scraped across the uneven surface. She landed with a resounding thud.

An answering crash came from up a single straight flight of stairs that ran half the length of the wall her head had been facing while on the cot. Another metal on metal clank of pots maybe, echoed down before Zach's leather boots appeared at the top of the steps.

More than almost anyone in the world Greer didn't want him to see her like this. Vanity had a little to do with it, but more than that she hated the disdain that rolled off him in waves. From the first day in training to the last day she'd deposited drinks to him and the other bouncer at the Stas' night club, Sable, before he'd disappeared, nothing she did won his approval. When others finished a course first it earned them the slightest nod from Captain Saulter. Every time she'd finished first his frown deepened.

When his shoes once again appeared inches from her nose she refused to meet his gaze. Part of her hoped he'd leave her there. The other part really needed to pee and forbid doing so in her—no, his—boxer briefs again.

"I need a bathroom, please."

Zach's large hands slipped under Greer's arms. His palms and fingers splayed across her upper ribcage and hoisted. Her feet found the ground. With his strength supporting her deficit, she stood.

Before she could revel in the accomplishment Zach slid his left arm behind her back and pulled her to his chest. Her bare right arm draped over his shoulder and traps. Only their T-shirts separated her breast and abdomen from his skin. An inferno sizzled everywhere their bodies pressed together. She'd been cold for so long, and he radiated heat. The move also forced her gaze to his. His chilly London-fog eyes contrasted so starkly with the warmth she pulled from him in greedy waves.

He bent at the waist. Panic rattled Greer's heart.

"I can walk." When his lips thinned she added, "...with a little help."

"Stairs," he said by way of explanation. His arm grazed the backs of her calves.

"I'm disgusting." She croaked more than shouted, but still she hoped he'd reconsider.

Zach scooped her into his arms, a place she'd been in plenty of fantasies, but a place she never truly wanted to be. He'd been a force beyond her reach. She'd recognized it immediately and been wise enough to steer clear. Yet, in her dreams she'd touched him, but not like this. Not tainted. Damn him for ruining the bright spots in her bleak nights. Damn him for...

Greer's gaze snagged on a ring of round red scabs that circled Zach's neck like a sadistic choker. The marks didn't make sense. They were too deliberate to be an accident. Maybe he was into some kinky stuff. And yet, she couldn't imagine him allowing anyone to have the upper hand, no matter how good some said it felt.

"What—"

"Don't," he bit.

Yeah, the barely-hinged rage in his voice told her all she needed to know, and it shot a fresh chill through her bones.

He carried her upstairs into another large room without sparing her another glance. Greer waffled between wanting to hide her face in his shirt and wanting to toss herself to the floor. She settled on accepting the ride. She looked straight ahead, trying not to show too much interest in the surroundings, and not meeting his gaze again.

They passed a well-worn oak desk at the top of the stairs and curiosity won out. Maps, a ruler, and an assortment of pens and markers littered the top. Across from it a king size mattress lay on a bare frame, its headboard the unpainted barn slats that blocked the midmorning sun. Tousled sheets hung off the far side, held up from the floor by a closed laptop in the center of the bed.

Light shone from three windows, one on the rear wall at the top of the stairs near the desk. The largest one had once been loft doors in between the desk and bed. A long rectangular window had been cut out over the small corner kitchen. Zach strode past a small dining table so unblemished and gleaming that it had likely never been used.

Zach aimed for a large rectangular partition at the end of the room bound by the railing on one side and a refrigerator on the other. He sidled sideways into the faintly lit box and bent. Greer's bottom and legs landed on terry cloth. His arms slid from her body, taking his heat with him.

She hugged her arms around her bent knees and held her breath. Less than a second later the flip of a switch accompanied light from a rustic silver fixture over a small sink. He stepped around her in the center of the floor. In order to follow his movements, she released her death grip and turned her head.

The shower curtain sang under Zach's hand. He scooted it all the way to the side and reached for the faucet. She thought he'd been searching for towels or something, but he looked ready to settle in to her bathing routine.

When he turned and reached for her the twine holding her heart in place snapped and the thudding organ dropped into her stomach. Acid splashed up, stinging her throat.

"I can clean myself."

Zach hoisted her off the floor like he had before, like a toddler incapable of bathing herself. He ignored her completely, his gaze on the open lid of the toilet. One step in that direction and instinct took over.

Greer struck at his exposed throat. Normally the move took a hundredth of a second at this proximity and inflicted maximum damage. Now her strike played out in slow motion, taking an eternity to leave his bicep where she'd held on for dear life.

Inches from her mark Zach's thumb pressed the pliable skin between her thumb and forefinger. His other fingers locked around her palm and twisted. Without his body holding hers up gravity sucked her down. Her knees hit the ground with a resounding crack. A cry shot from her lips. Her arms flailed in a feeble attempt to catch herself. The vice grip on her hand kept her from cracking her head on the toilet.

"God damn it." Zach snatched her off the ground in one arm and glowered. His gray eyes sparked. It was the first emotion she'd ever seen in them. "I've already seen you naked. Multiple times. Get over yourself. I'm not some barely-strung beast who's going to rip away your virginity."

Greer's mouth moved, but no words came out. For a minute she just stared at him in disbelief. No one knew she was a virgin. It wasn't something she talked about, and since she hadn't dated ever and quickly neared spinster territory she might never have to.

"How do you know I'm a..." She couldn't even say it.

One of his brows lifted. "Your price and white gown gave it away."

She remembered very little past the first day at the compound. The bits she did remember were blurry and disjointed, until Zach had appeared and given her hope.

"How did they know?" She breathed the word so quietly it sounded to her own ears like she really didn't want to know the answer.

Just like that the spark vanished. The cold curtain swung into place. "It's probably best you don't remember."

A thought struck her hard and fast. He'd said *price*. Her price had been high. He was a mercenary. So was she. Thanks to her daddy-issues. She had a savings account, but nowhere near the amount of money she'd seen some of the men throw around for the used girls that first night.

Greer gripped his forearms because if she didn't she'd fall on her face. And stupidly she needed his strength to be able to look him in the eye.

"You bought me to...to sate your—" a sob broke her sentence, but its message had been received. The spark returned and ignited into an all-out flame.

"If I wanted you, I could've had you for the cost of a condom six months ago."

She shoved at his arms, but he didn't budge. God, she hated being incapable of defending herself, incapable of caring for herself. She hated even more that he might be right. If he'd shown the least interest in her, what would she have done? His distant, occasional glances had been enough to reel her in to fantasies she'd only given life to in the depths of her psyche.

Rage bubbled. "Fuck you, Saulter."

"I should've left your ass there. Would've made my life easier."

Greer wanted to turn away and cower into a ball. This man took rejection to a whole new level. It hurt almost as much as detox. She forced herself to look into his antagonism. Beyond the anger, behind the steel cage of his muscles and the concrete wall of his demeanor, she caught a glimpse of suffering. It hung in the funny crook of his lips and in the strain of his jaw.

She swallowed her pride—the little bit that endured—and tried not to gag. Her grip eased. She quit fighting. Lord knew she didn't have the energy for it.

"I'm sorry."

For the first time in the nearly seven months she'd interacted with him in one capacity or another, Zach Saulter's hard gaze retreated.

"Are you going to let me help without a trip to the theatre? I don't care for drama." The vibrato of his voice rolled across her neck, leaving gooseflesh in its wake.

"Yes."

Zach exhaled long and low. He cinched one arm around her, glared somewhere over her shoulder, and bent. His fingers brushed her hip. He hooked the band of the briefs and tugged one side and then the other over her bottom before shoving them to the floor. Next he looped his free arm under the shirt. The hair on his arm tickled her back as he moved it into place and tightened his hold. He slipped his other hand under the front of the loose fabric and pulled it up to her arm.

Greer used every bit of energy to wrestle her arms through the sleeves. The shirt pooled around her neck. Zach grabbed the back and pulled it over her head. He undressed her with moves so clinical a nun would applaud.

Even with her breasts pressed and jostling against his abdomen he didn't react. He walked her backward and set her on the toilet. She'd never peed in front of a man before. Doing it in front of Zach twisted her stomach in an ugly bow, but what did it matter. He turned to the shower and adjusted the temperature, caring about her nudity as much as he cared about fashion magazines.

She took care of her business as quickly as she could, and then used the edge of the sink to stand, close the lid, and flush. A tiny part of her hoped he'd show some reaction to her standing on her own, the tiniest bit of encouragement for the effort she expended.

He wiped his palms across the seat of his jeans and straightened. His wet hands left a damp trail over his muscled ass. When Zach turned he pulled up short for a half a second before he rushed forward.

"Are you determined to scramble your brains?"

"What?" Greer hardly had enough time to get the word out before he scooped her post-wedding style into his arms.

"Your legs look as sturdy as a runway model's on ten inch heels."

A laugh closer to hysteria than humor shot like projectile vomit from her lips. There was nothing she could do to stop it.

Zach paused at the edge of the full tub. His chin dropped and he met her half-closed gaze. "What's so funny?"

"How would a guy like you know about heels and runway models?" She guffawed the words in between desperate breaths.

"A guy like me?"

"Macho, punch-you-in-the-face-as-soon-as-talk-to-you kind of guy."

From this close, with this inquisitive look on his gorgeous face, he didn't appear as old as she'd once thought. Not that she'd thought him old per se, but mid-thirties for sure. But when he lost the commander-of-the-universe bravado the years fell away, revealing a mid-twenties glow.

His eyes rolled skyward, causing her laughter to pitch as high. He eased her into the steaming hot bath. The heat melted her muscles in the best way. It stripped the last of her bluster with it and her laughter dissolved into sobs. She covered her face with her hands and waited for him to stand and go. He didn't. The hand Zach looped under her legs receded from the water, but the hand at her back stayed. Eventually her cries crescendoed, dwindled, and then eased all together.

"Lean back." His hand cupped the back of her neck.

Greer dropped her hands into the water and looked a question at him.

"I'm going to wash your hair so you don't drown yourself trying to do it, and then I'll leave."

Maybe it was exhaustion or the rawness of her pride, but Greer let go. Zach guided her back. The water eased up her neck and around her skull. When the water enveloped her ears her brain went silent. Her eyes closed. All the questions fell away. The pain ebbed. Her emotions calmed.

Zach gently brushed the loose strands from around her face. He skimmed the tips of her long hair, creating eddies in the water that caressed her shoulders. Tension grew in his hand and he lifted her to sit. She almost whimpered. Water sluiced off her in a cacophony.

Greer opened her eyes. Hands she'd seen down a drunk Russian three times his size, and then toss the lug out on his ass, poured a quarter-size dollop of shampoo in the center of one palm before rubbing them together. Calluses scratched like sandpaper, but bubbles oozed out from between thick fingers.

He started on the surface, gliding the minty cleanser from root to tip. Then he delved deeper. The tips of his fingers worked the sensitive skin atop her head. Greer's mouth dropped open. He seduced her with heavy circular strokes around her temples and easing toward the crown. Her breaths rasped across her lips. His fingers reached the base of her skull and a quiet moan shattered the silence.

Her body flushed with embarrassment and something richer and darker. To Zach's credit he didn't stop. Shamelessly she pressed into his touch. Her breaths came deeper, more punctuated. His right hand slid up the back of her neck, and then down her pony tail. He gathered it up and massaged it into the rest of her hair.

When her head dropped forward she saw the erect tips of her rosy pink nipples dipping into the water. Greer clamped her mouth shut tight to keep in the exclamation. The embarrassment had to show on her face. Her cheeks heated ten degrees.

Zach eased her back toward the water. Greer clamped her eyes shut. The last thing she needed to see was him noticing her arousal. He'd go back to hating her and treating her like crap on the tip of his boot. If he noticed, he didn't say anything or try to drown her. In short order he rinsed away the shampoo and set her up again.

She expected him to leave then, held her breath for it to happen, but he reached for a bottle of conditioner. Her lady parts pulsed with excitement while the rational parts of her shrieked in fear.

"You know about conditioner too," she blurted.

"And moisturizer. And panty lines. And periods." His fingers dove into her hair again. "I have an older sister."

"Oh." It wasn't eloquent, but it was all she could manage under the assault.

"I know about razors and shaving cream too. If you want to shave and can do it without slitting anything, there they are." He pointed to a small shelf next to the head of the tub.

"Oh," again was all she could muster.

"She read fashion magazines she swiped from offices and used them to teach me to read."

Half of Greer's brain cells had been fried in the brew of chemicals the Stas had forced on her. The other half drooled on themselves thanks to Zach's decisive fingers. Even still, one of them—or maybe a few held hands, joining forces to understand a bit of the enigma that was Zach Saulter—caught the unspoken hints he'd thrown. Zach hadn't had enough money for proper books and his parents hadn't cared enough to teach him how to read. If that didn't explain a thing or two, Greer didn't know what would.

All too soon he laid her back into the water. Greer mustered up the courage to look at him. He studied her hair, not her boobs. Stubble covered his proud jaw. Small specks of water ran a path from his sleeve end to his shoulder. The splash saturated the fabric, darkening a dozen tiny circles of the gray blue shirt.

His earlier words haunted her. *If I wanted you, I could've had you for the cost of a condom six months ago.* He didn't want her. She should've been relieved. Again that empty feeling nestled in between her rib cage damn near her heart.

In the past men wanted her, especially since she wasn't easily had. She'd been so hell bent on her career, and simultaneously terrified of getting pregnant or contracting an STD, that she hadn't given them much thought. When she watched her friends' relationships and marriages splinter and crumble she patted herself on the back for dodging the bullets. Why have a man when you can have dildos in every shape, size, and speed setting?

As though his mind followed her naughty path his lips pressed together. A hint of a smile curved one of his lips.

"When I was older I used them for different things." He said it so quietly had she not been watching his mouth she'd have missed it completely.

Greer swallowed. Part of her wished she had missed it.

He set her up and handed over a bar of soap and a rag.

"I'll come get you in a few. Don't drown." Zach moved to the door, snagging her soiled clothes off the floor, without a sideways glance at tits nor twat. He drew the door behind him, but stopped with it a few inches from the frame. His gaze swept her top to bottom.

Greer's pounding heart stilled.

"It'd be a shame to waste all my hard work."

If she'd had the strength to throw the large bar of lavender soap at his head she'd have given it her all. Her tongue lay like a dead fish in her mouth. Not that it mattered. Her brain couldn't conjure a comeback to save a saint.

Zach closed the door with a quiet click of the latch.

"Asshole." Greer buried her face in her hands, not knowing who she called asshole-him, or herself for wanting his admiration.

Chapter Four

The bathing process had been a hell of a lot easier when she'd been unconscious. Less pushback. Way less...temptation. Jesus H. Christ. Out cold she hadn't reacted to his assistance.

Great, now he lied to himself. Sure she'd made tiny mindless noises of pain the first day and pleasure the second when the drug's effects began to lose their hold. But she hadn't known her own name, much less that he was the one scrubbing the filth away. Today though... Her eyes had been open. Her acumen returned.

She'd reacted to his attention with embarrassment and irritation. And to his touch. Bloody hell. She'd responded with unadulterated lust.

Zeke stomped his way down the stairs, dumped the sullied clothes and sheets and several clumps of damp hay into the burn barrel with the ashes of the others he'd destroyed yesterday. He'd thought then that she'd be back to normal today, but he wasn't that lucky. Never had been. It had taken too long to get her right, and even still she couldn't bloody walk. He hadn't planned on her being doped.

At least she could do the actual scrubbing herself.

Zeke adjusted his pants, cursed, and hustled upstairs to see what he could salvage for breakfast. Judging by the charred smell when he'd walked through with the clothes, something hadn't survived.

He'd wanted a full English fry-up, but he'd learned a thing or two during his time in the States. One, Americans thought black pudding came in a snack pack. Two and three, fat as they were, they preferred their bread toasted, not fried, and they usually only ate one meat at breakfast, not three. So, he'd settled for bacon, eggs, salt and pepper tomatoes, and toast.

"Minus the toast." He rescued the slightly over-crisp bacon from the pool of warm fat inside the pan, and then placed it on a paper towel. The yolks of the sunny-side eggs had cooked through. At least the bottoms weren't scorched beyond recognition. Too bad the same couldn't be said for the black squares that had once been bread.

He chucked the lumps of coal, lowered the heat element, and pressed down two more pieces. After distributing the food between two plates, Zeke eyed the loo's door. His cheeks puffed. Slowly he let the air out between his lips. If only the tension gnawing on his skull—and elsewhere—-would discharge as easily.

Pussing out, Zeke set Greer a place at the table, taking extra time with the crease of her napkin. Like he'd ever folded a napkin in his life. He hardly used them. When the back of your sleeve worked well enough, why bother?

A loud splash sloshed around the barn. What sounded like a thousand droplets rained down inside the water-closet. Visions of Greer executing a cannon-ball in the small tub saturated his mind, but he knew she'd tried to stand again and had fallen. Zeke's boots churned toward the door before the waves subsided. He almost took the latch with him through the entrance.

Greer thrashed about, throwing beads of water across the already drenched floor. His blood ran cold. She jerked in stilted motions like she was in the throes of a massive seizure. Then he saw the quiver of her upper lip, the grit of her teeth, and the glint of pure rage in her eyes.

"Greer." He barked her name, but she continued abusing the water with all the coordination of a drunkard. "Are you done acting like a child?"

Her head snapped in his direction and her limbs stilled. The flames in her gaze threatened to roast him where he stood.

"I can't walk." Drops of water speckled her face, neck, and chest. Sheets of hair stuck to her breasts and back.

"Christ. It's not permanent. You'll be pacing by lunchtime."

"I know, but have you..." She shook her head. The movement created rivulets down her body.

"Have I what?"

"No." She dismissed him with a shift of her gaze. "I know you haven't."

"Haven't what?" Why was he pushing this? It didn't matter what she said. He needed to get her better and get her back to her family. The sooner the better.

She placed a shaky hand on the edge of the tub and centered his gaze. "You've never been helpless. At someone else's mercy."

"You don't know the first thing about me." Zeke's voice rebounded off the walls of the small enclosure more forcefully than he'd expected.

Greer looked at him, really needled deep with those big blue eyes like she did sometimes. Her shoulders slumped as though he'd knocked the wind from her. It didn't last long. Her jaw shot up. "You're right. I don't because you always have the upper hand."

Right.

"And you always have a hard head. No wonder they doped you." She opened her mouth to rebut, but he stepped forward, cupped the now-cool water into his hands and dropped it on her back. The little patch of frothy bubbles disappeared along with her gusto. "Your stubbornness probably saved your life. I'm sure you put up one hell of a fight."

Zeke braced his arms under hers, but her slack jaw and wide eyes stopped him.

"Did that hurt?"

She shook almost imperceptibly, but her expression stayed the same.

His head tilted. "What?"

"It wasn't exactly a compliment, but it was the closest thing to one you've ever said to me."

"That's not true. You finished at the top of your training class, you and Coen."

"I know, but you never gave me a word of praise." Her lips closed and curled into a frown. "You patted Derrick on the back and glared at me."

Well shit. He'd noticed Greer Britton from day one. Any man between the ages of birth and death would with her doe eyes, angel hair, and hot-as-the-devil body. He'd tried not to treat her special, tried not to stare at her perky breasts that'd fit just so in his mouth, lithe legs made perfectly for wrapping around his waist, and a high, tight ass he could think of all kinds of fun uses for. In doing so, he'd still treated her special...only especially badly.

"You hungry?"

She quirked a brow, but didn't push the subject. "I think I can eat."

Zeke helped her stand, lifted her over the edge, and then set her on the edge of the tub. He grabbed a towel and started on her hair.

"So, you bathed me before?" Greer's gaze shifted to the ceiling.

"Twice." He worked his way down her back and arms. "I don't do well with the stench of vomit."

Greer muttered a string of curses.

"I'll get your legs, and then let you get your middle while I grab you some clothes."

"Okay."

After he blotted her prickly legs and tried not to stare at them or the patch of hair above her cleft, Zeke evaced to the chest of drawers next to the bed. He snatched a T-shirt and a pair of underwear, dragged in a few ragged breaths, and then returned to the battle ground.

He had plenty of experience undressing women, but he'd never dressed one before. Cripes, he hardly stayed around long enough for them to dress themselves. There was something too intimate about the way Greer tucked her polished toes into the leg holes, and even more so when he tugged them up her thighs.

His knuckles grazed her hips. Greer drew a breath and held it. His cock lengthened unabashedly. Ah. Put him out of his misery already. Zeke barricaded his lust and braced himself for close contact.

"Up you go." He wrapped one arm under Greer's and lifted.

They stood chest to chest. He slumped to keep his dick out of the equation...and to reach her knickers. No, his underwear. It helped to think of them that way. Her arms wrapped loosely around his shoulders, pressing her breasts against his pecs. The softness nearly buckled his knees and plopped them both on their arses. Damn, he should've gone top first. Not that it'd help this next part.

Zeke looped his first two fingers inside the band. Greer's shallow breath quivered along his collar bone. Her skin warmed his knuckles. He pulled them over the swell of her bottom on his right side, and then reached across her back, across the crests and valley.

When he slid up the other side Zeke wanted to toss his hands into the air like he'd seen cowboys do after roping a calf and call it good, but blast if he wasn't home free yet. He eased her back to the ledge, which was better than against him...until he couldn't look away from what had been cuddled to him.

"The shirt," Greer whispered.

"Yep." Zeke moved as though he'd been shot at. He yanked the fabric hanging from his shoulder, found the bottom, and stretched it over her head. They worked together to maneuver her arms into the holes and cover her torso and upper thighs. The room seemed to sigh with them.

He held out his hands, ready to get out of the cramped space. "You ready to try walking?"

"Yes." Greer settled her palms against his.

Zeke grit his teeth and ignored the zing, the connection. She pressed into his hold. Her set mouth cracked under the strain. A grunt rumbled in her throat. The instinct to scoop her into his arms flared. He doused it in WTF and let her struggle through.

"You're almost there. Two more inches, then lock those knees out." He heard himself cheerleading, but couldn't believe it.

Her lips turned white under the pressure of her strain. She met his gaze and straightened with a heaved sigh.

No telling why, but Zeke bit back his excitement and exchanged it for a meager nod. "We're not done yet."

"I know." Greer pulled back her shoulders and took a wobbly, defiant step forward. She took another and another until they'd left the loo and lacked only three or four strides more to the table. Her weight shifted into his hands, relying on him more and more for each step. Two away she panted. "I'm not fuzzy anymore, but I just don't have the strength."

"You don't lack strength, Greer. You just lack energy." He wrapped his arms around her middle and shifted her to the waiting chair. "Hell, you haven't eaten in days. I don't know what they fed you, but I've been lucky to get you to swallow and hold electrolytes the past three."

"Three days?"

"Here. Nine there."

He lowered her to the chair, and then stood… or tried to. She caught his forearms in a pitiful grasp. He took a knee and met her gaze. Greer's long lashes lowered to her fingers, which caressed the skin just above his wrist. She studied the bruised, raw flesh and gnarly scabs.

Her lips parted. Zeke tensed. He didn't want to talk about it, wouldn't talk about it. No point.

"Where's Raisa?" She released his arms and shifted her gaze to the plate.

For a couple of seconds his feet didn't move while his brain processed. He turned away, grabbed two glasses, filled them with water, and then sat across from her. Greer's teeth sank into a piece of toast. She reached for a glass and urged him on with a wide glare.

"If she follows my instructions, she'll be fine."

Greer took several gulps. "Where?"

"At one of my safe houses."

"Why didn't you bring her here?"

"I didn't plan to bring you here, but you couldn't tell me what I needed to know."

She tossed the crust of a toast point onto the plate. "So why even save me? Oh wait, because you wanted information. Of course."

"I saved you because you were under my command when you were taken. I kept you because I need to know what you learned about the Stas' operation and if you saw Derrick Coen at any point during your abduction or imprisonment."

Her hands covered her sob. "No. They have Derrick too."

Well, that answered that.

When he didn't answer she composed herself. "You can't find him?"

"It's more difficult to find men."

"How'd you find me?"

"They only have two gentlemen's clubs in the city. That's where they put the women young and pretty enough to make them money. The men and older women they send to their packing and transportation hubs. They're scattered across the country."

Despite the gravity of their conversation, Greer picked up a piece of bacon and bit half of it off. Self-preservation took over. A breath Zeke hadn't realized he'd been holding eased from his lungs.

"My cover sucked. I was a waitress. Sure the men talked in hushed tones, but the minute I showed up their attention shifted to other things.

Sick sons of bitches." She pointed the piece of meat at him. "The only one of us who might've learned anything valuable is missing. I mean, you were a bouncer. You couldn't have learned much."

"A list of all the compounds."

"How'd you get in the club?"

"Submitted really nice fake documents, called with a Russian number, pretended to be a member of the old-country mob, and vouched for myself. Then I brought lots of money."

"Where'd you get all the money?"

"An account."

"Whose?"

"None of your business, Lilly Rush."

"What?" The eggs she forked into her mouth stalled mid-chew.

"You mean, who?"

She swallowed. "No. I pretty much mean what the hell are you talking about?"

"You've never seen the TV show Cold Case?"

Greer guzzled the rest of her water, wiped her mouth with the back of her hand, and looked at him as though he'd beamed in from outer space. "You have?"

"I moved here last year, left all my mates back home. What else am I going to do from sundown to sunup?"

"Sleep?"

"I don't need much."

"Back on target. Where'd the money come from?"

"You mean, who is Lilly Rush?"

"Fine." She shoveled in the last of her eggs and a crumb of bacon, and then chewed once before inhaling. "Forget the money, for now. How did Derrick manage to get placed as a runner?"

"They'd trust a man more easily than a woman." Zeke stabbed his eggs. "Well, that, and as a waitress he'd have made shit for tips."

"You do have a sense of humor."

Zeke winked, added more food to her plate, and put his in the sink. "I have some work to do. You can take the bed."

"We just had breakfast."

"Dinner," he corrected.

"What?"

Standing over the desk with his back to her, he could no longer see her face, but if she could manage it now she'd have a haughty hand on her hip.

"What if I can't make it there? What if I need to go to the bathroom again?"

"Your mouth works just fine. So, you can tell me when you need help."

"How do you expect me to sleep? I've been sleeping for three days."

"Greer?"

"What?" she huffed.

"No more questions until morning." Zeke tried to keep the pleading from his voice, to make the command sharp and final.

"What are you working on?"

Tomorrow he'd get rid of her and find Derrick Coen, but there was a massive load of hours until dawn.

Chapter Five

When Greer stretched, every fiber of her being got behind the event. The nerves that had throbbed yesterday sang in praise of freedom. Each muscle yawned with contentment. Her fingers reached. Her back arched. Her toes curled.

The haze of drugs, along with the need for more, faded into the background like a bad dream. As soon as her eyes opened though, all her unanswered questions stampeded with thundering hooves.

Zach Saulter lay three feet away. He dragged a lazy arm over his eyes, and then rubbed a hand over his mouth and sturdy chin.

Greer's hand flew to her heart on a two-fold mission. One, make certain she still wore clothes. Two, keep the thudding under wraps.

"Calm down. I didn't steal your virtue."

"I wasn't—"

"Sure you were." He turned those stormy eyes on her. "But I'm the one who had to worry about having his virtue stolen."

"Hilarious." Greer turned onto her side toward him, tucked her legs to her chest, and adjusted the pillow under her head.

"What?" His lips pursed. "You think you couldn't steal it because I don't have it or because you don't have it in you to do it?" He rolled onto his side and shrugged for emphasis. The move shifted the sheet. It fell off his bare shoulder. "Because those vicious limbs could fleece the kindness of a monk. I swear you kicked me in the kidney three times and the nuts once."

She tried to follow the line of conversation, but the hump of his massive shoulders and the swell of the top of his pec made breathing difficult.

"You said the bed was mine."

"I just wanted a two-foot strip." He held his hands two feet apart indicating the distance, but he'd lost her completely.

Bubbled, peeling skin jarred her more than his beautiful physique, which was saying something because his muscles caused a tingle in muscles she didn't know she had. The burn was an irregular shape just above his nipple. Her finger automatically lifted to her mouth to cover her shock.

His gaze lowered to the maybe week-old wound, turning to a scar. When he met her gaze again the drowsiness had vanished, along with the hint of playfulness he'd revealed. The wall rose into place, high and proud.

She couldn't let it go.

"How many days?"

He'd been imprisoned by the Stas. It explained his disappearance and his injuries. But as frightening and infuriating as her captivity had been, his had been worse. Much worse. Her fingers ached to reach out to him, this man who chained his emotions in tidy bindings behind a cold visage.

The warmth in his gaze fled. Zach eased to his back.

"Please." Greer couldn't stop the plea's escape.

His jaw twitched. He drew a breath. She held her own in preparation for his answer.

Zach yanked back the sheet, revealing a wide, lean torso. His feet swung to the ground and he stood in one graceful maneuver. The jaundice of healing bruises marred his sculpted back, the powerful globes of his exposed butt, and the robust columns of his hairy legs.

Oh, Zach.

She almost sobbed the words, but managed to choke them back for ones that might not chafe so much.

"Saulter?"

He sighed and gave her his facial profile. "It's just a body, Greer. I didn't get naked to put the moves on you. I can't sleep in clothes." He shuffled to the dining table and grabbed his jeans off the back of the chair.

Greer sat, tossed the covers off her legs, and shifted onto her heels.

"I don't care about that. It's your...bruises. Your scars."

"You don't?" Calling her bluff, Zach gripped the pants in his fist and turned.

Greer double-fisted the reins on the naive part of herself that smacked a hand to her forehead and fainted, as well as the hormonal one that fell to her knees in writhing moans of worship. She kept her gaze trained on Zach's challenging gray eyes and off his fully erect manhood.

"I don't."

She should care that a man had slipped naked into bed with her. Though, it was his bed. It should teach her to get into a man's bed at all. Not that he'd done anything presumptuous.

Her chest expanded on a fortifying breath. Meaningfully, inch by inch, Greer lowered her gaze first to the scar on his chest, and then to another on his abdomen. His thickly-veined cock twitched. Her lungs screamed for release. Her lady bits tingled in response, but she refused to swallow the saliva pooling in her mouth.

She continued down his body to the cuts and bruises on his legs. If only she'd had the wherewithal to journey back up his hulking warrior body without blushing. Instead, she shifted her gaze to his. Too late she realized his gaze was locked on the front of her shirt. More accurately, the points of her nipples that tented the fabric.

"You don't?" One of his brows cocked lazily.

"I want to know how long they had you and why. I want to know what they did to you, how you managed to suffer through it, and how you escaped. I don't expect you to tell me all of it. But at least the basics."

He chuckled, causing the etched lines of his abs to contract. The hollow sound echoed through her, nearly knocking her on her ass.

"Get dressed, Greer."

"You first," she shot back.

"It bothers you." He grinned, a trite showing of teeth. "At least I know there's blood in your veins and not ice."

Anger thrashed about inside Greer's chest.

"Me? Oh, you're one to talk about ice in the veins." Her hands flexed, keeping pace with her rage. "You've never smiled or yelled or cried. Not once in seven months have you shown a true emotion. It's all for show. Even when you get mad. It's fake. You're fake."

Ooh. She hit a nerve with that one. His eyes came to life, sparking as they had the day before. Red colored his cheeks. Striations shown on the tops of his shoulders and in his arms from the strangle hold he kept on the jeans.

"*I'm* fake? You've watched me like a bloody leopard ready to pounce on my cock at the first chance, and then I find out you're a virgin."

"Well, I already knew you were an asshole. Not hard to figure out. And I didn't watch you for that." She jabbed a finger at his junk.

"You can't even say it," he laughed.

"Oh, for the love…" Greer tossed her hands into the air.

"Why'd you watch me then? I mean, if you can't even say penis, you surely wouldn't know what to do with it."

"Fuck you and your big dick." Her voice rose an octave with each word.

That hiked both his brows. "So, now you're interested?"

"I watched you because I wanted to see something real from you, something honest."

They stood there for a full minute, descending from the height of frenzy.

"Well," he sneered, "sorry to disappoint you."

"You didn't."

Zach stilled with his thumbs hooked in either side of his pants, ready to step into them.

"I saw it yesterday when I accused you of buying me for your own pleasure. You were angry… and disappointed that I'd even think you capable of it."

His jaw firmed and something passed through his undecipherable gaze. It vanished before she could get a read on it. He shoved his legs into his pants, tucked his heavy balls and beautiful penis inside, and then zipped.

"Get dressed."

"In what?" Greer gestured to her ensemble. "And why?"

"You ask more questions than any person I've ever met."

He jerked his shirt off the other chair and shoved his head inside.

"It's the only way you learn things." She collapsed onto a hip. "So, why get dressed?"

"What if I said, so I'm not tempted to fuck you?"

Heat stained her chest, but luckily the T-shirt covered it. If only she could ignore the baking of her internal organs. "I'd say you were trying to avoid my question."

"Sod it all." Zach shrugged on his holster, secured his gun and extra mags. "I'm taking you to your dad."

"My dad! Why?"

"I have things to do and I can't babysit you any longer."

"I don't need you to." Greer scuttled to the edge of the bed, stood—thanked God she could finally—and jumped up and down to prove her point. "I need you to help me figure out why I was taken in the first place."

"Your dad can do that. He's powerful enough."

She stiffened. The entire United States knew her family. They saw her dad daily on the house floor and her uncle exiting Air Force One. But most people didn't know they were her family. As a security measure and memorial to her late mother, on her thirteenth birthday, Greer had taken her mother's maiden name.

"How do you know that?"

"It's my job to know."

"No one at US Elite knows."

"I know." He pointed at the dresser to her left. "Clothes are in the bottom drawer. They won't be great, but they'll fit."

Greer crossed her arms over her chest. "I'm not going."

"Why not?"

"I already told you. I want to know why I was taken."

"There's an old British proverb." Zach slid a long fixed blade into its sheath on his left side. "It goes something like...you don't have to go home, but you can't stay here." He tapped a finger on the tip of his lips. "Yep, that's it."

"I'm going with you to find Derrick."

"No, you're not. You're too skinny. You can hardly hold your own weight."

Greer's ire frothed again. "You're not my boss anymore."

Zach stepped forward. "No. But I'm bigger than you and in this world that's all that counts."

When he took another step in her direction Greer clenched her teeth and lifted her chin. "I'm not going."

"You can stay."

After all that it couldn't be that easy. Nothing with Zach Saulter was easy. "I can stay, if..."

Lids narrowed around his turbulent eyes. "Tell me why you really don't want to go home?"

Greer's arms fell at her sides. He saw through her, at least as well as she saw through him. Enough to know that there was more to the story.

"I don't want my dad to know I was taken. That I was put on the market to the highest bidder."

"It wasn't your fault."

"It wasn't his, but he'll feel that way."

"Why?"

"He's my dad."

Zach tightened his stare. “The truth this time.”

“Because he recommended me to US Elite.”

Chapter Six

Zeke had a crap ton of things to do and not one of them included chopping fire wood. For cripes sake, the sun beat down hot enough to sear his back and shoulders, and he wouldn't be here when the season came to use the split logs. But it was either plow logs or Greer mother-fucking Britton. With each swing of the axe sweat spattered the splitting stump like shrapnel. Pretty soon he wouldn't have any perspiration left. He hadn't grabbed a canteen or even his laptop when he'd stormed out four hours ago. An hour in he'd found out the hose water tasted more like metal than water. At least his computer had a password from prying eyes.

When his vision tunneled an hour later—with no better idea for how to get rid of Greer or find Coen in the pile of compounds—he dropped the axe and headed inside for a cold arse shower. He'd challenged her, tried to cow her into submission with his body. Boy, had that backfired. She hadn't turned away. She'd met him boot to boot, so to speak, and dressed him down as though he'd been fully clothed.

He'd never been so rock hard in his entire, sordid life. He'd never been so near taking what he wanted, consequences be damned.

Calculate the repercussions. Minimize them. That was his job. Only when he stood too close to Greer she dulled the ramifications of his actions to background noise.

Despite her innocent eyes, Greer saw more than most. She knew he hid things. If she knew half of what he beat into his closet every morning, she'd have fled when she had the chance. Seeing exactly what she did to him should've made her run. Her stubborn little feet hadn't moved.

Zeke secured the barn door, smiled at his car parked in the far corner—see, he smiled—and then climbed the stairs to his safe house, which didn't feel quite so safe with Greer here.

At the sound of clanking glass his senses prickled. What was she up to now? Probably rigging a booby trap or looking for tools to hot-wire the car. He ascended the last three steps more slowly. His head stayed on a swivel, ready for her attack. Only he wasn't quite so ready. This woman's booby trap outdid all the scenarios he'd conjured.

Greer stood on her tiptoes. Her left arm gripped the edge of an open cabinet, while the other reached the top shelf. The hem of her shirt caught at the ample swell of her bottom. His black boxer-briefs clung, exposing every dip and curve. She stretched and grunted from the effort. Her finger grazed a drinking glass and pushed it farther into the recesses.

He definitely should have sent her packing. His feet carried him into the kitchen, while better judgment urged him back to the chopping block.

"Oh, hey."

She whipped around with her hand over her heart like she had many times in the past day and a half. Like he scared the shit out of her. That couldn't be right though. She stood up to him when grown men and wiser women had doubled down on retreat.

"What are you doing?" he snapped. *Ever the charmer.*

Onions, spinach, carrots, mushrooms, and chicken littered the counter, along with pots and pans, cutting boards, and a big-arse knife.

Huh?

"Cooking lunch." Her nose scrunched. "Dinner really. It's almost four p.m. I mean, only old people eat this late, but since you didn't have breakfast or lunch..." She bobbed her tiny shoulders and swatted a strand of white blonde hair from her brow. "I just figured you were hungry. I am, and I ate breakfast." Her fingers toyed with the hem of her shirt. "I ate some lunch too. I didn't know when you'd come back. Or if you'd come back at all."

"You're rambling."

"I know. I felt bad for running you out of your own home."

"It's not my home."

"You know what I meant." Her hands bracketed her hips. There was the gusto.

"You felt bad?"

"Yes."

"Bad enough to leave?"

Her pretty pink mouth formed a thin line.

"Guess not." He nodded to the cabinet. "And there?"

"Oh, I can't reach the glasses."

Greer gave him a doe-eyed, please-help expression that looked totally out of place on her usually determined features.

Zeke stepped back, grabbed the back of the dining chair, and dragged it between them. "Problem solved."

She flashed him a crooked smile and hopped onto the chair. Too late he realized her round bottom would be within biting distance. Damn her, but she still had to stretch to grasp a glass in each hand. His extra-large shirt flagged with the movement, giving him a clear peek of her abdomen.

Still on the chair, she turned with both glasses hugged between her breasts and stared down at him. “Thanks. You go get cleaned up and dinner will be ready soon.”

“What are you up to?”

Her head canted. The shorter strands of her hair fell over her forehead. “Are you always this hesitant when someone does something for you?”

“Yes.”

“No surprise there.” She hopped off the chair and hurried around him to the sink.

Zeke’s gaze followed her. She filled one of the glasses and then extended it to him. He stared at it for a long time.

Greer put the cup to her lips and took a hefty sip. “It’s not poisoned.” She grabbed his hand and put it in his palm.

“I can get my own drink.”

“Good for you. Can you wash your own ass?”

His eyebrows rose on that one.

“Well?” Her hand flipped palm-up in question.

“I can.” His gut burned, but he couldn’t decide if it was with annoyance or amusement.

“Good. Go do it. You stink.” She fanned the air between them and crinkled her nose.

“Fine, woman. But I’m locking the door.”

“I’ve already seen you naked.” A smirk skewed her pretty mouth. “Get over yourself.”

“Tossing my words back at me. Cute.”

Her mouth formed an O and she covered it with her flitty hand. “Cute? Was that a compliment?”

Zeke turned away and stalked to the bathroom. He deflected. It’s what he did. The coping mechanism had gotten him through some dire shit. Yet somehow, Greer penetrated that shield. That revelation and the chilly water kept his dick at bay during his shower. He liked puzzles, was good at them, really good, but this one required more hands-on manipulation to figure out. A bad thing for them both.

When the cold reached the marrow of his bones Zeke cut the water and grabbed a towel.

“Hey?” A thin knock on the door followed the reedy, feminine voice. It obliterated the numbness he’d worked so hard to attain.

“What?”

“Your clothes.”

Zeke looked at his damp body, and then at the door. He’d never lived with anyone, not since childhood anyway. He’d never had to account for nudity.

“What about them?”

“I brought you some...so you don’t have to traipse through here in your towel to get them.”

He scrubbed the towel over his head and face on his way to the door. The lock *snicked* under his hand and the door swung wide. Greer jumped. Again her hand clutched her heart, only this time a neat stack of his clothes lay between them.

“Who said I’d use a towel?” His hung in front of the goods. By the look on her face no one would know it.

Greer launched the stack at him like a javelin. They bounced off his wet chest. He caught a pair of pants. The underwear and shirt plopped to the ground.

"I was trying to help." She yanked the knob from his grasp. The door rattled against the frame.

Zeke wiped the grin off his face. Why was disarming bombs, hand-to-hand combat, leaping from airplanes, and tormenting Greer Britton so much fun? A shrink might have an answer, but it wouldn't be the right one.

He dried, dressed, and left the bathroom, heading for his desk. The dining table arranged with two settings and a full spread pulled him up. Greer's expectant gaze nailed his bare feet to the floor. She stood between the table and kitchen counter with her hands folded meekly in front of her—his—oil splattered, food-stained T-shirt.

"Salad. Sautéed chicken and vegetables. And an apple crisp for dessert." She gestured to the table.

His stomach grumbled, but his intuition howled louder.

"What are you up to, Greer?"

"Helping out."

"You keep saying that."

"Because it's the truth."

"But are your reasons altruistic?" Zeke shook his head.

"Whose ever are?" Her arms went wide.

"Fair point."

Bull's eye. He'd saved her, but only to spare his conscience—which already had plenty to deal with—and to cull information.

Reluctantly, Zeke sat. He waited for Greer to do the same before picking up the utensils she'd ordered on a precisely folded napkin. They ate in silence. She cut little bits off the hunk of meat and pulled the tender morsel from her fork with her lips. She blotted her mouth. She sipped from the glass. The difference between Greer Britton on the training grounds and the woman before him made chewing difficult.

"You said your dad recommended you for US Elite, but why the military to begin with?" She opened her mouth, but he couldn't hold back any longer. "A woman like you has no place in the military."

Greer dropped her fork and knife. They clattered onto her plate. "Really? Well, just get it off your chest. Tell me how you honestly feel, then maybe I'll get to the heart of your scornful—"

"It has nothing to do with your ability as a soldier."

That quieted her tirade, but did little to dull the resentment in her blue gaze.

"You performed better than 97 percent of the men who applied for Elite's top ops."

"But?"

"But Elite is 98 Percent male. Male soldiers. Male trainers. Male officers. The military is at, what, 85 percent these days? You have no business being surrounded by a horde of battle ready, horny bastards months away from their last proper lay, and miles away from the families and responsibilities that separate them from base instincts."

Zeke shoved away his plate. "If Chad had been your trainer at Elite, things would've been bad for you." Just speaking the man's moniker raised his hackles.

"Worse than getting abducted by the Stas, drugged, and sold to the highest bidder?"

"Much worse." That son of a whore had collected bids on who would bag Greer first. Fifteen men brazenly scrawled their names on the dry erase board in the men's locker room, while the rest dropped green. By bag, they didn't mean have sex with. They meant blind her with a black bag, constrict the cord so tight that it almost strangled her, while he—the winner—raped her.

Maybe she saw the rage in his eyes. Maybe she figured out that the rumors were true. Either way, the taut line of her mouth relaxed.

"I always wondered how a man trained as well as Chad could shoot himself in the leg while cleaning his sidearm." Her breaths stabilized. She caressed her narrow throat. "Thank you."

Warring emotions coursed through Zeke's veins. Veins that normally felt little except the adrenaline of battle quaked under the offensive her words and her manners provoked. He wanted to throttle her and kiss her, hold her and run for the hills, all at once.

"I have work to do," he said.

Zeke didn't flee the barn, but in short order he put the room and desk between them. Wisely she didn't follow. The chaos of the kitchen kept her busy for a while. Long enough for him to get lost in the maze of information at his fingertips.

During his days as a bouncer he'd hacked into the Stas database under the guise of reviewing security footage to look for a thief. The information didn't do him a lick of good without the key. His hope had been that Greer would have that and more information from her time undercover. After all, she'd...

She walked out of the loo with a towel wrapped around her head and wearing the sleep clothes he'd bought for her before he'd gone to the club to extract her. He popped the top onto the highlighter, immediately pushed it up with his thumb, and snapped it again, in a ritual he hadn't been aware he'd undertaken. Why he'd bought her spaghetti strapped camisoles and tiny cotton shorts he didn't know, but he could castrate himself for it. His suddenly tight jeans might just save him the effort. He dropped the marker and folded his hands together.

The noise drew Greer's attention. "Always with you and those looks." She scoffed and continued on toward the bed. "What now?"

"You made nice with the head of security at Sable."

"And?"

"I find it hard to believe you two spent so many hours in the control room not screwing and you still managed not to get any information from the deal. You must give marathon blow jobs."

"And you must be the biggest asshole I've ever met." Greer yanked the towel off her head and tossed it onto the pillow he'd used the night before.

"So what did you two do in there?"

She muffled a scream with both hands. When the noise died her fingers spread wide. Her palms lifted to the sky as if evoking the powers that be to either strike him down or give her strength. Finally her clear gaze found his.

"We talked."

"He's a fifty-year-old bald Russian. What did you have to talk about?"

"I know it's hard for you to understand, but some people talk to hear the sound of their own voice. Yep." She nodded. "Shocking, I know. Some people even talk to work through a problem."

"Did Buzzy?"

"His wife of thirty-two years found out who he worked for. She threatened to leave him and move to California to be near their daughter if he didn't get out. Buzzy knew they'd never let him leave, not alive anyway."

"So why didn't you help him?"

She waggled a finger at him and grinned. "This you'll get. It took me three weeks of just talking about nothing, inane things, to get him to trust me enough to open up." The finger stopped its back and forth. "Nope, take it back. You wouldn't know about that last part."

"And then Buzzy and his friends delivered you to the gentlemen's club."

"No. He wasn't with the guys that...dragged me from my bed. I was about to broach the subject of helping him leave when I was taken."

Greer walked to the desk and fiddled with dog-eared edges of plans for the club where she'd been held. "When I was taken, I wondered if they'd heard our conversations. Mine and Buzzy's. I wondered if..."

"He's fine. I looked him up."

"You did?"

"He has the system key."

"Not much good it would do without the database." Greer sighed.

Zeke turned the screen overloaded with open windows to face her.

"Oh."

"Yeah." He pulled the laptop back around, enlarged a screen from the ten or so across the bottom, and committed the address to memory.

Before he could stop her, Greer skirted the desk. "No." Her yell shook the screen. She leaned over him and reached for the computer.

His hands shot out and encircled her wrists. "Don't."

Her wide blue gaze left Buzzy Loren's address and met his stare. "You can't bring him into this."

"He's already in this. He's the bad guy, Greer."

"He's not a bad guy. He—"

"He's killed people. He's a bad guy."

"You've killed people." She didn't try to escape, but instead pressed into his hold.

"I never said I was a good guy." On the contrary. Right this second the only thing he could think about was pulling her onto his lap, burying his hands in her hair, and kissing her mute, ripping the knickers off her bottom, and ramming himself home again and again until she found her voice in the throes of orgasm.

"But you are."

"Am I?" Zeke let his gaze rake her bent legs, her hips, her torso, her breasts.

"You are."

"Not hardly, but I'm good enough that I'll give you the chance to stop right here and walk away."

Her too-proud chin jutted. "When I have a mission I don't stop."

Zeke stood to get the thought of her legs around his waist from his mind. He pulled her arms wide and pressed his chest over her, trying his best to daunt her. His voice dropped a thick octave.

"Is your mission to get good and fucked on this desk tonight?"

Pink lips parted, but she suppressed the gasp. Her gaze sliced to the desk, and then back to him. The black of her pupils trampled onto her innocent blue irises.

Fuck.

He needed her to screech at his crude words, not stand her ground.

"That's not going to work on me, Saulter."

"It's not a bloody tactic." Zeke shoved her left hand against his throbbing erection. He held her wrist in a vice grip, ready to remove it if she latched on in anger.

Greer didn't move. She didn't clamp down. She didn't shrink back.

"If we're going to find Derrick, if we're going to get answers, you have to let me in just a little," she breathed.

"Are you going to let me in first?"

"Yes, but not in the way you want… or the way you think you want."

She lifted her hand from his crotch. Zeke released her, but her tiny hand encircled his wrist and guided him toward her chest. Her heart thumped under his fingers. He just stared at her, unable to speak or think.

"You see, I say I'm a virgin, but my cousin raped me when I was twelve."

Zeke jerked as though she'd socked him in the jaw. Something earthy and raw fought for life inside his chest. It burned hotter than the oils they'd poured on his chest. It seared deeper than the fire that had licked his bubbled skin and charred his nerve endings.

"Why are you telling me this?" His hoarse rumble hardly formed a coherent sentence.

"I'm giving you a very secret, very personal part of me."

Conflicting emotions battled inside him. On one side retreat sounded the only route for survival. On the other, invasion lit the only path for redemption.

"In hopes that I'll help you?" he whispered.

"Or maybe that you'll see sharing is cathartic. Or maybe in hopes that you'll trust me."

"Trust isn't easily earned." And habits weren't easily broken.

"I know." She gave a hollow chuckle. "I think with you it's never earned."

There was a hell of a lot of truth in that. But wait... "You said your cousin raped you, as in your cousin the president's son?"

Chapter Seven

Greer may as well have sliced her heart open and let the blood trickle out one drop at a time. She didn't talk about this, not with anyone, but nothing short of an equally grand gesture would get Zach on her side.

"Yes." She whispered the word to keep the bile churning in her gut from erupting.

"Then..." The striated muscles in his jaw danced. "How did the Stas think you were..."

And it could get worse.

The heat drained from her face. Her extremities grew numb like the drugs plunged into her vein again. The answer lodged itself in her windpipe. Sheer will forced it out one rusty word at a time.

"He didn't choose the path that would get me pregnant."

Zach's hand lifted from her chest. The trickle turned into a waterfall. His hands latched onto his dark hair, straining the roots. He drifted from her on slow backward steps, and then turned and retreated to the large window. The grips on his head eased from his hair. He braced a hand on the edge of the wall.

Tears stung her eyes. Color and heat continued to siphon away. She wanted to run to the bathroom and lock herself inside or hide under the covers, but what good would that do? This confession, the first and only one she'd given—until tonight—couldn't go any worse.

Muscles strained the back of his shirt. They bunched with each bullish exhale. His head started on a slow back and forth that gained speed. His palm snapped out, smacking the frame. The panes rattled.

Greer's skeleton jumped. She held her ground. There was no place to go. When she'd joined US Elite she'd sublet her apartment in DC and placed all her things in storage. Besides, she wouldn't leave her partner in the enemy's hands.

"You joined the military to protect yourself."

Zach had turned. His growled statement washed over her and seeped into her soul.

Was that the reason she'd joined? It had been a perk. A major perk.

"Joining the Marines was a family tradition all the way back to my great-great-grandfather Gunner Boone Stockton, senior. All except my father were highly decorated."

"Did you tell your father?"

For the first time, she couldn't look at him. Her chin drifted left. Out the other small window the sun slipped behind the trees, turning the sky as dark as her memories of that day. Not of the act. Not of the horrible pain of grunted thrusts. But of seeing her own father's face darken with rage...at her.

She'd done everything right. She'd said no. She'd tried to fight. She'd screamed. She hadn't showered after. She told a trusted adult. He'd made her feel responsible. He'd shoved her into the shower and demanded she remove her shame and never speak of it again. He'd ruined her more than Greeson had.

Zach's gentle grip on her chin turned her to face him. "Did you tell your father?"

"Yes."

The lightning in his cloudy eyes could only compare with a tempest rolling in off the shore. Rage billowed off him in silent waves that decimated the banks.

"And he didn't do a fucking thing."

"A scandal would have killed my uncle's road to the White House. And I..." Greer hauled in a breath.

"You what?"

"Tempted him with my revealing swimsuit."

His grip on her chin tightened. Every finger made its own impression. His gaze narrowed.

"You tempt me in full gear and a gun strapped across your chest. You tempt me naked and vulnerable and every which way in between. You have no idea." He ground the words between his teeth. "But that doesn't matter. No amount of undress, no amount of spread legs and bare pussy gives anyone a right to violate someone. No invitation, no fucking way."

He lightened his grip incrementally, and then brushed away the marks before releasing her. Neither of them moved.

"What about your mother, did she know?"

"She died when I was a baby."

Zach nodded ever so slightly.

"I told you something. Now tell me, how did you have enough money to buy me and Raisa?"

"No."

The refusal deepened the cut in Greer's exposed heart, but it told her something too. He'd been deeply hurt. Was that what turned him into a bad guy? Zach said he was bad. Perhaps he was on the wrong side of a line. Maybe he took money for favors, bad favors. He certainly had the crass, cold manner for it. And yet, at the heart of this brutish, beautiful man hid a protective and just soul.

"Now that we've got that out of the way, will you let me get back to it?" He stepped away from her, straightened the chair, and yanked on the belt of his pants before sitting.

"You plan to stare at the screen all night in hopes that you catch a pattern you haven't over the past three days?"

"I had a better idea. You didn't appreciate it."

"You had an idea. Not a better one."

Zach braced his palms on the desk, hissed a breath, and glared at her. "Do you have a better idea?"

"Yeah, I do."

Chapter Eight

They ghosted through the shadows outside an abandoned warehouse complex that hosted too many delivery trucks and too much off-grid wattage to really maintain its deserted status. With no more than a half nod they split up as they'd planned. Well, he'd planned for her to stay at the barn, but logistics swung things in Greer's favor. Her camo-clad form disappeared around the corner and he suppressed the urge to follow. The drug's major effects had waned two days ago. She could handle herself.

Zeke sidled to the building's brick face, leapt, and pulled himself onto the fire escape. He hustled up the brittle steps of the southern exterior wall, scanning the dark surroundings and even dimmer interior through the grey matte of an infrared monocular. His shoulder pressed against the butt of his rifle, while his left hand cradled the barrel.

Just beyond the defunct chemical company's fortified fences, gleaming glass high-rises partitioned into luxury condos in various stages of completion speckled the horizon. The occasional car rumbled past, but never closer than four blocks away. Construction ran during the day, which left the Stas the perfect opportunity to package and ship their illegal wares in the cover of night.

Rounding the third floor Zeke stopped. His heart beat oxygenated blood through his veins. Two round eyeballs stared back, unblinking. His right hand drew the rifle to ready. A carnival-character smile graced the painting's otherwise naturally painted face. Beyond the propped canvas, brushes and old paint cans cluttered the space. A couch missing three seat cushions and the stuffing from the center's back squatted in the corner.

"In position. Two low." Greer's voice cracked through the comm link in his ear.

"Copy."

He continued, encountering a room that doubled as a crack house at some point and a rather neatly arranged space that may have sheltered a family. Graffiti coated the building's roof. It added a little something to the desolate space. His boots whispered across the artwork and headed to the elevator shaft that crowned the building with a copper top and ornamental spires. The architecture provided easy footholds onto the weathered metal.

Zeke lowered his chest to the eagle's nest, eased his elbow over the roof's crest, spread his feet, arches down, and settled into position five stories high in the breezy Long Island night. He ignored the panoramic view of distant New York City and the shimmer of the few visible stars. Why look there when what the row of windows at the top of the adjacent building revealed was so much more interesting?

"In position and locating."

Shipping crates lined the far wall. Two assembly lines split the remaining area. Open boxes sat at each end and at stations in between. Gunmetal black pieces assorted in different sizes and shapes filled them. Bedraggled men and women stood along the line, adding essential parts to AK-103s.

Derrick Coen leaned against an orange shipping container.

How the hell she'd found him, Zeke hadn't a clue. She'd shooed him away from the computer last night and started clacking away on the keys. Greer didn't think she had any of his trust, but it had taken an inordinate amount of the stuff to keep him from snatching away the laptop. She could've kited an SOS to anyone. In the six hours it had taken her to complete the task a SWAT team could've descended on the place and he would've been SOL.

The openness of her confession, in her safeguarding Buzzy, of her determination to find Coen had kept him at bay. That and she'd finally told him she'd coaxed Buzzy's password from him before she'd been taken.

A day, nearly 200 miles, and a trunk load of weapons later his patience and confidence in Greer paid off.

A man with a rifle across his chest gestured wildly at Coen. Zeke couldn't see the guard's mouth, but he bet it gaped wide enough to invite a fly inside. Coen's head hung, studying the clipboard in his hands.

Another guard paroled the line, while two more ambled back and forth on a narrow catwalk thirty or so feet in the air. All of them carried the mark of the Stas visible on the hallow where their clavicles met. The very tip of a cupola cross peeked out from behind the shirt that often hid elaborate tattoos of the Kremlin.

Zeke's lips parted to confirm Coen's location, but the bloke's expression stopped him. His lazy stance and cocked brow read irritated more than scared. And why wasn't he on the line? The guy had organizational skill, but something about the scene trampled up Zeke's spine and left ice in its tracks.

The guard shimmied in rage once more. Coen held up one finger and pointed to a flat of crates against the south wall. The guard turned, yelled at a man at the end of the nearest line. The assembly worker grabbed two rifles from the people around him, stuffed them into his crate, and closed the lid.

A modern ice age started in Zeke's veins and flowed outward.

"Located?" Greer begged, but her words drifted into the background.

He stared at the seal on the top of the crate. He'd have missed it from the ground or north wall. At this distance the stamps on the pile of crates looked like a Rorschach blot. But this one...

They heaped completed weapons into crates stamped with the US Elite seal.

"Z? Located?" Greer snapped.

That pulled him back from the edge. Only his sister called him Z.

"Two low in. Two high. Target located, quadrant one."

"Ready to move," she chirped.

"On my mark."

Now, more than ever, Zeke needed this to go off without a hitch. He fished the detonator from the front of his vest and depressed the button. A boom echoed through the complex, but he'd rigged it for effect more than destruction. The northeast door buckled, drawing the guard's barrels.

Screams seeped through the walls and rose into the night. Workers ran. Metal parts bounced across the concrete.

"One and two down," Greer said.

"Sea of workers headed your way."

"Target in them?"

Zeke pocketed the device and found Coen in his scope. He crouched next to the container. His gaze swung left and right, low and high. The chap's brown eyes centered Zeke's sights.

"No."

"I'm going in."

"Negative." Zeke growled.

Something wasn't right.

He swung the barrel to the left. Greer bulldozed her way upstream through the crowd. She looked like a pebble in a raging river. Somehow she burst onto shore, her cheeks red. Her mouth opened, forming Derrick's name.

Coen shoved himself away from the container. His hands lifted palm up. He waved Greer away. Stubbornly, she charged forward.

Zeke swept the warehouse. Three of the guards had vanished out the door. The fourth sprinted in Greer's direction. He yanked the deadly point of his gun around from the blown door.

"Bogey, quad six." Zeke shouted in the quietest voice he could manage.

Greer sank her fingers onto Coen's sleeve and hurdled him around the open end of the container. But she wouldn't make it in time.

Zeke focused his crosshairs on the guard's temple. His fingers found the trigger with ease.

The world shook. He lost sight of his target. He lost sight of Greer. Night took hold. The bite of metal and blood filled Zeke's mouth.

A string of shots roused him from the depths. *Greer.* Zeke struggled to his elbows to find his rifle and Greer. Weight planted itself against his kidney and pressed.

"Who are you?" The bur of a Russian accent swam in his ear.

His reply came out as an incoherent mumble.

"What?" A hand pressed against his collar and rolled him.

One of the guards from the warehouse leaned close, assessing the amount of weapons strapped to his body. "Alexi Basov," Zeke wheezed.

Shock widened the man's features. He straightened just enough.

Zeke kicked out, aiming for the knee cap though he couldn't see it. The man's howl reverberated at what seemed a distance. He rolled to the side. The boot that had crushed his kidney disappeared over the side of the building.

He sat, scanned the empty roof, grabbed his rifle, and turned back to the warehouse. His heart lodged firmly in his throat.

The splat-crunch punctuated the end of a life.

Left to right, Zeke scanned. No bodies littered the warehouse floor. Footfalls pounded up the building's north end fire escape. He righted his brains with a shake, wiped the blood and grime from his lip, slid off the elevator shaft roof, and ran for the south escape.

He gripped the rails and lifted his feet. Gravity did the rest until each landing. A spray of bullets pinged off the metal barrier between him and the Stas guards. His cheeks puckered, but he didn't stop.

Zeke tossed himself through a window and into the painter's lair. He rolled to his feet and pressed on toward the interior stairs. The farther he moved into the building the dimmer it grew. His monocular read like a cracked cell phone screen. A regular ol' flashlight guided him through the trash laden stairwell and to the main entrance.

"Greer?" Zeke whispered into the comm link.

When several precious seconds passed without an answer he hunched and bolted for the car four blocks away. He expected to dodge bullets again, but none rained.

The longer he ran with no answer from Greer the harder breathing became.

"Greer?"

Where the fuck was she?

"Greer?"

"Shut up and move." She nearly plowed over him around a blind corner. Coen's legs pumped just behind her.

"Are you hurt?"

"No." Greer snapped like a crocodile. "You are."

"Na."

"Oh, I'm great. Thanks for asking," Coen panted.

They pushed ahead on seasoned legs, falling into a fast even pace, covering ample ground. But not ample enough. Tires squealed behind them.

Zeke bailed left into an alley and pulled Greer with him. Several long strides in, his gaze deadened into a brick wall. His gaze shifted, looking for a way out. They collectively slowed. The roar of the approaching engine grew.

"Fish in a barrel." Coen danced on the balls of his feet.

He refrained from telling the bloke to sod off, mainly because his attention locked on an alcove a few feet away. Zeke shifted the rifle onto his back. "There."

They crowded into the shallow space and stilled.

The rumble reached a pinnacle. Greer's hand moved to her sidearm, while Zeke tried the door knob. It didn't budge. He pulled a multi-tool from his belt and worked blindly on the lock.

When the engine revved on down the street Zeke, turned, worked the mechanism, and opened the door.

"They left." Coen tossed his arms wide and cocked his wrists in question.

Greer followed him into the back of a furniture manufacturer based on the amount of wood, fabric, and stuffing cluttering the place.

When Coen stepped inside Zeke launched himself at the man. He double fisted his collar, yanked him forward, planted his feet, and popped his hip. Coen grabbed Zeke's wrists, but hit the floor before he could do anything.

"What are you doing?" Greer shrieked.

Zeke smashed his forearm into Coen's throat, pinned his legs with his own, and jerked down his shirt. Bright colors and the elaborate design of the Kremlin's tallest cupola decorated the center of his chest. The black outline continued under the fabric.

"No." Greer stepped back and covered her shock with a hand.

"It's not what you think," Coen choked.

"Never is, is it?" Zeke patted him down expecting to find a wire or at the very least a gun. He found a cell phone, which looked almost as bad. He tossed it to Greer.

She removed the battery and smashed the device into splintered pieces.

"Why weren't you on the line?" Zeke hopped to his feet and put himself between Greer and Coen.

The ponce hacked and sputtered. He rolled onto his side and wheezed breaths with his cheek against the sawdust covered floor. Finally he clambered to his hands and knees.

"I had an in with them." His head lifted. That murky gaze found Zeke, and then Greer. "Before you started disappearing like planes in the Bermuda." He patted his chest. "They trusted me, but when you two came into question I did too bec —"

"Because we all started about the same time." Greer supplied.

"Don't." Zeke shot her a warning glare.

She glared back.

"Yes. Two weeks wasn't enough lag time between our starting for them not to get suspicious," Coen answered.

"How'd they—" she started.

"Greer," Zeke yelled.

"Then ask some damn questions." Her arms knotted across her middle.

"I will when he finishes answering the first one," he explained.

"They asked me if I was loyal to Stas. If I was willing to prove it," Coen continued.

"What made them suspicious in the first place?" Zeke demanded.

Coen lifted a palm. "I don't know. I asked. They told me to mind my own business or I'd join you."

"Did you prove your loyalty by selling us out?" Greer snarled.

"No." Coen looked at Greer a little too long for Zeke's piece of mind. Zeke stepped closer, commanding his attention. "I got a stupid tattoo and they let me run the floor. I just drove a delivery truck before."

Zeke's lifted a brow. "So you weren't held against your will?"

"I was, but I was told it was for my own good, for the good of the brotherhood." He braced a hand on the wall behind him and stood.

"The Stas would have to kill me before they tattooed that shit on my skin. And corpses weren't worth tattooing." Zeke searched Coen's face for a reaction.

A twinge of a smile played on his lips. "I guess I value my life more than you do yours."

"We'll see about that. Why'd you look straight into my scope?" Zeke demanded.

His gaze rose to the warehouse rafters, and then settled on Zeke. "It's the best vantage point for an invasion. I was trying to warn you, or whoever created the explosion that they were coming."

"It could have been a rival gang." Greer gasped.

She apparently found it impossible to keep her mouth closed. He'd like to put something between her lips to keep them busy, but that wouldn't happen...not ever. Not after what her own flesh and blood had done to her.

"Their bomb would have killed people. Yours didn't." Coen pointed at Zeke.

"He has valid answers." Greer tugged on his sleeve. "Can we go now?"

The bloke had all the right answers, yet another reason Zeke didn't trust him. Derrick Coen was an opportunist. When he was honorably discharged for extremely dishonorable conduct he ran to US Elite. When US Elite left him in the lurch he ran into the Stas's open arms. In short, he pledged loyalty to whoever kept him alive. Frivolous loyalty damaged more than an outright enemy.

Light filled the alleyway. The glow filtered in through the door no one had bothered to close. A car door slammed close enough that none of them dared whisper.

Zeke signaled for Greer to head for the car. She jogged on silent feet through the unfinished sofas and chairs, but stalled at large double doors. Her eyes and waving hand ushered them to follow. Coen did. Again Zeke signaled her to leave. Before waiting to see if she obeyed, he eased the door to its frame, secured the lock, and pressed his eye to the peep hole.

Two seconds passed. A guard with a rifle in his hands prowled into view. He stopped at the alcove and hiked the gun against the front of his shoulder. One tedious step at a time the Stas allegiant approached. Zeke snugged the barrel of his Glock to the door and breathed, slowly, steadily.

The knob wiggled under the guard's hand. When it didn't open he straightened and turned to leave. His steps halted. He pivoted back to the door. The oval shape of his faced elongated as it neared, taking him from arsehole to alien. He edged his eye to the peep hole for an eight count.

He backed out of the alcove, tossed his hands up, probably to the driver, and hollered a negative that hardly made it through the heavy door. Zeke hurried through the maze of furniture with little more than filtered moonlight to discern the path. The front door on the north side had been propped open. He ducked through it and sprinted across the street to the parking garage where he'd left his car, to where Greer waited with Coen...alone.

When he reached the well-lit structure he slowed to a casual walk. His heart hiked in his chest more now than it had when he'd been in danger of having an AK-103 pierce his belly button. Cars filled the lot near capacity, but no one idled about at one a.m. Not if they knew what was good for them.

Zeke took the north stairs, opposite the plant. He wanted to observe Coen from a distance. As expected Greer watched the south stairs, between her pacing the width of his car. She pinched her lower lip with her thumb and forefinger and swayed with each change in direction. The corners of Zeke's mouth pitched skyward at her manic concern for him. He had to remind himself to watch the one he'd come to see.

Coen watched the door, but his gaze lingered on Greer far more. Whether on her shapely hips or the Glock holstered at her side he couldn't tell. Though, neither sat well.

"Greer?" Coen said.

It jerked her attention from the door and stalled her pacing. "Yeah?"

The bastard closed the distance between them and cupped her pale cheeks. "I thought you were dead or worse."

To hell with observing. Zeke moved from behind the truck he'd used for cover and walked toward them.

"I thought you were too." Greer cupped his hands. Zeke's chest constricted. She pulled his hands from her face and released them. The bands loosened.

"I was." She smiled. "But Zach saved me."

Fuck, he hated hearing her call him by a name that wasn't his own. He hated more that he couldn't do a damn thing to change it.

"Oh? Zach is it? I thought he was Captain Saulter?" Coen's bushy brows hooded his eyes.

"He was until he saved me."

"Well, thank you for saving me." Coen's hand lifted toward her face once more.

"She removed your hands from her body once. If they have to be removed again, they'll no longer be attached to your body. Clear?"

Both of them spun to his voice. Greer did the chest grab thing he'd come to enjoy. Derrick did a slack jaw, eye-roll thing he liked too.

He recovered quickly and tossed up double peace signs. "I was just saying thank you for saving me."

Zeke advanced until his boots hit the other man's sneakers and patted his own cheeks. "You want to cup my face too?"

"Nah. But thank you." Coen spread his arms wide. "Really."

"Can you two kiss and make up later? I'd like to get out of here." Greer tried stepping between them, but settled for standing on her tiptoes and staring from one to the other.

"Greer, back seat. Coen, front."

They both fell in without a word. Zeke closed the rifles into the trunk and hopped behind the wheel. They drove in silence through Long Island. As they sped through Queens, Greer stiffened just as she had on the way to the Stas held warehouse.

When they reached the outskirts of Hackensack Zeke pulled the car to the side of the road. He tugged two stacks of cash from a pocket and handed one to Coen. He held the other out to Greer.

"Go. Let your families know you're safe, but don't go home. Hide for a while. I'll get to the bottom of this as fast as I can."

Greer jerked the money from his fingers and offered it to Coen. "I'm finishing this. You should go."

Zeke opened his mouth to protest, but her fingers gripped his bare forearm. The touch alone weakened him.

"Please," she begged, "I need answers."

"I'll happily keep the money, but if she's staying," Derrick winked at Greer, "I'm staying."

Chapter Nine

"So you've been hiding out all this time." Derrick's head swiveled, taking in the large barn and the haunting hickory trees that danced in the dark on an invisible breeze. "You leave us without so much as a heads up. You draw all kinds of suspicion down on me and Greer, so you could what, commune with nature?"

"He hasn't been—"

Zach's gaze caught hers. Just the corner of his eye and a shake of his head and the explanation died on her lips. The double barn doors opened automatically. This place was more high tech than she'd originally assumed.

"I don't get to know why I was abducted, why my captain abandoned me, abandoned *us*, on our first mission?" He didn't face either of them with this rant, but faced forward, like he asked the whole world. "I want to know, damn it." Derrick's fist popped against the roof of the car.

Striated muscles in Zach's arms clenched. It seemed he strangled the steering wheel to keep from choking the life out of Derrick.

"I know you want answers." Greer sighed. "Acting like an ass won't get you any closer to them. We're all tired. We've all been through a lot over the past few weeks. Just relax. We'll get to the bottom of all this, just not tonight."

"You mean this morning?" Derrick propped his elbow on the door and looked out the window into the darkness.

She plopped back onto the seat and waited. Zach drove inside and the car stopped. The engine quieted. Zach climbed out and propped his seat forward.

The scents of earth and hay relaxed the knots at her nape more than the plaster and fresh paint fumes of her generic DC apartment ever had. Greer crawled out the back and stretched her arms toward the aged wood of the second floor. She might have fallen asleep on the three-hour drive back to the farmhouse had the blanket of tension inside the car not proved too thick. It sucked spare oxygen from the interior even with the windows cracked as they'd zoomed down the interstate. She'd fought for every drowsy breath.

By the time they hit the trampoline of pitted and rocky backroads she'd moved from sleepy to bone weary. Not that she'd speak a word about her discomfort to Zach. He'd dealt with her at her worst. She wanted to show him her strength. Taking out two guards and extracting Derrick should've gone a long way to that end, but he hadn't said so. He hadn't said anything since he tried to kick her out. Her and Derrick.

Zach stepped back, giving her ample room to decompress. Yet, he didn't go far. He cataloged Derrick's every move. Derrick inspected the piles of hay and a tool bench on the far wall she hadn't seen until they'd headed out nearly nine hours ago.

"What is this place then?" Derrick stomped his foot on the hardened ground.

"Safe." Though Derrick had asked the question, Zach's gaze met hers when he answered.

A gooey smile mushed her lips. Zach returned a version of a smile. Greer nearly fell over. Seriously, she wobbled and grabbed the open door to steady herself. He placed a hand behind her back, but kept a few inches between them, guiding her to the base of the steps.

"I'm sure you're tired. Why don't you go get cleaned up?" The tips of his fingers pushed against the small of her back and urged her onto the stairs.

He'd cradled her in his arms, scrubbed her naked body, but somehow that brief, light contact electrified Greer's skin unlike any touch before. Now she stood confidently on her own two feet. Now she could take out the enemy. Now he had no reason for physical contact, except that he'd wanted to touch her.

The tingle followed her to the suite, to the chest of drawers, and into the bathroom, though Zach stayed below. Since she had her full faculties back, Greer took extra care with herself, conditioning her hair and combing away the knots. She reached for the razor, lathered the legs she'd lacked the strength to shave last time, and grazed the blade up her calf. No more than a quarter inch of growth came off. After more than a week not in control of her mind and body, she expected to look like one of those au naturel movement chicks with leg hair long enough to braid or color. Only a few shave-less days' worth looped and eddied its way toward the drain.

Outrage and revulsion translated into a sob. Greer trapped the animalistic sound behind her hand. Those sleazy fuckers had not only drugged her. They'd violated her while she'd been unconscious. It wasn't rape. And yet...the realization battered her with emotions in the same zip code she'd been dragged through all those years ago. She folded in half. Water beat her nape. Hair and water flowed over her face. Her knees hit porcelain.

Greer curled into a ball and cried. The rushing water buffered the noise. It drummed in steady droplets. Her tears did too.

Exhaustion, not resolve, forced Greer to her feet. She shaved her body with disinterested swipes. Maybe there was something to the no-shave movement. After all, men didn't have to shave.

When she turned the water off Zach's and Derrick's muffled voices filtered through the wall. She dried and dressed with an urgency that told her being held prisoner in her own body was bringing up a landfill's worth of shit from her past. Odds were good she'd die a virgin. Nobody liked baggage.

She scooped up the pile of clothes, sidearm, holster, extra clips, and knife and held it against her chest. The boots standing in the corner could wait. She braced for reentry and then turned the knob. If the guys noticed her red eyes or bare legs neither said a word. She had opted for an extra baggy T-shirt tonight—this morning—and wondered why she hadn't done the same last night when Zach's eyes had been the only pair on her.

"Bacon. Eggs. Toast." Derrick sat at the kitchen table, shoved soupy eggs and half a wedge of toast into his mouth, and chewed. "If I'd known the man cooked, I would've kept my mouth shut." He pointed his loaded fork at Zach, who sat across the table, before scarfing its contents.

"Food always was your weakness. And girls." Greer smiled, thankful to see both men chowing amicably at the table.

"And running my mouth." Derrick mumbled around the other half of his toast.

"Truer words." She skirted the table and set her heap on the chest, not knowing where else to put them.

"Hey."

Greer turned back toward the two men.

Derrick's lanky arm reached across to the everyday ware heaped with food. He shook the dish from side to side. "He even made a plate for you. Come on, you have to be hungry after waxing some guards and running a couple of miles."

She tugged on the hem of the shorts and hurried to the table. Her stomach flipped and fluttered enough that she had no urge to eat, but she wanted to hear more about Derrick's abduction and time at the compound. "I didn't kill them."

"Crying shame," Zach mumbled.

Derrick chimed in with, "too bad," at the same time.

The men's gazes met. Both rocked back, Zach to his chair back, Derrick to his elbows.

Orange juice sloshed around Derrick's cup as he carried it to his mouth and took a deep swallow. "I know you don't trust me. It's your nature." He plopped the empty glass onto the table and braced his forearms on either side of his nearly demolished plate. "Now, it's mine too. I was a spoiled kid with too many gaming consoles. I played war games since I could write my name. The adrenaline rush, the frustration of losing, the elation of winning. It seduced me."

Derrick shoved away his plate. "When I enlisted they shipped me off to Afghanistan. I still played war, shooting the bad guys from a distance, advancing levels. It had no meaning. None of it. Not until I was chained to a factory belt and the enemy stared down at me. His spit rained on my face. The cold barrel of his gun clogged my throat."

The more Derrick talked the further Zach withdrew, folding his arms over his chest and reclining into the chair. Greer reached out and covered Derrick's warm hand with hers, wishing it'd be that simple to touch Zach. No one deserved what they'd been through. It could've been worse. At least she didn't have a mark on her body. Derrick had escaped with a hideous tattoo. Zach hadn't been so lucky.

"I thought I was tough until that moment." Derrick squeezed her fingers. "I caved. I gave them my loyalty to save my life."

"Live to fight another day," Greer whispered.

"Those bastards—" Derrick began, but a shrill beep halted all conversation and Greer's breath. Her gaze flew around the room looking for the source of the noise. When she couldn't pinpoint the siren that seemed to radiate from the walls she looked to Zach. His piercing gaze honed in on the computer.

"What is it?" Greer forced the sentence one syllable at a time.

Per usual, Zach didn't grace her with an answer. He shoved back the chair and ran for the desk. Greer followed, determined to find out what the hell was going on. Derrick brought up the rear. "Is the place on fire?"

Again he didn't answer. Greer's stomach dropped into her big toe.

Zach unlocked the bottom left drawer of the desk. His gaze narrowed on Derrick while he yanked open the drawer. He pulled out the laptop, set it on the desk, and wrenched it wide. Finally his eyes left Derrick and shifted to the screen. He typed in a password that would make the Department of

Defense proud. She'd only caught two letters in the long sequence and they'd help as much as having an Italian translator in a North Korean court room.

"You bloody mind?" Zach eyed them, turned his laptop away, and continued clicking.

"Yeah, I mind that you're keeping me in the dark," Greer snapped.

"I don't know what's going on yet," he popped back.

"You know what the noise is from though," she pointed out.

"Christ." His grey eyes rolled before he continued, "It's a tripped parameter sensor."

Greer considered that for a second. "Wouldn't the woodland creatures trip them all the time?"

"If they were in the woods, yes. These are on the main road and driveway." Zach used the mouse pad to click several times.

Derrick moved to the old loft doors turned large window. Yellows and reds congealed in the distant sky, outlining his lean body like a shadow profile she'd done in kindergarten art class. "It's still pretty dark out, but I don't see anything."

Greer eased back from the desk toward her gun on the chest.

"Fucking teenagers," Zach snarled.

"What?" She stopped.

Zach turned the screen. A video clip reached the end, but immediately started over. The Jeep that had been exiting the frame when she'd first seen it now entered from the left.

A young boy drove. His gaze—which should have been on the bumpy road nearly three miles from the barn—lit on the girl in the passenger seat. More accurately on her bare breasts. The girls, one in the front seat and another in the back, stripped their shirts overhead and whipped them around in the breeze. In the back seat, the boy not driving helped himself to a taste.

"I don't understand," Greer croaked.

"You don't?" Zach's gaze dropped to her breasts.

Heat traveled from her nipples up her chest to her cheeks. "I don't understand why they're out here."

A genuine smile crooked his lips. "There's a lake on the property. Kids, brave enough or drunk enough, come out to get naked in the formerly-abandoned barn." He gestured to the walls around them. "Or they go skinny-dipping. I can show you later, if you still don't understand."

"Man, backseat is a nine-point-five." Derrick leaned between them and gawked at the constant loop of boobs.

Greer hugged her arms around herself and stepped away from the screen.

Zach clicked and typed. The video disappeared.

Derrick straightened. "Come on, man. I've been pent up for weeks. The least you can do is let me watch."

"The least I can do is not punch your nuts into your nostrils." Zach's gaze slid to Greer, and then back to Derrick. "Have some respect."

"Aw." Derrick swatted the air with his hand. "She's used to my mouth."

"I reset the system, but I need to go scare these kids away." Zach closed the computer and returned it to the drawer. "I'll be back soon."

"I can help." Derrick stepped toward the stairs.

Zach stopped at the top of the banister. "Great. Clean the kitchen." His head disappeared below the floor.

Greer didn't hear the door open or close, but dual relief and grief over his absence plagued her.

Derrick clapped his hands together and turned to her. "About the—"

"If you say cleaning the kitchen is really a woman's job, I'll use that frying pan to beat you to death in your sleep."

"I wasn't. That talk was just a diversion." Derrick rushed to the desk. He pulled on the drawer, but it didn't budge. "The computer, did you catch the password?"

"What are you doing?"

His lanky arms tensed. He pried at the handle with gritted teeth. "Help me."

"Help you what? What the hell are you doing?"

"I'm trying to save us."

"Save us from what?"

"There isn't time." His hands slipped off and he stumbled back. He moved to the center drawer and pulled so hard the drawer winged from the desk. Paper clips, markers, and pencils scattered across the floor, along with a long silver letter opener.

Derrick dropped to his knees, grabbed a paperclip and the opener, and went to work on the drawer.

The desperation with which her partner worked on the lock sent a wave of gooseflesh rolling over Greer's skin. Greer stepped backward, toward her gun.

"Why do you think we got grabbed?" His determined gaze left the drawer and found her. The laser line of his gaze zipped to the chest of drawers, and then centered on her. He stood. "Why do you think?" His sharp tone reverberated around the room and smacked her in the face.

"I don't know. That's why I'm here, to find out."

A hollow laugh rolled from his belly. "He's the reason."

"He?" she managed to rasp.

"Zach Saulter isn't his name."

Greer's legs rubberized. She'd never seen him as a Zach, but she hadn't expected it wasn't his real name...or maybe she had. The floor softened under her feet, threatening to swallow her whole.

"He runs a rival gang out of the old country, the Rhyke."

"Who told you this?"

"The Stas."

"How can you even begin to believe them over your own—"

"What, captain? He's not a real captain. He's a gun for hire."

"Just like you and me," Greer hollered.

"He played us and the Stas for information. We were pawns, Greer."

Her head shook in a constant back and forth while she tried to calculate the situation from every angle. The partiality she had for Zach couldn't come into play. But it already had. He said he wasn't a good guy, but he acted like one. Derrick said he was a good guy, but didn't act like one.

Derrick went back to work on the lock. Metal scraped metal and her nerves.

"They took him too," she finally blurted.

"Yeah, to find out what he wanted from them. I don't think they got it."

"Because he doesn't cave." Accusation hardened her voice.

Something shifted on Derrick's face. A slip of the mask. Hair at the back of Greer's neck stood on end.

He dropped the paper clip on the floor and abandoned the lock. “I think they’ll come after him again. He’ll be back soon. We need to go.”

Derrick clutched the opener in his fist.

“Why didn’t you go earlier?”

“Because you didn’t. But you’ll come with me now. Won’t you, Greer?”

Chapter Ten

"Take a step and we'll see how well you breathe through your brain." Zeke trained his Glock on Derrick's temple.

The man stopped a foot from rounding the desk toward Greer. Her blue gaze found him, but snapped back to Derrick's hands too quickly.

"Drop it." Zeke whispered the order and mounted the stairs.

A letter opener Derrick must have found in the old desk clattered to the wooden top.

"Well, it didn't take long to chase those kids off, Alexi." Derrick held his hands up in surrender and turned toward him. "Almost like there weren't any kids. Just like there isn't a Zach Saulter."

"There were kids," Zeke countered, "six months ago. I never knew the footage would come in handy." He shrugged. "Well, for more than the obvious. And Zach Saulter exists. He's just a lawyer in Dallas."

Greer's jaw dropped as though he'd pissed on a Bible.

He'd expected as much. He just hadn't expected the weight of her reaction to sit on his chest like an angry gorilla. His breath hitched.

"I told you." Derrick shifted his jaw toward Greer and his left foot shifted ever so slightly in her direction.

If she noticed, she didn't give any indication. Her gaze locked on Zeke's, waiting for an explanation he couldn't give. Especially not with a rattlesnake coiled between them. He needed Greer to recognize Derrick for what he was—and for her to hold on to the misplaced trust she had for him a little while longer.

Zeke squeezed the steel between his palms and used it to harden his voice. "How'd you know?"

"They questioned me for hours, chained in that damn warehouse. The Stas wanted to know about you. When I said I didn't know anything, which was true..." Derrick jabbed a finger at him. "You didn't show us shit and told us even less." A snort spewed from the wanker's razor-edged nose. "They tried to turn me against you. So they told me that shit. What they didn't know is that I never had an allegiance to you."

"Well, you did the British Academy proud. Truly, a moving performance." Zeke dipped the end of his Glock and tipped his head. "I'd clap, but I might blow your lying ass off."

Greer stayed unusually quiet. Her gaze bounced back and forth between them.

"Say what you want, but she already knows the truth," Derrick said.

"Yes, she does." Zeke fisted the front of his shirt in his left hand and yanked it up, revealing the ravages of his captivity. "She knows what a questioning from the Stas looks like." He released his shirt. "You have a pledge of loyalty. I don't. They didn't question you. What would they gain? You're a lowly pissant who doesn't know anything."

Derrick flung himself around so quickly his shirt flapped in the breeze. "Greer, did they do that to you?"

That primitive desire to protect Greer flopped around in Zeke's chest once more. Someone mercilessly held defibrillator paddles to it, forcing it to life inside him.

"They didn't question her," Zeke growled.

Derrick's brown gaze sliced back to Zeke. The top of his lip curled into a hideous sneer.

"How do you know for sure?" Greer voiced the man's question in a whisper. "There's so much I can't remember."

He held Derrick in his periphery, but centered his gaze on Greer's soulful blue eyes. "You'd remember every hit, every cut, every lost breath, every burn. There also isn't a mark on your body."

"He's seen you?" Rage cracked Derrick's voice and his carefully constructed facade. His pecs puffed with rapid breaths and he stepped in her direction.

"Careful." Zeke's index finger eased down the trigger guard, itching to take a shot.

Had they been a couple before all this? Had they been intimately involved? Zeke entertained the notion for no more than a second before deciding they hadn't. Not because he figured Greer had been saving herself for him, but because Derrick Coen's brash and irreverent personality didn't lend itself to intimacy.

His didn't either, now did it?

Greer stumbled back from the sudden outburst, but caught herself. Then everything changed. A certainty he hadn't seen in her demeanor since training straightened her spine. Her gaze sharpened to the fine point of a blade.

"Those bastards abducted me. They drugged me for nine long days. Zach…" Her gaze bobbled for a fraction of a second before firming on Derrick.

She pointed at Zeke. “He, whatever his name is, he saved me. He dealt with the aftermath.” Her finger shifted to her sternum. “And my body isn’t your concern.”

Sweat beaded on Derrick’s flushed forehead. His mouth formed a hard line. “Sure it is.”

The dip of Derrick’s temple begged for a bullet. It took ounces of reserve to keep from hugging the trigger and giving it to him. He didn’t need the son of an Irish whore much longer, but he needed to know where he’d gotten the information he’d told Greer.

Her eyes widened, but the set of her jaw firmed. “The hell it is.”

“You’re my prize.” Derrick’s smile grew. He lunged.

Zeke’s index finger tightened on the trigger. Instead of Derrick’s head, he lifted the barrel and aimed for the blacked-out figure skirting the roofline with an automatic rifle snugged to his chest. The man’s arms flew back. He teetered and then fell backward off the tin roof.

Another shadow shifted on the far end of the barn past the kitchen window. Derrick’s hands gripped Greer’s shoulders.

A roar erupted from Zeke’s throat. He’d only heard anything like it once before. The first time his father had beaten his sister with a closed fist. He’d been five, a boy, completely incapable of helping. Now, he could do amazing, terrifying things with his hands.

Greer caught Derrick’s chin with a punch. His head jerked, but his grip held. He shoved her toward the far wall, near the chest of drawers—and her gun.

Zeke holstered his Glock and—

A deafening *boom* echoed in his skull. Invisible force shoved him to the floor. Bits of wood and glass hailed, pinging off his prone form like angry hornets. Black lapped at the edges of his consciousness.

Greer?

He had to find her. The need pushed him forward more ardently than the blast. The black tide receded. He blinked. Crimson laced his field of vision. Zeke used the back of his arm and swiped at the blood. He pressed to his hands and knees. Blood blinded. The floor swayed.

"Greer?"

Zeke listened for her answer. A distant ring replied. Again he wiped at the stream, and then forced his eyes wide.

Derrick dragged Greer's limp body across the debris-laden floor. Her bare feet scraped over splinters of tin and chunks of glass.

A possessiveness completely foreign gulped its first heavy breath. Zeke pulled a knee to his chest and struggled to stand. He searched for solid ground, but floundered, finding only the hard edge of the kitchen table.

"No!"

From too far away Greer's voice cut through the haze and disorientation. He grabbed the hand towel from the table top and dragged it across his eyes. The smoggy room developed like an old Polaroid. Using the chair for balance, Zeke straightened. A large hole gaped in the front of the barn. The blast had been made for distraction, not destruction...except for his car, which seemed to be at the epicenter of the blast. He couldn't see it. That was a good thing for Derrick. Maybe when he caught the fucker he wouldn't kill him.

Grunts of a tussle and the smack of flesh meeting flesh filtered in through the gaping hole. Greer yelped. Nope. Derrick was already dead. He just didn't realize it.

Rage drove him forward. He ran full tilt toward the old loft door. The rusted hoist chain hung from the large round pulley and weathered wood post he'd kept through the updates. Zeke leaped into the open air. He looked right, expecting to meet the bullet of the shadow he'd seen ghosting across the barn roof moments before the blast. His left hand clamped the rough metal. Blood had snaked down his arm. Several links in the old chain slipped through his grasp. He redoubled his effort. His grip held. No shots rang out. Gravity went to work.

Chain screeched through the un-oiled wheel. The baler hook at the bottom of the circular length soared. Before it met the pulley—*shit*—before it passed him knotted links jammed into the pulley's slender opening. His fall stopped with an abrupt jerk. The chain slipped from his fingers and he fell toward the earth.

A tuck and roll saved his ankles from total decimation. His shoulder took a hit. Blood trickled down his face once again. Zeke anchored himself on a knee. He yanked his sidearm from the holster.

Greer stood over Derrick. Crimson oozed from the man's nose. Her knuckles whitened around the letter opener she held high in the air. Determination tightened her features. Her fist drew for the strike.

A shot split the air from the right. *The other shooter.* Zeke swung toward the barn. He focused a bead on the gunman.

Greer screamed.

Zeke's stomach followed his bullets across the yard. The man grabbed his neck, fell forward onto the tin eave. He was up and running before the thought registered. His barrel swung back around and found Derrick, ready to obliterate the man, but completely unprepared to see the horror of what had happened to Greer.

Brain matter and blood clung to blades of grass.

She hunched forward. Her white blonde hair cascaded over her shoulder. Slender fingers hid those beautiful blue eyes from the annihilation that was Derrick Coen.

The tip of his Glock wavered. Muscles in his entire body rubberized and he actually stumbled to the side. Whether from the blood loss or relief he wasn't sure. But he had time for neither. He moved forward, blocking Greer from the line of the barn. The setting sun cleaved into his sensitive vision. Zeke squinted against the dying light and surveyed the perimeter. Branches swayed in the light breeze. Bugs accosted the kitchen window, beating themselves against the glass, trying to get to the florescent light.

No one scaled the roof. No one moved in the woods. It didn't mean they were safe. It just meant they wanted them alive. Zeke had endured his last day in captivity and would die before he returned.

"We need to go."

She looked at him with wet, blood-shot eyes. "You're bleeding."

"I'm not dead yet, so it'll keep for now." He held out his hand. When her fingers wrapped around his they grabbed something else deep in his chest.

Chapter Eleven

"Who shot him?"

Z—she'd taken to mentally calling him that, since she didn't know what the hell his name was—hiked his other foot into the truck, slammed the door shut, and plopped a motel key on the seat between them. "I was beginning to think you'd succumbed to shock." His big hand wrapped around the shifter and yanked the relic into drive.

"I couldn't get a word in edgewise, for all your muttered cursing."

"Men don't mutter," he groused.

"I'd say let me check your pants, but that won't be necessary." She flashed him a smirk. Her nerves vibrated from the non-stop rollercoaster, but this mindless banter with him—whoever he was—made it tolerable.

He slid her a sideways glance, but didn't even crack a smile.

"I didn't peg you for a materialist. I mean, we're both alive," she pointed out.

The old pick-up wheeled into the back parking lot with a long series of groans and squeaks. Z parked the vehicle behind a motel two hours away from the Pennsylvania farmhouse and closer to New York. "It wasn't just a car they destroyed. It was a symbol, a..." He let the words fall off with a shake of his head. “Just wait until I find them.”

“A symbol of what?”

Z opened the door and leaned out, but stopped. He surprised her by turning back and slumping against the seat. A sigh drained from his lips. It expelled the tension in his shoulders. “Freedom. It was my freedom.”

It might be the first real answer he’d given her. The subject matter meant something to him. His willingness to share shifted something between them. A grimace creased his blood-crusted forehead. He grabbed the wheel with his left hand and shifted toward the door.

Greer held her breath and dove. After all, it couldn’t be any more terrifying than hearing that shot rip through the wilderness and thinking that Z’d been shot. She reached out slowly, giving him time to escape if he wanted. He watched her hand stretch the distance for his. Her finger slid over the top, smoothing over the large ridges of veins, tendons, and coarse hairs. It was wider than she’d imagined, warmer. She didn’t so much hold his hand as shield it.

“Even when they held you captive, they didn’t take your freedom. You’re stronger than that.”

A cloud drifted through his stormy gaze. Had she taken him back to those awful days? Had she over stepped the tentative bounds of their budding…who knew what it was? For that matter, was it anything? The knot in her throat said it was something, on her part anyway.

“They—whoever they were—targeted Derrick. They shot him before you or me. Derrick knew something valuable. I don’t know who took him out, but if we figure that out we’ll figure out why we were taken.”

Greer lifted her hand. “I didn’t say that so you’d—”

“I know.” He trapped her hand against his palm. “I’m telling you what I can.” His lips compressed and then released. “I just can’t go back there.”

No wonder he couldn’t rehash the days of imprisonment and torture. “More than most, I get that.”

Z nodded. “Back at the barn, why didn’t you run when Derrick gave you the chance?”

She looked at their hands, at his strong fingers, capable of crushing hers in their grip, capable of cuddling hers in their grip. “You wouldn’t hurt me.”

“According to Derrick, I’m the leader of a notoriously violent gang.” The firm line returned to his mouth.

“And yet, you risked your life to save mine. You did the same for Derrick.”

Her eyes clamped shut at the memory of his body at her feet—the body of someone she’d thought of as her friend. “I’ve never killed anyone.”

“You still haven’t.”

She looked at him, really took in his hard jaw and proud nose, his troubled eyes, and she slipped a little. The precipice was steep and threatened her life as truly as the Stas had, but the urge to throw herself over the side livened every cell inside her.

“I would have.”

“Good. When it’s you or someone else, always choose them.” He squeezed her hand.

The hole in the side of Derrick’s skull haunted her again, but she pushed past it. “Did the Stas turn him?”

“Did he work for them all along?” Z asked. “Or did he work for someone else? All questions we need to answer. I had my suspicions before...about both of you."

"What the hell?" Greer yanked her hand from his as though his touch burned.

"When you were taken I thought I was wrong. I wasn't wrong about Derrick."

"I can't even..."

The notion steamed its way down her esophagus and she nearly hacked it up, but what did it matter. His opinion of her didn't matter, not even enough to finish the thought. She jerked the handle and shoved the door with everything she had. Good thing too. The bottom of the damn door ground against the metal frame, lamenting its order to open. Her sturdy backside helped in closing the thing. The sneakers Z had bought for her whined as she hurried by a parked Cadillac across the wet asphalt. When the hell had it rained?

Z grabbed her left arm. She pulled it away.

"You're walking through urine."

Her shoes stalled in a shallow puddle. She whipped around and glared at him.

"Hey." He lowered his hands and spread them wide. "I didn't do it, but I'm betting the guy taking a piss on the building did."

Sure enough a man in dirt-trimmed clothing aimed his sizable penis at a motel room door and created a pool at the threshold. Her cheeks heated. She'd seen more man parts in the last two days than she'd seen in her entire life. At the other end of the building a narrow breezeway sheltered a faded rucksack—digital woodlands print—the kind that never quite blended into the sands of Afghanistan—a dog, and a bag from the fast food chain a few blocks away. Tears stung her eyes without warning. She blinked them away. Looking at the puddle of piss she stood in helped. It and the one forming at the corner of the building were the only wet spots as far as the eye could see.

"Let's go." Z reached for her arm again, but she side-stepped him.

"You go. I'll be there in a minute." Greer rubbed her soles on the dry ground, and then headed for the large black dog.

"What are you doing?" Massive pectorals and a frown blocked her path.

"I'm going to talk to that gentleman." She pointed to the still-peeing man. "When he gets finished."

"It's just pee. Don't get your knickers in a twist."

Greer smiled. "Stay here or go to the room. You'll make him nervous."

"You're making me nervous."

"Good." Before he could say more she hurried toward the breezeway.

The pup stood. His head canted and one half-masted ear flipped up to a point.

"Hey, sweet boy. What's your name?"

Intelligent eyes sparkled with curiosity.

"I'm Greer." She sat across from the pair's territory, leaned her back against the wall, and stretched her legs out in front of her.

Light glinted off the dog's onyx nose as he sniffed the air.

"Hey?" A deep, hollow voice barked.

The man had zipped his jeans. He stood at the edge of the sidewalk. His dirty blond hair flopped back and forth as his head swiveled between her and Z, who leaned against the old truck with his arms crossed over his massive chest and a scowl on his sexy face. The gash on his forehead only added to his brutish appeal. Though, this guy probably didn't think so. Her attention returned to the dog.

"I take good care of him."

"I can see you do." Greer gave a soft smile, careful not to sound condescending. She pointed to the nook across from her. "Please, I just want to talk for a minute."

He hiked a thumb over his shoulder. Shrapnel scars speckled his lean bicep. "Look, that asshole had it coming. He tried to strong arm Poppy into his Caddy after she told him she wasn't open for business tonight."

"Poppy?"

"She...uh..." He scrubbed a hand through his scruffy locks. "She works at the motel some nights."

"In an unofficial capacity?"

"Don't try and cause trouble. She's just trying to get by."

"I'm not here to make trouble."

"Well, God hasn't done much for me lately, lady. So, thanks for trying, but don't waste your breath, trying to save my soul." The man moved to the corner of the breezeway and leaned back, keeping Z in his line of sight. He gave a little nod and the dog rushed to his side. His gleaming black muzzle found the guy's hand and they exchanged a familiar greeting.

"He hasn't done much for me lately either. So, don't worry." The man's gaze narrowed, but she pushed forward before he could say anything. "My name is Greer. I'm a marine."

The man snorted. "They make 'em prettier than they did a few years ago." His gaze found Z. "Then again, maybe not. He a marine?"

"He's a lot of things. How long have you been back home?"

"Just ask what you want to know. How long have I been a bum? Why don't I have a job? Where's my family? Why don't they help?"

Greer offered her palm. "I don't want to know your business. I just wanted to know if maybe we served at the same time, in the same hell hole. But it doesn't matter."

His brow hiked at that. "Oh no? Look, I'm not into threesomes either. At least, not with another dude."

She laughed. It lifted the burden on her shoulders for the barest of seconds. Full breaths filled her lungs for the first time in too long. "I'm not here for that either. Look, I have a friend, a woman I served with. She's trying to do something good. She's trying to make a place for veterans." His lips parted, but her quelling look stopped him. "It's not an institution or anything like that. It's a ranch. I think she's calling it the Big Brass Ranch. I think you could help. I think it could help you."

Greer leaned forward, ripped a piece off the paper bag, and then stood. "Do you have a pen?"

The guy let out a long, weighted breath. He looked at the dog, at her, and then at Z. After a string of seconds he leaned down, plucked a pencil from his bag, then handed it over.

Grooves had been carved to make the fine point she used to scrawl a phone number onto the scrap. She extended it to the man. "Her name is Emerson. Tell her I sent you."

When he took the paper she skirted him and headed for the room number she'd seen on the key.

"What's the catch?"

She stood only a few feet away from the ruggedly beautiful and empty man. "Don't let me down."

"Letting people down is what I do."

"Not people. Only yourself. It's what we all do."

"That's some pep talk." Lines formed a bracket around his shallow smile.

"I'm not a cheerleader."

Greer dipped her head and walked away. Z met her at the door. His shoulders drooped as though the pride had been knocked from him. He stared at her shoes and started to look at the man in the breezeway, but his gaze didn't quite make it. The key slid easily into the slot. He opened the door and waited. She thought to toe her shoes off before entering, then thought better of it. This wasn't a Marriott. The place made a Motel 6 look like a Hyatt. But it was as off the grid as they could get tonight.

Z's lips parted like he wanted to say something, but words didn't follow. She halted on the threshold and met his eyes. Still his gaze dragged the floor. When she didn't move ahead he grumbled. "Why'd you do that?"

"Why'd I talk to that man?"

"Yeah." He may as well have been a kid hiding his hands and kicking the dirt. The mightiness of his height, girth, and brawn paled. Something small and vulnerable shuffled into its place.

Emotion thickened her throat, but she swallowed. "Because I thought I could help." She walked to the far bed and sat.

He closed the door, locked it, and wedged a small black mechanism between the door and jam. After depressing a button on the flat surface a small red light illuminated the side facing the wall. She wondered if it was meant to keep her in, others out, or both. The luggage he carried in one hand plunked onto the other bed.

“Look.” He propped both hands on his hips and rose to all his egomaniacal glory.

“No, you look.” She flopped back onto the bed and stretched her arms out. “I’m still mad and I don’t want to talk about it. Go take a shower. You’re a bloody mess, and I don't mean that as a cute British colloquialism.”

“So you think I’m cute?” One brow furled.

“I think you’re an insensitive, distant ass covered in blood.” Only she didn’t believe it, not any more. Greer hid her eyes with the back of her arm. He’d begun showing her glimpses behind his wall that made her question the hard and fast opinion she’d formed about him so long ago. Seeing it whipped her up inside.

She needed to lighten the mood. Her arm slipped off her forehead and she looked him up and down. Cracked, crusted blood stuck to the edges of his face and the sleeves and chest of his shirt. “What did the clerk think of you?”

“I told her I was an MMA fighter. She said she’d be by at the end of her shift,” he deadpanned.

“Of course she did.”

“What does that mean?”

“It means you better go get a shower before she gets here.”

Z sauntered to the bathroom door with his hands still on his hips. When he reached the partition his arms dropped and he met her gaze. “My life…hasn’t evoked confidence in others. My career reinforces mistrust.” His head bowed, but his gray eyes held. “I know I was wrong about you, Greer. You’re not like anyone I’ve ever met. You trust me even though I haven’t done anything to earn it. You trust me even though your trust has been broken.”

A tear slipped across Greer’s temple.

"Thank you."

She couldn't respond, couldn't breathe. Her lungs ached. The lights above his head contorted. Z disappeared into the bathroom and the door closed with a quiet *click*. Damn him. Her heart pounded under her hand. She didn't want to think about the past. She didn't want to think about Derrick. She didn't want to think about why she wanted to believe in Z, why she wanted to know him better, why she wanted to make him see how honorable, how worthy of trust he was.

Greer jumped to her feet and used the hem of the large, grass stained, dirt smudged shirt to swipe at her tears. No way could she sleep. An old-school television sat on a short dresser that stretched from the doorway to the rod hanging on the wall meant to represent a closet. On the night stand the digital clock read 8:45 p.m. Neither looked particularly inviting. She was here for answers, right?

Her feet carried her to the bags. The zipper screamed open. Guns, ammunition, wires, and C-4 peeked out. She shoved them aside and reached for the laptop. Since it hadn't been facing the blast it had fared better than Z's Barracuda, which they'd used to mount the bomb. How she'd ever thought him incapable of emotion she didn't know.

The laptop yawned and a white password screen popped up against the black backdrop. Of course. She typed *pain in the royal ass* and pressed enter. Shockingly it didn't grant her access. The cream-colored bathroom door stared at her in challenge. Not to be outdone, she stalked to the thing, computer in hand, and flung it wide. She grabbed a handful of the thin shower curtain and pulled it to the side. Plastic rings scraped along a cracked plastic rod.

Z's knees bent and his back hunched in a desperate attempt to fit under the spray. Suds slid off the ridges and slopes of his glorious body. His head tilted. One eye surrounded by bubbles squinted open.

"Do you want to earn my trust?" she yelled over the water.

The bulge of his pecs expanded. Both hands ran through his dark hair, over his face, and around his neck. He rose to his full height and turned his back to the shower head. Water sluiced off his abdomen, the intricate dagger that stamped his left side, and down his full penis. Greer swallowed, and then licked her sensitive lips. His biceps bunched and he tugged on his nape. The striations in his forearms leaped. His jaw joined in. When his gaze slid to her it may as well have been a sonic blast. It chopped her brashness off at the knees, leaving her a bumbling fool.

"Yes. In fact, in trying to earn it, there's something I've kept myself from doing." He stared at her mouth.

Her lips swelled at his attention, both sets.

"But you want my password?"

She gripped the laptop so hard its metal edges bit into her fingers. "Yes." Her voice cracked, but she didn't withdraw.

His hands fell to his sides and he faced her. She glanced at his heavy length. No way to avoid it. Her fingers itched.

"Is that all you want, Greer?"

"No." She surprised herself with the truth. She wanted him.

His exhale edged with a groan. It filled the room, cocooning her in desire. "I guess one honest answer deserves another. Two-thousand, in numerals, and the shroud is my loyalty 2011. No spaces. No capitals."

The shroud is my loyalty?

"Don't try to figure it out. Just put it in the computer and close the door on your way out."

Lost for words, she nodded and backed out of the room, making certain the latch on the door caught. She plopped onto the bed, dazed and too aroused for anyone's good. Greer put her fingers to work with the password. The thing took too damn long to cycle through the start-up. It gave her time to think.

He'd given her quite the show. Her lady bits pulsed under the heat of the laptop and the mental picture of his abused, exquisite form.

The screen brightened, ready to work. Greer crossed her ankles, but the move pressed her thighs together. She abandoned the proper gesture, afraid it would have her looking quite unladylike in a few minutes. A few clicks later she found the Stas system she'd been eyeballs deep into the previous day. This time she ignored the warehouse locations. Instead she searched the books for Derrick Coen. The list scrolled on forever, containing upward of five thousand names. Luckily, they'd been listed in alphabetical order.

When the air shifted in the room she knew Z had opened the bathroom door with his usual stealth. His scent sneaked across the room. Her gaze locked on the column of last names, but the letters blended into alphabet soup. The thud of her pulse sped. Dewey moisture slicked her palms and her fingers slipped on the mouse pad. Why the hell did he have this effect on her?

She clamped her eyes closed, breathed, and then opened them. Lust hadn't made her see double. The names were coded in an indiscernible mix of letters and numbers. Her shoulders slumped.

"What's wrong?"

There were so many ways to answer that. *You're emotionally unavailable. I like you and I shouldn't. My hormones won't listen to reason. We haven't gotten any closer to finding out why we were taken. You almost died tonight and that scared me. It scares me more that I care so much.* She settled for, "Stas records are coded and I don't recognize a pattern."

"It's another layer of protection. There's a key and only the top guys have it."

"Could we trace them through the warehouse list?" She continued to scroll through the list, looking for anything familiar.

"Doubtful. They don't frequent these places. Can't get their hands dirty."

Powerful thighs strode past the screen, slaughtering her concentration. "Could you put on some clothes?"

Greer shouldn't look, but not even self-preservation kept her gaze off the sturdy globes of his ass or the dimples above. Corded muscles wrapped either side of his spine in a stunning contour.

Z leaned over the open bag and dug inside. Then she noticed he held a towel to the top of his head. Her irritation fled. Blood smeared his cheek and droplets dotted his chest. Dread tamped her arousal. She tossed the computer to the side and hurried to him.

"Damn it." Blood dripped off Z's nose into the bag.

"Sit." Greer shoved him to the side and dug through the contents for the first aid kit.

The bed groaned under Z's weight.

"I can't believe you listened."

"Not easy to see through blood."

"You did it at the barn." She ripped open the pack, found a roll of gauze and a stack of butterfly bandages.

"Didn't have a choice. Coen was taking you… where, I don't know. My sensors didn't register movement. On our way out I looked for rut marks off the main road to see where the shooters came in, but it was dark."

"And you were bleeding. Let me see." Greer stepped between his legs, grabbed the towel, and held pressure on the wound. She caught a loose end and smoothed it over his eyelid with slow, gentle strokes. Red soaked the once-white point. Blood streaked his skin, but it would do for now. "How's that? Can you see now?"

Long lashes lifted and closed a couple of times before opening wide. A smile pulled at the corner of his mouth. His gaze zeroed in on her breast scant inches from his mouth. "Yes, I can."

A blast of heat worked its way up the curve of her back. She firmed her mouth and pushed the desire away. If only Z would do the same.

"Zach never suited you."

"No?"

She shook her head, reached for the roll of gauze, and then handed it to Z. "Roll about half of that off for me and rip it."

"You're bossy tonight. 'Stay here. Do this.'"

"In my head I call you Z."

The white roll fell to the bed and unraveled to the approximate spot she needed.

"Are you okay?" She'd never seen him fumble anything, not even after he'd crashed to the ground from the second story. He'd lined up his shot instantly and fired while almost blind.

White fibers ripped under his controlled violence. He handed her the narrow roll of gauze. She quickly tossed the towel to the bed, carefully lifted the hair off his forehead, and laid the dressing lengthwise over the three-inch gash.

Greer held it in place, then found Z's gaze. "Who are you really?"

"Derrick told you." His jaw flexed.

"I want you to tell me the truth."

He wore another layer off his teeth, but held his tongue.

"Z?" She pleaded.

Still nothing.

She pulled back the gauze and examined the wound. "You could use stitches."

"The strips will work." He grabbed four off the bed and offered them to her one at a time.

"I might have to shave some of your hair. The end of the cut is in your hairline."

"Don't even think about it."

"Tell me the truth and I won't."

"You don't believe him because you don't want to. You don't want to think of me—the man who saved you—as a vicious monster capable of destruction. Truth is, I am."

"No."

"Yes." The heat of his hollered breath penetrated her shirt and warmed her belly. He thrust the strips at her and she obliged, placing them a half-inch apart across the cut.

She dropped the gauze, bracketed his face in her hands, and forced his face up. "No," she insisted. "I know you're capable of violence. I've seen you kill." His gaze dropped. Her hand under his chin coaxed it up once more. "But you're not a gangster. You're a loner. Gangsters are about the score, the brotherhood, the power. You're not driven by money."

"I'm not a good man."

"You don't think you are."

The tempest in his gaze broke. His hands plunged into her loose hair, locking her in place. He inclined the sharp cleft of his jaw and yanked her down. Her hands landed on the unforgiving rounds of his shoulders. Her lips crashed into his. His jaw forced her mouth open and his tongue delved inside. The hard points of his teeth gnashed her delicate skin. He kissed with punishing force as though trying to prove his point.

Outrage should have fueled her fight, yet sadness overruled it. If anyone got too close to the truth, he shoved them away. No doubt he expected her, especially in light of her past, to run screaming. For the first time in her life, she didn't want to run. As crazy as it seemed, she wasn't afraid of this man who could snap her neck with a flick of his wrists or force himself on her without breaking a sweat.

Greer filled her hands with his cropped hair and tangled her tongue with the silk of his. She stepped closer. His firm, satin length bumped against her thigh. A moan one part surprise and two parts awe siphoned into his mouth.

"Fuck, Greer." The muffled curse filled her ears. He shoved her to arm's length and released her hair. Pants and muttered curses flew between his swollen lips. "I know what I am. And your purity can't erase my sins."

"I don't want to erase them." Though her racing heart tried to course her around the room she stood her ground. "I want to ease their hold on you."

"You can't."

"I can try."

"Why? Why waste your effort? And if you say it's because you want to help, I'll have you air lifted to your dear old dad before the sun comes up. To hell with finding out why we were taken."

She swallowed her pride and squared her gaze. "Because I want to know you more than I've ever wanted almost anything."

Z leaned back, but he had no place to go except flat on his back. He must have figured that out because he straightened and fixed his jaw. His gaze danced around the room. Her chest and cheeks sizzled. Still she didn't budge.

"You said almost anything. What did you want more?"

"When I was a little girl I wanted my mother back so much that I bargained with God. I told him if he'd give her back he could have all my toys."

"Guess he didn't like Barbie dolls."

"I had Legos and Play-Doh, thank you."

When he found her gaze again the tension ebbed from his taut shoulders. Greer reached for the towel. She dragged a clean corner of it over the side of Z's chin. Faint scars marred his complexion. There were new ones too, besides the obvious pink on his chest. A hideous row of small round marks circled his neck like someone had fastened a dog collar, spikes in. A puckered laceration roughened his trap. If he had this many scars on the outside, he had far more on the inside. Her heart broke.

One by one, her fingers grazed the macabre necklace. Fresh, smooth skin whispered under her touch. Z's neck bent and arched, allowing her to follow the line. His gaze cemented hers. Clouds rolled and lightning cracked behind them. Her breaths grew shallow as though a hand reached inside her chest and pressed her heart back together. She knelt between his spread thighs and washed away the blood on his chest, carefully blotting his tender scar.

His pecs rose and fell in steady waves. Greer dropped the towel. She released the hold she'd had on herself for most of her life and allowed emotion to rule, not emotions of the past, but of the here and now. Her fingers grazed the large discoloration on his chest. Need pulled her closer, to the edge of total surrender, to the heat of his skin. Z stilled. Greer moved slowly forward as though this virile man were no more than a puff of smoke that would dissipate with the slightest breeze. She wanted to grab him and hold him as resolutely as he held her moments ago, but she wouldn't force it.

Her lips pillowed against the uneven scar. Z exhaled a tiny noise. She clamped her eyes shut to savor the sound, the scent, the feel of him. His skin tasted like danger. Her head spun. Her pulse skittered. She continued the tour of his battle wound with her fingertips and mouth.

At the ridge of his pecs small, nearly translucent scars dappled his left side. She followed the trail. The thud of his heartbeat throbbed against her mouth. Her lips pressed more firmly and she lingered over his heart before working her way to a bruise on his shoulder. Before long her hands grew more adventurous, fanning out over the pleats and ripples of his arms and torso.

The tip of his dagger caught her off guard. She'd seen it from across a room. Up close the intricate scrawl of ink inside his flesh menaced. A thousand questions rattled across her brain, but she kept them locked away. Her tongue flicked out, catching the point of the blade and his flat nipple in the stroke. He arched in response. Like a chain reaction her nipples stiffened against the loose fabric of her shirt.

Greer's fingers found the dimples on Z's back, and then slipped down to the curve of his ass. She dipped her head and ran her tongue from point to hilt along the blade. Her hands rounded his hips, following the pointed V of his abdomen. When they reached the apex she stalled and sat back on her heels. His cock stood proud. The silky skin that had grazed her thigh earlier was lined with light blue veins. Its head wept clear liquid that threatened to slip down the flared top. Saliva pooled in Greer's mouth. She licked her lips and stared transfixed.

She knew what she wanted, but didn't know how to ask.

Chapter Twelve

Greer touched him with such reverence. Plenty of women had touched him over the years. Always for their own pleasure. Yeah, he'd gotten off every damn time. But this... This was the first time he'd been touched with loving hands. He'd hexed the word long ago. He hated even thinking it, and yet, it poured off of her in untamable waves. They crashed against his chest, suffocating his cynicism.

Why hadn't she run from his icy demeanor or bruising kiss?

She saw the ugliness in him and embraced it. Hell, she tried to heal it with every touch of her lips. The caring poured off her. His palms itched to plunge into her hair again, but he didn't know if he'd try to stop her or urge her on. He didn't know which he wanted more. This was Russian roulette with both their lives. No question, he should stop her.

When her tongue branded the tip of his dagger he lost the battle. Until then he'd kept his cock at bay. Now it starched, ready for whatever was in store. Dumb thing. Greer was the marrying kind and he had nothing to offer. Stability? He didn't know the meaning. He was buried in so many lies he often forgot what was real.

Her red, wet lips were real. She sat back halfway to her heels. The shirt she wore—his shirt

—hung loose at her neck, giving him an unobstructed view of her clavicle and the barest hint of breasts. Her hands rested on his thighs, awfully close to his prick. The question and desire in her eyes were real too. Lord help them.

That sparkling blue gaze lifted from his stiff length. Her throat worked. A gasp broke her lips. Zeke held his breath, waiting.

"May I," she breathed.

Brain and organ function must have stalled as well because he nodded and shifted his hips forward, giving her better access.

"I need to hear you say it."

He understood her need for consent. It smacked him over the head like a falling brick. He almost scrambled back onto the bed, but her exposed gaze fused him in place.

"Yes."

Before he could change his own mind the pads of her fingers caressed the side of his shaft. It was no more than a breath on his sensitive skin, but the exquisiteness of her touch shot endorphins through his veins like atomic missiles. He lost his grip on the severity of the situation and sank in the pool of deep-rooted lust he'd hidden since the first time he laid eyes on her.

Greer's lips parted and a pure-as-sunshine smile tugged at the corner of her mouth. She caressed each side, gently exploring the ridges and texture of his sensitive skin. God, help him. She was a virgin. A twenty-something-year-old virgin who'd also been abused. Zeke set his jaw and tried not to feel.

She fisted his girth in one palm and stroked slowly from base to the bell of his cockhead. Not feel? Who the fuck was he kidding. His sack tightened. The bead of pre-cum rolled off the side of his head and slipped over three of her fingers. He prayed it would send her packing. Her lower lip disappeared inside her mouth. When it came back it was wet and wedged between her teeth. The points of her breasts scratched the front of her shirt. Rapid breathing billowed the fabric.

Her other hand reached forward, middle finger extended. It landed on the stream of clear cum, pulled it off her fingers, and then smeared it across his crown. She played in it like finger paint, examining the composition. Zeke fisted the comforter, hoping he could keep as firm a hold on his lust.

"Is this okay?" She asked the question with no guile. This wasn't a game to woo him. She honestly wanted to know. He could see the sincerity and trepidation in her gaze.

"Fuck, yes," he groaned.

His unbridled answer emboldened her. The grip she held on his cock tightened. Her strokes grew steadier. She continued the torture of his cap, slicking his own arousal around and around over the flared skin. Soon her hips rolled with the movement of her hands, as though she'd found her own arousal. Zeke watched the sway of her clothed ass. He wanted to strip her and show her true pleasure, but he kept his hands and jaw clamped tight. This was her show. Whatever she wanted he'd give, if she asked. But sod it all if the swell of her hips weren't asking to be thoroughly fucked.

Again her tongue traced the line of her pretty mouth. His cock twitched. Greer lowered to her heels and dropped her lips inches from his prick. Her gaze met his with molten lust and a question.

"Greer, you're killing me."

The pout of her mouth defiantly plunged over his crown and slid to the tip of his shaft. Her shiny lips plumped over his bell and slid off the tip. She licked the crease of his head, repositioned her hands at the base of his cock, and lunged for more.

Her breasts bumped against her folded arms, coaxing her nipples into sharp peaks. Several times the unforgiving edge of her teeth found his flesh. Not even that or her discordant rhythm kept him at bay. His hips rolled in time with Greer's. It helped settle the beat of her sucking strokes.

He redoubled his effort not to orgasm...until her gaze locked on his. She boldly, adoringly, bathed and sucked him with her mouth. Her pure, sultry eyes undid him. It sent shocks of orgasm flashing up his spine. As gently as he could in the throes of the most tumultuous upheaval of his life, Zeke cradled her jaw and pulled his prick out of her mouth.

"I'm sorr—" She started to apologize for Pete's sake.

Zeke fisted his cock and clamped it tight, but he was too late. Bursts of cum launched from his heavy sack and darted up his shaft. Thick, white cream discharged onto her neck, the top of her chest, and onto the shirt. It came in wave after wave from seven long months of pent-up angst for this woman, this amazing, too-good-for-him-on-his-best-day woman, who treated him like he mattered.

Her mouth formed a surprised O as she watched him lose himself. He panted like he'd run a thousand miles uphill. He wanted to say something poignant, but he couldn't speak. His insides formed rows and rows of neat little knots. His palms sweated. Never had a sexual experience unsettled his calm. They'd been a release with no emotion behind it, never any caring, never...no fucking way. He couldn't go there. But still he knew without a shadow of a doubt that he'd take a bullet for her, and there weren't many people he'd do that for. Just one, really, and they were bound by blood and hell and love.

Greer stood, opened her mouth to speak, closed it, and then opened it again. "I'm going to go shower. Thank you." She pressed a hand to her swollen lips and turned toward the bathroom.

When the door shut Zeke smacked a hand over his face and collapsed onto the bed. What a sodding loser he was.

Chapter Thirteen

Drugs had never interested her, but that intoxicating sense of power could become a real problem. “Amazing.” Greer breathed the word from her tender lips onto her fingers for maybe the fifth time since she’d brought Z to the point of total release. A grin contorted her mouth. She flipped forward. The towel fell from her head, but she caught it and hugged it to her chest. Her thumb rubbed over the dip at her throat where he’d lost himself all over her.

Enough gloating and stalling. It was easy to be brave behind the bathroom door, but how would she feel facing him again? One way to know. She hung the towel on the back of the door, tugged at the hem of her camisole, checked her cotton shorts, and turned the knob.

The clack of keys filled the room. So, he was still awake. Her heartbeat spiked. On the vanity beside the sink sat the hair brush and toiletry kit he’d given her when she’d regained her wits at the farmhouse. Z must have grabbed them before they left. She’d been too emotional to think so logically. Her stupid grin returned. She’d dreaded finger combing her hair and wiping off her teeth with no more than a wash cloth. Time and again, he told her what a bad guy he was, but time and again he showed her kindness. She diverted to the vanity, grabbed the brush, and pulled it through her hair.

Her reflection caught her by surprise. She'd expected to look different, stronger or more mature maybe, but no. Aside from her red lips she looked remarkably ordinary. Stringy blonde strands clung to her cheeks and back. The curve of her nose still flared a bit too much at the sides. A hint of a blemish edged the bottom of her jaw... All things she would've complained about before offered comfort. She still fluffed the roots of her hair, brushed her teeth, and examined her chin, but she did so with new appreciation.

Unable to stall any longer, Greer straightened the mess she'd created on the vanity, and then turned. Z's wide shoulder rested against the headboard of the bed where she'd explored the frontier of her sexuality and him. Fists that had threatened to rip the fabric covering the bed thirty or so minutes ago relaxed into agile tools for seeking information. Light glared from the laptop screen casting his chest in an eerie glow. His head hung and his eyes squinted with single-minded concentration.

The carpet pricked her bare feet. She would have grimaced, but like Z's inattention, what did it matter? Awkwardness usually reserved for the high school lunch room on the first day at a new school —in a new state or maybe even a new country—nor the overused carpet would make her regret what she'd done. Z hid behind a fortress, but for those few minutes she'd reached beyond it. She'd reached him, and had enjoyed every second of it. Withdrawn or not, bad or not, when he let go there was a lightness that stole her breath—and maybe her heart.

Greer crawled onto her designated bed, yanked back the covers, and crawled inside. Whether they rented by the hour or not, the motel sheets coaxed the trace of embarrassment from her muscles and molded them into putty. She pulled the plush pillow from underneath the scratchy, awful tropical patterned one that matched the coverlet, and wedged it under her chest. Her face met it with a sigh.

Z continued to type, scroll, and then type more. Every breath he drew accentuated the contour of his lower back and muscled bottom. The man had no qualms with his naked form. Neither did she for that matter, except he provided a visual road block to sleep. With him otherwise occupied, she drank him in from the tips of his hairy toes to the top of his head and everywhere in between. Memories distorted the view. His arms strained against the comforter. His abdomen rolling in time with her mouth. His hips pistoning his cock inside her. His scent. His taste.

Blood pumped like roaring waves through her, obliterating her inner ear with the rush and recession of its consistent battering. Her most intimate parts throbbed, making her a near-writhing ball of need.

She clamped her eyes shut against the onslaught of his body. She was at the mercy of her imagination though, as she had been since she'd first seen him strapped into an officer's uniform, standing proud and imposing, commanding a team of deadly men, and her.

A light touch grazed her hand. She shot upright, ready for battle.

"I'm sorry I startled you." Z crouched next to her bed.

How had she not heard him? Had she fallen asleep or had she been so deep into her own fantasies she honestly hadn't heard him?

"Make some noise or something." She pressed a hand over her flailing heart and drew a heavy breath.

"In my work noise gets a man killed. In yours too," he reminded with a hitched brow.

"Could you put on some clothes?" His naked forearms rested on the comforter just in front of his bare shoulders and chest.

"I put on pants."

Greer leaned onto her elbow and peered down. By pants he meant black, muscle-hugging briefs. Her insides bloomed and contracted greedily.

"You said your dad recommended you for the job. What did you mean?"

He obviously hadn't caught the please-fuck-me face she'd been unable to hide. All for the best. "I was an active marine," she explained.

"I know." The corner of his mouth pulled into a lopsided grin. "Would you look at that? We have something in common."

"There was nothing royal about my posting." Her gaze dropped to the Royal Marines Commando dagger on his abdomen. "You were elite."

"Still am." He winked. "But I want to know about you."

She ignored the flutter in her belly, but damn, it was hard. He let this flirtatious part of himself show so seldom.

"I started straight from college as a second lieutenant. Four years and three tours later I made captain." That time in her life had been terrifying and freeing in the same labored breaths. She missed it more than she let herself think about.

"My comrades resented me, of course. They were mostly men, who started just before or after me."

"It's a fast advancement."

"Not terribly. They thought I was promoted because my uncle and father were in the senate. When I called to tell my dad, and make certain they didn't have anything to do with the pace of my rank increase, he cut me off." She rolled onto her belly and rested her chin in her hands. "He said he was surprised by my rash promotion, and all but hung up on me. It seemed like he resented my advancement more than the men I'd passed over."

"Why would he begrudge your progress? Other than he's a total piece of shit, which we've already established."

"He's not that bad."

"He's rat shit. Let's move on."

"Military service was a must in my family. My great-grandfathers were starred, two brigadier generals. My grandfather was a major general."

"No shit?" Z's shoulders straightened.

"None." A grin struck her by surprise.

"That's impressive."

"They were impressive men." She nodded.

"Your dad couldn't hack it?"

"He was sent home two weeks into his first deployment, given an honorable discharge, and to this day I have no idea why. He wasn't injured. Not that I've been able to discern from his medical records."

"So you've been snooping?"

"I had questions he refused to answer."

"I have plenty of those too." His thumb grazed the curve of her jaw. "You going to start snooping on me?"

It took a few seconds for her brain to register the question. She chuckled. "Already have. Imagine—there was nothing on you, Mr. Z."

His hand left her chin. "Your dad cut his foot on a rusted nail in camp, developed tetanus, and was sent home."

"What?" Greer scrambled to her bottom. "How do you have access to that information?"

"It's all bullshit," he said, not answering her question.

Her head cocked.

"It's a cover-up. Something else happened outside Al-Wafrah. What? We'll probably never know. The commanding officer who signed off on the report died in a car accident the day he landed in the States."

An ominous chill rolled over Greer's neck, creating an outbreak of gooseflesh across her arms and legs. "My dad knows."

"He's the only one who would."

She wrapped her arms around herself and chafed them with her hands. "That's one hell of a coincidence."

"So, your father recommended you..."

"He knew a guy with US Elite. He said they were doing groundbreaking work, less red tape, more results. He told me they were really making a difference, helping more people." A huff erupted from her throat. "My dad scheduled the interview. I got the job."

"And you didn't turn it down, even though you wanted to."

"How'd you know I didn't want to take it?"

He aimed his steady gaze on her and shifted his knees onto the ground. "When you talked about your rank your face lit up."

"Yeah, I didn't want to, but I didn't want to let my dad down more. I'm a pleaser."

Z braced his hands on the bed, hung his head and shook it slowly back and forth, as though trying to work it out in his head, but coming up empty.

"I like to see people happy. If I can do something to facilitate that, what's the harm?"

"There's no harm...unless you're the one whose happiness pays the price."

"It doesn't." She turned toward him and pointed toward the door, trying to get him to understand. "The man outside—"

"The homeless guy." Z's head jerked up as he spat the word.

"Yes, the homeless guy. If he accepts my help, he'll find his purpose again and he'll help my friend out in the process. If it works out, I'll have changed people's lives for the better, mine included. My happiness grows with his."

"He's not your responsibility."

Z's face reddened to the shade of her night-on-the-town lipstick. She'd seen him angry, but never so visibly moved by it. His calm had vanished like a waitress when you're so hungry you could eat your arm off. She suddenly wondered if they were talking about the man outside or the one kneeling in front of her, but reason didn't temper her reaction to his disregard.

"Why not? He's a person. I'm a person." Anger lifted Greer to her knees. She cleared the gap between them. Her voice rose to meet her indignation. "Just because I have a place to live and he doesn't, doesn't make me better than him. It just makes our circumstances different. Do you think you're better than him—name with no name—because you had a fancy car and cash to throw around? I mean, you see how quickly that can all change."

"I was him," Z shouted and stood. His hands found his hips. He stood over her now. His chest puffed, but his head hung low. "Only I was a kid."

Realization rocked Greer onto her heels.

"Nobody gave a fuck about me or my sister. The only thing they were interested in was how to use us to get what they wanted."

The crack in her heart shattered wide. Greer wanted to pull him into her arms and hold him close. Tears clogged her throat, but she gagged them down. He'd never forgive her pity. She wanted to protect the child he'd been and heal the man he'd become, but she held perfectly still.

"Nobody is going to take care of you in this world, but you. It's time you learned that shitty fact. I figured you'd have learned it when your dad blamed you for your cousin's crime when he should have been at the kid's doorstep beating the life out of him."

Greer covered her mouth. Her cheek throbbed as though he'd slapped her.

Z drew up. His grousing and huffing died on his open lips. He didn't take the statement back. Why would he when it was true? She should have learned her lesson. But it was high time he learned one too.

"That's not true. Your sister cared. You cared for her. If no one had cared, you wouldn't be here today, taking care of me. If no one cares, you be the one who cares, the one who makes a difference." Greer lifted to her knees again. "You still don't see it?"

"See what?"

"That you are the one who cares? It's not just me."

His hands squeezed his knuckles white for an eight count, before he lifted them to his nape and tugged. All the while his gaze roved her face. Quiet war raged inside him like he wanted to curse her and caress her at the same time.

"Say it," she demanded.

"What?"

"Say you care."

He stayed stubbornly silent.

Greer stretched her arms wide, daring him to release the thought that caused him so much trouble. "Say something."

"You sucked me off to put me in a better mood?"

Her mouth fell open. A squeaky amalgam of confusion, protest, and outrage leaked out.

"I refuse to be your charity case."

"Charity case?" She leaned forward. Her chest bombarded his space. "It would be more than what I am to you. To you, I'm simply the means to an end. But no, let me salve your ego. I went down on you because I wanted to feel you, to experience your taste. I wanted to draw a reaction from you for purely selfish reasons."

"Selfish?" He stared down at her.

"Yes. I don't regret it. If you do, I'm truly sorry." A cursed tear slipped down her cheek. "I didn't expect it to mean much to you, but it meant something to me."

Z's head bent. His lips pressed against hers, silencing her outrage. The hard mouth he'd punished with earlier now forgave with a tender embrace. Hot fingers splayed across her jaw and dipped into the hair at her nape. He cradled her head. His full mouth grazed delicate kisses along her lips. Sun-weathered skin around his eyes crinkled with each caress. That hypnotizing grey gaze never left hers. She'd never kissed with her eyes open. The closeness added a layer of vulnerability. There was no place for either of them to hide.

Her fingers craved the touch of his skin, but she didn't move. She surrendered. His lips grew more insistent on her mouth, parting her lips. The eager tip of his tongue slipped inside the edge of her mouth. He coaxed her upper lip into his heat. The point of his teeth abraded her already swollen skin. A surge of desire roared low and rolled through her. Z pulled back, panting, but held her fast.

"Fuck me to my grave, Greer, I care about you." His lips formed a tight, menacing pout.

She stared at him in awe for too many pounding heartbeats. He cared about her. He didn't sound the least bit happy about it, but he did. "Why is caring so horrible?"

"It means I've given my enemies a weakness to use against me."

How many enemies did he have and why? She wanted to know everything, but wouldn't ask. If she bombarded him with questions, he'd shut down. So, she stuck with the one she needed to know as desperately as she needed her next breath.

"A weakness?"

"You...you're the worst tactical move of my life. I can't seem to protect myself from you."

"I won't betray you." Greer placed her hand over his heart. "Not ever."

"I know." His long lashes nearly hit his cheek as he zeroed in on the center of her sternum. After a long pause, he pressed his hand against the very spot. His fingers spanned practically her entire width, absorbing the surge of her heart.

She watched the pulse in his neck increase. Hers matched it with wild swells. His hand moved with the rise and fall of her breaths. When his gaze lowered to her breasts the waver of her chest became shallow.

Z's tongue slid across his bottom lip, leaving behind glistening skin. His hand climbed one tantalizing millimeter at a time. The sturdy touch roved up her chest, to her collar bone, and up the side of her neck. She hoped he'd tug her hair again and kiss her, but his hand lowered to where it had begun and started up the other side of her chest and neck. He explored and examined her skin. Once again his hand found her heart, and then ascended until his fingers rested at the base of her throat.

"You trust me."

"Yes." She whispered through nerves and eager lips, though he'd made a statement.

His gaze found hers. "If you want me to stop, you say the word and it's done."

Greer nodded.

"I'm not going to fuck you."

Greer's heart dropped into her big toe. Her cheeks flamed. She'd wanted him to, had been silently begging for it.

He put his thumb under her chin and raised her gaze. Only then did she realize it had dropped. Again he wet his lips. "You deserve someone who'll make love to you. I don't know how to do that. But...fair is only fair."

She was about to protest that she was no man's charity case either. His fingers wrapped around the width of her neck. He pulled her forward and speared her mouth with his tongue. The argument died on the steady strokes of his thick tongue against hers. Her grip banded his forearm, holding him close. The tension in her knees gave. She bowed under the onslaught of Z.

His other arm banded her lower back. As the kiss wore on, it also wore down her budding anxiety. His kiss pushed everything aside except his command over her pleasure.

He sucked at her mouth, pulling her lower lip out and nibbling on the edge. Molten sensation dripped through her veins straight to her core. She moaned against his mouth. If he wasn't going to screw her brains out, what was he going to do, kiss her into a coma?

Z leaned back, dropping the hand that had slipped to her hips. "You with me?"

Greer couldn't speak or even nod. Arousal limited her physical capabilities to gulping air.

"Looks like you're a little bit behind. I'm going to have to slow this down so you can keep up." A crooked smirk tilted his mouth.

"I can keep up," she panted. Her knees had rubberized somewhere along the way. A wine-like buzz slowed her reactions. It also made her brazen as hell. If he stopped now, she'd probably strip and demand he continue.

"I don't want to rush this anyway."

That knowing smirk returned. Z's free hand grabbed the comforter and yanked it onto the floor. Using the hand at her neck, he pressed her back. When gravity took over his grip shifted to her nape. He eased her to the bed. The fitted sheet cooled her overheated skin. His gaze roamed her arched body, lingering on her bent legs. The tension at her neck broke. His fingers dragged over her neck and chest. His flesh hid the swell at the top of her camisole. On instinct her back rounded, pressing the proud curve into his hand.

His neck rolled. A guttural vibration rumbled in his chest. The pressure of his hand increased. Greer watched his other hand join in. He molded her breasts to fit his palms. The rough sides of his thumbs chafed the thin white cotton again and again.

While Z coaxed her nipples to beaded points Greer morphed from a virgin soldier into a carnal being. Low moans and exclaimed breaths poured from her lips. Her bottom rocked, giving squeaky voice to the coil spring mattress.

"Yeah, you can keep up."

Z's firm touch anchored at the bend of her knees and tugged. His deft fingers lit a path down the back of her calves to her ankles, straightening her legs. He spread them on either side of his hips. The chilled air coasted over the crotch of her damp shorts. Then he yanked. Her bottom hit the edge of the mattress, while her core buffeted his fully erect cock.

"Ooh, gah." Greer's toes curled and her eyes clamped shut.

He gripped the back of her ribs and urged her deeper into the arch. She went willingly, letting the crown of her head scrape the sheet and her arms fall by her sides. One of his arms held her in place. The other danced along the rim of her camisole. Moist breath teased her chest. His fingers dipped below the right strap, and then slipped it off her shoulder.

"Please, Z. You won't break me."

She didn't know what she wanted, but she wanted it now. If he couldn't make love to her, she needed to feel the unbridled desire that kept him from the care and intimacy he now showed her.

Z drove the strap off her other shoulder and jerked the front of her shirt to her belly button. The fabric gave under his strength, scraping the skin at the small of her back. Her eyes flew open and her head shot up.

Grey eyes smelted to liquid metal. They stole every thought, except *fuck me*. Luckily, she didn't say it. It would take two shifts of material for their most intimate parts to meet, to mate. Z leaned forward. His lips sealed around her pink areola. When he sucked her hips rocked, pressing her wetness against him. His tongue slapped her nipple. His gaze locked on hers.

Full lips parted over her pointed flesh. He plucked her deeper into his mouth and sucked. The electric sting of his tongue traveled through her body and lashed the tip of her clit. Greer's hands clamped onto the coarse strands of his hair. She tugged him closer, which drove her hips forward. They undulated, rubbing against the full crown of his head. The voltage multiplied.

His fingers bit into the lushness of her bottom. He urged her strokes harder and deeper. The frantic pace he set with his hand matched the suckling of his mouth. Frenzied breaths dried Greer's throat, but her inner walls slicked. She grabbed at his shoulders and banded her legs around his hips. Her eyes closed.

"Yes, Z. Yes."

A pop and the sudden immoveable bar of his hands shocked her eyes wide. His mouth left her flesh. He untwined her legs from his middle. Ragged huffs of air left his thick lips.

"What'd I—" Greer stammered.

"You didn't do a damn thing wrong. You do it all too well. That's the only problem."

He stood. A pang of alarm jarred her pre-orgasmic bliss. The look of pure animalistic lust in his gaze tamped down her rising concern. She'd gotten to him, Mr. Closed Off and Concealed. He filled his hands with her bottom, shoved her up the bed, and then climbed on. His fingers hooked the shirt wadded at her waist. The camisole and boxers too moved down her body under his coaxing hand.

Both nipples throbbed, but the one he'd paid such close attention to swelled larger than the other. Rubbed red skin covered her pubic bone. A dimple the size and shape of Z's thumb marred her hip. The inner muscles twitched. He tossed the clothing over his shoulder and spread her knees wide. His head tilted for a better view of her everything. Her cheeks should've burned, but the only thing aflame was her desire for this man.

"Cor blimey, beautiful." The front of his boxer briefs twitched and the dark circle at the tip of his penis expanded.

Z lowered himself to all fours. His head hung low like a hunting wolf as he crawled toward her. When he nuzzled his wide shoulders between her legs Greer's neurons liquefied. His gaze held her in place. A velvet swipe of his tongue sang across the swollen tip of her tender nub to the base, and then over the crest of her pelvis. Her fingers clawed the bed sheets. Her senses overloaded. Heavy breaths rushed in and out of her lungs.

"Easy," he warned. "I can't have you passing out. You'd miss all the fun."

His voice thundered an inch from her lady bits, vibrating her from inside out. It did nothing to slow her breathing. Her breasts surged to the ceiling, and then lulled so quickly her extremities tingled and the room narrowed to a shallow tunnel.

"Greer?"

"Hum?"

"Are you scared?"

"No. No." Her head whipped back and forth, tousling her hair. "I just can't catch..." She panted.

Z's mouth encircled her clit and sucked.

Greer gasped. Her lungs locked. His hands pulled hers from the bedding and entwined with her fingers. The comfort anchored her to the earth. It pulled the room and the slow strokes of Z's tongue into sharp focus. Her pulse regulated. She clung to his sure grip and bowed to his skilled mouth. Each lap of his silky, taunting tongue drove her higher and higher, while his hold encouraged her fall. Greer held tight to Z, closed her eyes, and let go of everything else.

A shot of ecstasy unlike any orgasm she'd experienced licked its way through every nerve ending in her body. Her back curved off the bed. Her toes pointed and her legs quivered.

"Oh God. Oh God. Oh Gooo..." Her chant disintegrated into moans and throaty whimpers.

His strokes kept pace with her vocal symphony, and then tapered, matching her breaths. When her taut form uncoiled from the stringed instrument of passion it had become Z whispered kisses up to the crown of her pelvis. His fingers slid from hers. An acute moment of bereavement jarred her bliss. Her bleary gaze found him.

He pushed his chest off the mattress. A fine sheen of sweat clung to the ridges of his pecs and darkened his tousled hairline. His kisses continued up her centerline to the tip of her chin. Her lips parted to accommodate his, but they jumped over her mouth to her nose and finally her forehead. The bed creaked under his shifting weight. He settled beside her thrumming body.

The popcorn-speckled ceiling came into view. They laid diagonally, closer to the foot of the bed than the head. At the end nearest corner the bare mattress peeked out, the sheet meant to cover it ruffled near her feet. Her hum ebbed, overtaken by a chill. Greer turned toward Z, fully expecting to be patted on the head and told to go to sleep.

Why provide him the opportunity? She dove into the crook of his arm, wedged her head under his chin, and cuddled her legs around his hairier ones. The unfamiliar texture of hard muscle and itchy hair should have kept her on edge, but contentment warmed her. After a long silent heap of seconds, Z's arm nestled against her back. His hand covered hers over his heart. Every muscle in her body noodled. Euphoria and exhaustion combined with his heady scent proved a lethal concoction. Her gaze lingered on the bump of his pulse at the base of his neck as long as it possibly could before succumbing.

Chapter Fourteen

One. Two. Three. Four. Jesus, 116 more seconds to go. Zeke tore his gaze from the poorly-calibrated wall clock and tried to calm his heart rate. He inhaled for ten seconds, and then exhaled for ten through the first minute. The persistent muscle jammed into his sternum like a rising alarm clock. He focused on using his diaphragm to move breath in and out of his lungs. It always worked in the field, but this was unlike any mission he'd ever endured. The jittery pounding continued. *Fifty-six. Fifty-seven. Fifty-eight. Fifty-nine.*

Zeke lifted Greer's limp arm and head, held his breath, and slipped from under her with the same care he might show a depressed landmine. When his backside cleared the bed he lunged to the far corner of the room. His hands found his hips. He hung his head between his shoulders and huffed as though he'd run across the Afghan desert...again.

For a bird who weighed 135 pounds sopping wet, Greer knew how to wallop a bloke's feet out from under him. The damnedest thing was she didn't know that she knew how to do it. It came as naturally to her as the sway of her perfectly curved arse. No schemes, no pretense. The arm and leg that had been sprawled across his body retracted close to hers, accentuating the bow of her lower back and pert bottom.

“Kill me now.” He stalked to the bed, snatched the comforter off the floor, and dropped it across her soft skin.

She tugged the covers over her shoulder and tucked them under her chin without blinking. Zeke backed away and paced the edges of the room like the caged animal he was. What the bloody hell was wrong with him? He’d managed captivity in an outhouse on an Alaskan glacier better than this. But how?

He never lost sight of the goal—hold out until he found a way to get out. The same could work here. He needed to find out who had ordered their abduction and why. Once he had those answers he and Greer could go their separate ways. His calluses scraped the length of his face.

Zeke sat on the edge of the other bed, as far away from Greer as the queen sized mattress allowed. The bag lay at his feet. Beside it the first-aid kit gaped, its contents strewn about the faded greens and pink of the patterned comforter. He reached for the single packet of antacid tablets, ripped into the foil, and popped them in his mouth. While he ground the chalk into barely consumable paste, he pulled the laptop in front of him.

Five windows cluttered the screen. He scrapped each of them. Right now, the list was useless. The code didn’t follow any known cyphers. He opened the list of Stas holdings Greer had unlocked.

Each entry listed a physical address, property value, inventory value, and site “manager.” After scrolling through the extensive list until his eyes crossed and his lids threatened to shut without proper caffeinating, a pattern materialized. Values for the arms warehouses, "gentlemen's" clubs, and transportation centers correlated with others in their category to within ten to twenty thousand dollars. Transportation took the largest sums. They bought officials throughout the state in which they operated, in addition to the cost of vehicles—planes, semis, trucks, cars, boats—and the insurance they carried to cover the hauls. Warehouses came next because of their inventory. The paltry amount assigned to the gentlemen's clubs proved that they weren't in the business to make money, but for their own personal power trips.

Dip-wads.

Several listing values stood above the rest. Each lacked any name attached to the property. Using live satellite feed, Zeke pulled up the addresses in individual windows. The grit of sand and froth of ocean marked a beach house on the Outer Banks of North Carolina, while the green of a golf course sidled up to the Miami mansion. There was an air strip in California and an estate in upstate New York. He didn't have a clue what it meant, but the familiar spark at the base of his pituitary meant the sliver fit into the multilayered puzzle somehow. The same way he knew Greer fit into this equation, somehow.

She huddled under the blanket in a tight little ball. Her long lashes rested easily on her cheek. He needed to figure shit out and fast. The more time he spent with her, the more jumbled his insides became.

Zeke turned back to the screen—trying his damnedest to ignore the uptick in his chest—and logged into the black screen. He typed the address for the air strip into the white search box, and then pressed enter. A white line ran from one side to the other only four times before the windows offered one result—Gibraltar Investments.

President Grieves W. Stockton's campaign slogan and the irritating music that accompanied the commercials paraded through Zeke's mind. *Stockton, steady as Gibraltar.*

"No fucking way."

He uncoiled his fists and drummed away on the keys. Every address he entered cycled back under the same holding as he'd expected. Time to dive deeper into the rock. The link took him to the information page for Gibraltar Investments. A blanket on anonymity cloaked the owner or owners, but that had never stopped him before. He searched every bank account tied to the holding.

A sea of numbers sloshed onto the screen. He scrolled through the three ledgers and found more than 500 pages per account. The first deposits and withdrawals began two years ago, six months after the president had taken office. They also matched the amount on the Stas books for each of the properties. Beyond those entries, daily deposits and withdrawals populated the registry. None of the amounts exceeded ten thousand dollars nor repeated the same value. Whoever had set this up either knew just enough to get by without getting flagged or, more likely, never expected anyone to look.

Zeke grinned while he entered the routing number for one of the deposit transactions and hit enter. The white line zoomed across the screen once, twice, ten, twenty, fifty times. His grin fell. After too damn long the white words, *No Results*, flashed at the center of the screen.

Fine, maybe they knew a little more than he'd given them credit for, but he had a hunch and he refused to stop until it panned out or proved him wrong. Sweat gathered on his upper lip. He accessed the high-powered sequencing software, pulled in the account reports, and ran a diagnostic. The program estimated a four-hour run time. It always took at least thirty minutes longer.

He needed to talk to the president, but he couldn't, not without blowing all his covers. How many were there now? Who the fuck was he today? In truth, he'd never known who he was, a punching bag, a street kid, a kid taking orders from Her Majesty's Royal Marines, a dagger, and then what? A rogue.

The clock on the top right of the computer read two-oh-eight a.m. Where had the night gone? His gaze slid to Greer. Her lips puckered in steady respiration. Slowly, he eased his back against the headboard, and then opened the information he'd downloaded from the US Elite database. He stared at the registry, at the 1.2 billion dollar entry that had doubled the private security firm's budget last year, at the red flag that signaled his involvement and embroiled him in a world of shit.

He patted the pistol next to his leg, saw the light flashing on his homemade security system, doubled checked Greer's calmed breaths, and then propped his head against the wall. Nothing to do now but catch some sleep and dream about the end of this nightmare...not the pain he'd endured through it. His arms folded across his chest with his palm covering the throbbing scar.

***

Greer's sharp cry ripped through his subconscious like a wraith in the night. Zeke bound to his knees on the saggy mattress, lifted his weapon, and scanned left to right for the intruder. Sunlight filtered in through the cracks between the window and the thick curtain, but revealed no Stas.

Greer sat on the floor between the two beds. The camisole and shorts covered her body and her own small hand sealed over her mouth. Light from the laptop on her straight legs revealed wells of unshed tears.

Zeke set the gun on the rumpled covers, kickstarted his heart again, and climbed onto the floor in front of her. He expected her to scream. G*et away from me. How do you have all this information? Who are you?* Her head swung back and forth in denial. He sat in front of her for a full minute, but no protests poured from her lips. Tears fell over her clamped hand. He reached across and pried her hand free one finger at a time.

"Can you zoom this in?" she whimpered.

His fingers hooked the computer and turned it on her thighs. The satellite feed of the upstate New York house filled the screen. He clicked on the diagnostic. It showed ten minutes remaining. After returning to the estate, Zeke magnified the sprawling house with its circular drive, court yard, pool and pool house, and pond, barn, and attached horse paddock out back, and then turned it toward Greer.

Her lips pressed together. Streams formed on either cheek. She slapped them away, but fresh ones cascaded in their place.

"What is it?" Zeke's hard voice cracked. He hated the tell, but damn the terror in her eyes sliced him in half.

"It's..." She drew an uneven breath, and then started again. "It's the place."

"What place?"

"My father and uncle took me and my cousin on their business trip. Dad always left me with a nanny, but agreed to bring me at my cousin's request. He got to go to the country house all the time. I was excited to go. There were horses, a pool, a pond. I thought we'd go riding together, fishing. My dad and uncle locked themselves in the study the entire time. On the third day..." Her quivering finger lifted to the green-roofed barn. "After, I hid in the stall with one of the horses until the housekeeper came calling for dinner, and didn't leave my room the rest of the trip."

He pulled the computer from her lap and shoved it onto his bed. Her knees drew to her chest. White-blonde strands curtained her back and legs. Muffled sobs leaked from the human cocoon. He sat next to her like a useless fool with no tool or weapons with which to fight her sorrow. Plans to slaughter her family formed in his ripe mind, but what good would that do her? As kind-hearted as she was, she'd probably mourn the fuckers.

Zeke eased his hand onto her shoulder. Her cheek nuzzled his fingers. The move bolstered his resolve. He slid his hands under her arms and lifted her into his lap, giving her every opportunity to protest. She clutched her hands and knees to her chest and burrowed under his chin. Her small body shook against him for a long while. The longer she cried the tighter his arms held her. Without conscious choice, he quietly sang the song his sister sang to him when he was sad.

"One for sorrow,
Two for joy,
Three for a girl,
Four for a boy,
Five for silver,
Six for gold,
Seven for a secret,
Never to be told.
Eight for a wish,
Nine for a kiss,

Ten for a bird,
You must not miss."

The sobs morphed into hiccups around seven, and abated by nine. Her fingers rubbed across his pectoral several times. She sat and grimaced at him.

"Singing's that bad, huh?"

"No." Her mouth formed an exaggerated O. She swatted the notion away, and then went back to drying his chest. "I soaked your chest."

He placed his hand over hers, pinning it in place. Her wet gaze found his. It sucked him under the current. Without calculating, Zeke placed his hand at her nape and pulled her close. His lips slid over hers, again and again. He loved the taste of her, the feel.

The computer beeped. Zeke tipped her head to the side and looked at the screen. The debited sums minus the property sums from all three counts equaled exactly 1.2 billion dollars.

His will power joined forces and he pried his lips from her pliable mouth. Her head swiveled to the laptop screen, and then back.

"What do all those numbers mean?"

"They mean I have to question your father."

Chapter Fifteen

"My father?" Greer jerked upright.

Z didn't respond to her shriek. She'd heard him and he knew it perfectly well.

"You mean interrogate him?"

"I do hope he resists." Z shrugged.

"Why?"

"Because I'd quite enjoy torturing him." His eyes darkened to a shade of hell.

Greer swallowed her fear. She prodded his chest with two fingers. "That's not what I meant and you know it. Why do you have to question my dad?"

"You know why. You just don't want to believe it. Just like you don't want to think I'm a piece of shite."

"I'm beginning to change my mind on that." Her arms crossed into a knot over her breasts.

Z levered his forearm under her bottom. She closed her eyes against the rush of ecstasy that overtook her outrage. He held her to his chest, stood on his knees, and moved to the edge of his bed. If he tossed her on top she'd probably forget about the argument in five seconds...or less. She swallowed the excess saliva in her mouth and tried to ignore her musk on his lips.

He sat with her still in his arms, turned the computer to face them, and then clicked each of the properties in turn. “These properties are all in a holding named Gibraltar Investments.”

Panic she’d tried so hard to bury over the years bubbled over. Greer’s hand caught the cry that shot from her throat.

“I can tie your dad and uncle to this house, but I can only question one of them right now.”

She struggled with the terror thoughts of her uncle and cousin conjured. Her hand fell away. “That’s the Stockton family motto.”

“I know. I was in the States for part of the campaign.”

Greer’s stomach flipped again. She pressed her nose to Z’s neck and breathed long, deep breaths until the gymnastic event ceased.

“Better?” he asked.

“I guess. How do you have access to all this information?”

“Don’t ask.”

She smirked. “I already did.”

“How’d you get the computer off my lap without me knowing?”

“In my work noise gets a woman killed. Nice diversion. Now, spill.”

He dumped her onto her bottom, stood, and dug clothes from his bag. “I could divert you, if I were so inclined.”

Greer let her gaze drop to the erection popping his boxer briefs. “So, you’re not inclined?”

“I’m hungry and…” His gaze raked her front.

“And what?”

“I can’t roger you, and then off your father, if the need arises.”

“Roger me?”

Z shoved his legs into his pants and yanked on a T-shirt. “You know what I mean. It wouldn’t be proper.” He shoved several bills into his back pocket, his pistol into his waistband, and headed for the door.

"Where are you going?"

"To get some food." He disengaged the device on the door. "Shoot anyone who comes to the door, except me, and don't call your father."

"You trust me not to call him while you're gone?"

"I trust you'll do the right thing. Once you really think about all the things we can piece together, you'll know what that is. Oh, get dressed. We're leaving in thirty." He opened the door, slipped through the opening, and then disappeared behind it.

That was hardly enough time to dress, much less contemplate her loyalties. She slumped against the bed and stared at the computer screen. The metal frame dug into her spine. It didn't compare to the painful memories that innocuous picture wrought. Her cousin had pressed her face into the lounger's cushion, suffocating her objections while he violated her. But more heart wrenching than that had been her father's refusal to take action against him. The man supposed to protect her from all things had turned the tables and placed the heavy burden of fault on her slender shoulders. Strike one.

Greer stood and moved to the vanity. She dragged the brush through her hair, starting at the ends and then working her way up. When the bristles finally smoothed through from base to tip she pulled it back into a low ponytail, and then brushed her teeth. The reflection looked nothing like her ruddy cheeked, round faced father; her father, who'd convinced her to quit her job and join US Elite for a noble cause that didn't exist. Strike two.

She splashed water on her face, and then blotted it away with the hand towel. At the bag she pulled out a pair of jeans and a snug, light-purple T-shirt. In all her years, she'd never seen her father in a T-shirt. He couldn't abide casual clothing, but apparently had no problem concocting a scheme with her uncle that involved properties in New York, South Carolina, Miami, California, and New Mexico. All strategic locations for trafficking drugs, weapons, and women across the United States. Strike three.

While she slipped her feet into her shoes the door lock clicked, and then opened. Z strode inside with a paper bag pinched between his pinkie and palm, and a coffee in each hand. He crossed the room and extended the Styrofoam cup to her. She remembered the last time a man had given her a cup of coffee.

Cold sweats iced Greer's body. Her hands quaked. The oxygen in the air dissipated.

Z's hand clamped her nape. He drove her to the edge of the bed and shoved her head between her knees. "Long, deep breaths."

Minutes passed before her lips cooperated, but finally they did.

"My father didn't only recommend me for US Elite, but for the team to infiltrate the Stas. I think he was trying to get rid of me."

Chapter Sixteen

Beyond the weepy oak branches stood the house of Greer's nightmares. If Zeke had any doubt as to whether the place and its memories haunted her he had only to look at the white-knuckled grip she held on the leather armrest of the black BMW he'd switched out at one of his storage units on the way. Out of the way, really, but what was one more hour?

"I won't let anyone hurt you, Greer."

"I know," she whispered.

"If anyone's home, they can't hear us."

"I know," she whispered again.

When Khani had pulled off his bandages she'd yanked them without warning. It helped him get over the shock. They'd talked this plan to death over the four, no, five-hour trip. He pressed the phone button on the steering wheel, and reminded, "You've got this."

A dial tone filled the car a second before the loud ring. Greer released the handle, reached across the console, and shoved his shoulder. It rang once, twice, three times.

"Hello," came a haughty voice.

"Dad?" Greer almost choked the word.

"Oh my God, Greer? Are you okay? Baby? Where are you? I've been frantic trying to find you.

None of your friends knew where you were. Do you know you've been out of touch for days?"

With each question Greer's shoulders straightened. When the questions turned to accusation her jaw hardened.

"I'm fine, Dad."

"Where are you? I'll come get you."

"I need you to meet me at your house."

"Well, I'm here. I couldn't go into work with you missing," he scoffed, and then added, "Come home, baby."

Greer's furious gaze met his. He nodded.

"Meet me at your upstate house."

Silence whined through the line.

"4087 Winding Lane. The place where Greeson raped me, remember?"

"What are you talking about, baby?"

"Cut the bullshit. I know everything. I'm just giving you a chance to explain before I go to the feds."

Another noiseless spell whirled across space. Stockton cleared his throat. "What time would you like to meet?" The man asked the question with as much concern as he would a tee time. It told Zeke he didn't give a shit about Greer's threat.

"Four hours will give me enough time to get there. How about you?"

"I'll take the plane and be there when you arrive."

Greer leaned across the car, ended the call, and then slumped against the seat. One arm rested on the door. The other splayed across the armrest. Her head rolled to the side. "Now what?"

"We wait and watch."

"For four hours?" Her arms shot into the air.

"I expect it won't take that long."

She turned to the passenger window, staring out at the thick curtain of leaves. A hearty sigh filled the car. Another blasted no more than a minute later. She adjusted the vent to blow directly on her face. Two minutes later she turned it away, and then flipped down the visor. She didn't look in the mirror, but slid the guard back and forth. The light above flashed on and off in time with her idiosyncrasy. Five minutes into the ritual she gave up, straightened, and turned to face him.

"I guess we could make out in the back seat. I've never done that."

Her words and the devilish look in her eye stroked his prick. "Jesus, Greer." He shifted the binoculars around his neck and adjusted the laptop being attacked by his crotch.

"Fine." A spark lit behind her blue eyes. "If you're going to be a prude, tell me who you work for."

Zeke removed the lanyard from his neck and computer from his lap, plopped them on the dash, and leaned across the console. Greer nibbled on her lower lip. Part of his brain exploded on the spot. He buried his fingers in her hair, pulled her within an inch of his mouth, and held her there. She arched into his hold, trying to complete the promise of contact. Her breasts swelled against the cotton of her shirt. The pink of her lips opened to receive him. Still he held her there. Her palms molded to his chest. She drove him to the brink of self-control.

"Kiss me already," she panted.

"You weren't kidding about the backseat?"

"Not really."

He tilted her head and whispered kisses around the edges of her mouth. "We'd never fit. Too bad I don't have a panel van. Or maybe it's for the best. I wouldn't want to steal your virtue in a bloody car."

"You can't steal something freely given."

His other hand found the crook of her neck, molded to it, and eased her forward. Their lips met in a tangle of heated flesh. Gone were the soft, tentative kisses. In their place, unhinged passion. Her hands roved his neck and chest, clutching and playing over the uneven topography. His knuckles brushed the side of her jaw, grazed the thrumming pulse in her neck, and dragged across her stiff nipples.

Greer moaned into his open mouth. She sucked his tongue, coaxing it into her mouth. Her lips slid off the tip, then slid slowly back to the base. The imitation of sex on his mouth ratcheted his need and busted through his reserve. His hand slipped under her shirt, yanked the cup of her bra to the side, and rubbed her bud hard in a counter-clockwise circle.

Her hips jerked off the leather on the second rotation. Air from her gasp rushed across his face. He seized the opportunity, continuing with his assault on her nipple and regaining control over the kiss. His tongue lashed at her lips. She opened to him, her head lazing to the side in an attempt to recapture the lead. Dominance probably comforted her. He'd show her abandon could be so much sweeter.

Zeke dipped his fingers into the front of her jeans. He jerked the material toward her belly, driving the crotch against the front of her pelvis and straight to the heart of the matter. Greer stopped seeking control all right. She bowed off the seat and cried out. Her fingers dug into the rounds of his shoulders. He pulled again, shimmying the coarse fabric left and right.

“Oh my. Ah.” Her hands found his hair and tugged.

“Do you want more, Greer?”

“Yes.”

The certainty in her voice knocked him back a step. He recovered by popping the snap of her jeans and dragging the zipper low. Of all the clothes to wear while necking, trousers were the worst. It took three sure jolts to drag them over the swell of her hips. Thinking trousers around her ankles would make her feel too exposed in the light of day on a suburban street, he left them high on her thighs. His first two knuckles coasted over her pelvis and down between the heat of her legs. They dragged over the damp lace of the panties he’d chosen for her.

Their kisses slowed. Zeke pressed against her swollen clit, and continued the descent of his knuckles across her labia. On the way back up, he paid extra attention to her distended nub, circling and strumming. Her hips undulated in time with his hand in the most erotic dance he’d ever witnessed. Sweat beaded on his forehead. His cock throbbed for attention. He ignored everything but Greer. Not the safest move in their current situation. Fuck if he could do anything to rein this in.

He shimmied her panties to the side. She moaned against his lips.

“Greer?” His voice cracked like a pre-pubescent chit.

“Yes.” Her tone answered to the question he’d yet to ask.

He cleared his throat. “Do you want me inside you?”

“Yes,” she breathed.

It was the quietest she'd been since they started this dance. Zeke stilled his hand just above her dewy flesh. "You can tell me no. I can make you come without milking the silk of your sweet pussy."

"I think you could just by looking at me and talking to me, but I want you inside me and all around me. It's just new."

"And terrifying?"

"Exciting." She smashed her lips to his mouth. Her hand smoothed down his arm to his hand and pressed it against her most intimate flesh.

He needed no more encouragement. His fingers slicked in her arousal. They glided over her lower lips and found her clit. Zeke forced his eyes open against the ecstasy of her skin, needing to see her reactions to his touch. When he circled the bundle of nerves her hips followed his finger. A massage to the base forced the breath from her lungs in quick heavy pants. Not ready for her to blow, he shifted to the point and rimmed the V of hooded skin. Her eyes clamped against the sensation. He lightened the touch and her eyes flew open. She was easier to read than a topo map.

Once more his fingers danced to the foundation of her clitoris and then split, landing on either side of the nub, and stroked her to panted breaths. His other hand tweaked her pointed nipples.

"Please, Z. More." She writhed in his carnal embrace.

Zeke smiled against her sweat-slicked neck. He nibbled a path to her mouth and twisted his hand. The V of his fingers pointed toward the sky and spread wide, exposing her swollen red clit. His middle finger extended. Throbbing in his crotch doubled in battering rushes of blood. How he wished he were burying himself balls deep inside Greer, but this wasn't about his pleasure. Though, watching her come apart at the seams in rapture, as opposed to sorrow, pleased him immensely.

One velvet inch at a time he discovered the hot, sweet feel of her. When he hit the second knuckle he had to back out to the tip. She was so damn tight. He whirled his finger around her silken walls, and then pressed deeper.

Greer wrapped one arm around his neck and another around his invading arm. With a toss of her head the platinum hair fled her rosy cheeks. Her body arched. She rocked against his arm. He pumped his middle finger slowly in and almost out of her warmth, before burying to the hilt and rasping her inner flesh with long steady drags of his pad.

"Oh, yes. I can't stop. I can't..." Her wide gaze found his.

"Don't you dare stop. Come apart for me."

Her hips undulated. She drove her sensitive clit onto his knuckles. The bite of her nails sank into his tricep.

"That's it, baby. Come for me." He released her nipple, allowing the blood to flow into the tip once more, and then plundered her mouth.

Moans filled his ear. Her body constricted around his finger for nearly an entire minute. Mumbled words and gasps crashed against his lips. Spasms took hold of her inner muscles.

Zeke pressed deep, but quit stroking. When the pulses stopped he dragged his finger from her body, broke their kiss, and sucked it into his mouth. Her mouth fell open on an inhale.

"Since I quit, I've been dying to taste you again."

Her throat worked on a swallow, but she couldn't seem to get a word out. She pulled him down and licked his lips with languorous strokes. He allowed himself one last kiss, and then straightened.

"I've been wanting to taste you too." Greer leaned on the console.

He framed her face with his hands to stall her. "If you put your mouth on me right now, I'd blow your brains out the back of your skull." His lips grazed hers. "Pull up your pants before we get caught or I lose my self-control."

"I lost mine." She dragged her swollen lip into her mouth.

"And it was..." He let the thought fall away. No need to get sentimental about bodily functions.

"Was what?" Those clear blue eyes stared up at him with lusty admiration and he couldn't deny her.

"The most beautifully erotic thing I've ever seen."

"And you're sure you don't want to crawl into the back seat?"

"I'd bust the windows and rip the seats out, trying to fuck you proper."

Her cheeks reddened further. She turned away, wiggled her panties and then trousers up her flushed hips, and fastened them. Zeke bumped up the air flow. He adjusted the snugness of his pants, not that it did a lick of good. Thinking the word lick certainly didn't help. His balls tightened. In a desperate attempt to shift the direction of his thoughts, he snatched the binoculars from the dash and aimed them at the house. Despite the brilliant mid-day sun the grounds hid behind a light fog on the windows.

They passed nearly half of an hour in the silent wake of their fervor. It took every one of the minutes for his raging hard-on to ebb. The windows didn't take as long to clear. He scanned the horizon in every direction, paying close attention to the ton of bricks and mortar. Birds and squirrels milled about. A nanny strolled down the tree lined street with a fat-cheeked infant swaddled in a prison of cotton.

"Why did they take you?"

His gaze swung from the chubby baby to Greer. He lowered the binocs on the snappy turn. "Seriously?" As he had before, he leaned across the console and dug his hands into her hair. "You want to go again?"

She pecked a kiss on the tip of his nose, and then retreated to the opposite side of her seat. He let her go.

"No, I just wanted you to know I'm not so easily distracted."

"If you think that was easy, I suppose I did it right."

Her smile broke the tension at his nape.

Zeke collapsed into his seat and reclined it a few degrees. Greer trusted him with everything, her life. It was time he started trusting her...just a little.

"They wanted to know who I was and who I worked for."

A robust laugh shook the car. She tossed her head back and covered her mouth. Between sighs her statement poured out a word or two at a time. "They'd have better luck getting a tree to talk."

"They'd have had better luck if they'd used you to get me to talk." He grabbed her, pulled her to his side of the car, and laid a kiss more sweet than seductive on her red lips. When he released her she stayed perfectly still. Her hazy gaze searched his.

The urge to squirm took hold with both hands, but he didn't move. Instead, he let her scour his soul for whatever it was she sought. She wasn't likely to find it, but he let her all the same.

"I thought I'd made some fatal mistake and they'd caught me," he rambled.

"Stealing the data?"

Zeke bobbed his head. "But that didn't make sense. They never produced or even talked about the evidence they had against me. Now, here we are, still trying to get to the bottom of it."

The soft pads of Greer's fingers traced his jaw. "What did they do to you?"

"Doesn't matter. I'm alive. They're not."

"How long did they have you?"

He ignored the chill that crawled up his spine. "Eleven days."

"Eleven days?" Greer's indignant shout reverberated off the glass. The whites of her eyes grew two-fold. Her inflamed lips curved into a frown. "And you were conscious for every minute of…" She shooed away the thought with violent shakes of her head. When they slowed her fingers laced his.

The tender gesture and her vicious outrage on his behalf shifted something inside his chest

"How did you escape?"

For a heavy minute Zeke waffled about how much to tell her. He must have waited too long. Her gaze left him and wandered down the street.

"My sister."

"How?"

"Let's just say she has skills and she put them to work."

Greer hiked a knee in her seat and then turned toward him. "I like her already. Now, if I ever meet her, I might have to slip her the tongue."

She said it with such nonchalance, holding her innocent face in a dead pan, that he lost it. Surveillance or not, his uproarious laughter might have chased away the birds. It definitely threaded a stitch in his side.

Her hand smacked over his mouth with enough force to silence him mid-breath. The tightness in her jaw and focus of her gaze through the windshield transformed him from cackling idiot to the warrior he'd been since his eighteenth birthday. He lifted the binoculars and spotted her cause for concern immediately.

A black SUV pulled into the garage. Six men poured out of the vehicle, donned full tactical gear, gleaming AK-47s, and mean mugs. Three entered the house with the hustle of battle. Two more fanned into the woods, disappearing in the thick brush. The last one stood guard at the open bay door.

"Where's my dad?"

"Don't know." Zeke pulled the laptop onto his thighs and opened it.

"If he doesn't show—"

"There's still time."

Fifteen minutes passed in edgy quiet. The sentinel's head maintained a swivel. Finally, his lips moved. His head bobbed once, his chest puffed, and a smirk pulled at his cheek. The molten rush of battle coursed through Zeke's veins. His breathing sped. They were so close to answers and so far away. If Stockton didn't show, they'd lose their only chance at finding the truth.

"We have the pieces of the puzzle. If he doesn't show, we can go to the FBI."

"Right," he snorted. "If we accuse the president of the United States of trafficking, amassing his own army, and using federal dollars to do it with shattered pieces of a tightly woven enterprise, we'll die before the sun sets."

"What about the media?"

"Do you plan on having kids?"

She jerked as though he'd hit her with fifty-thousand volts. "I...don't know. I've never really thought about it. I mean, you have to have sex to get pregnant. I'm twenty-six and it hasn't happened yet. So..." Her shoulders bounced. "Could I see myself as a mother? Sure. Though, how terrifying would that be. I could also see myself..." The ends of her mouth formed a frown. "You know, just me forever and ever."

Zeke let that sit for several seconds. As detail oriented as he was, he hadn't seen where that question would lead her. It made his point seem stupid now, but it needed to be made.

"If you did have kids, would you throw them to the wolves?"

Both her cheeks ballooned with air, and then steamed out in a drawn huff. "So, you meant figuratively." Her arms crossed over her chest, unraveled, and then crossed once more. "If I had kids, no, I wouldn't throw them to the wolves."

"Media is out of the question."

"Then what—"

The whirl of HELO blades cut Greer off.

They watched the sleek black bird glide through the blue sky, and then descend at the center of the lawn. A man with salt and pepper hair exited the side. Constant gusts blew his black suit jacket wide, revealing an intricately gold scrolled Walther PPK and about fifteen extra pounds that the coat concealed rather well.

"Dear old dad?"

"Yeah, dear old dad."

Chapter Seventeen

The death of the longest relationship of her life should illicit, at least, some errant tears and, at most, heavy weeping. Greer watched her father cross the lawn, stroll past the shimmering pool—the very spot where her cousin had violated her—and then enter his study through the veranda. Her eyes remained dry, but her vision clouded in a haze of red. Fury beat itself against the front of her skull, creating quite the headache. She gripped the handle and prepared to rip the door off its hinges. To hell with subtlety and tactics.

"You'd never make it to him." Z's heavy hand settled on her shoulder.

Why did he always have to be right? Her fists shook with the weight of her burden.

"Let it out."

"If I do, they'll know we're here."

"We're far enough away, they can't hear you."

"They could today."

"Fair enough. Channel it, then. Turn all that rage into focus."

Recycled air tinted with pine filled her lungs. He was right. No losing it now. When she turned toward Z his stormy gaze hovered intently on hers.

"This could go sideways on us in the blink of an eye. I need to know you're with me." His five o'clock shadow had turned into a seven or eight o'clock burgeoning beard.

"I'm with you." She placed her hand on her shoulder atop his.

"Good. Here we go." His thumb depressed the phone button. Again it rang throughout the car.

The pulse in her ears thundered.

"Greer?"

"Tell your men to leave," she ordered.

"What?"

"Is it time for a hearing aid, dad?"

"Listen here, little girl."

"No, you listen. Tell your men to leave or I walk."

The line went still, but the call time continued ticking. Forty seconds elapsed. Two men materialized from the brush and headed for the garage. The man at the back door met them at the side of the SUV. One by one they slowly piled inside.

"Happy now?" her father snapped.

"I wonder if the FBI would be happy with only half of the evidence."

"God dammit, girl. Let me talk to the man calling the shots right this minute."

Z's chuckle sounded rich and imposing. "How small minded of you to think your daughter isn't in charge, Senator."

"Who the hell are you?" Her dad asked with such force she wondered if he choked on the receiver.

"That's a question many have asked over many years," Z said. "None found the answer. Now, if you don't mind the sight of dead bodies and have no regard for your own suffering, continue disrespecting your daughter. If you do mind, listen to her." He smacked the steering wheel and ended the call.

She leaned toward Z. On the top left of the subdivided screen Greer's dad beat his cell phone against the large mahogany desk. His mouth opened wide and held for what she guessed was a hearty bellow. In two of the other screens guards ran to the noise. He hollered and pointed some more. One hired gun shook his head in vehement opposition. Her dad drew his gun and aimed it at the man's head.

"No." Her hand clasped her heart.

The hired gun let his rifle fall to the end of the strap at his side, offered his palms, and walked backward out of the office. His friend beat him out. They grabbed the man making himself at home in the kitchen, spilled out the side door, ran across the wide lawn, and met the SUV half way down the rear drive. After they shuffled in the vehicle lurched forward. It rounded the corner and left a whirling cloud of leaves in its wake.

Greer eased back into her seat and caught her breath. "Have you checked—"

Z pointed to the screen and the feed for the camera he'd set up on the main road through the neighborhood. "They haven't stopped yet." He closed the computer and tossed it and the binoculars into the backseat. "I have the motion sensor set on the driveway. If they come back, it will trigger the alarm on my phone." His hand slid to the handle. "Are you ready to get this wanker?"

"Yes."

"Are you prepared to hear the answers to your questions?"

"Probably not, but I can't live with the lies any longer."

"Then let's go. If the alarm trips we'll have thirty seconds to make it out the French doors and behind the row of statues. We stay put until they're in range, and then light them up."

"What about my dad?"

"Let me deal with him."

Greer had witnessed Z's indifference at taking a life, but could she be dispassionate about him killing her father, if it came to that? The truth, since that's what she wanted from now on, was she didn't know. Regardless of her feelings on the matter, she trusted Z. "Okay." She climbed out the car, placed the Glock from the glove compartment in the rear waistband of her pants, checked the backup at her ankle, and met Z at the front of the car.

They jogged around the edge of the woods, staying just inside the tree line until necessity forced them into the open. From the uptick in Z's pace she could tell he didn't like the exposure any more than she. Still he positioned himself in between her and the house. Their path intersected with the east side, the side with the fewest windows, farthest from the garage.

When they reached the house Z slid open the window they'd unlocked during their earlier trip inside, peeked his head in, and then gave her a boost. She placed one foot through the opening and onto the countertop of the master bathroom. After ducking inside, she darted through the bedroom to the hallway and waited. Her ears strained for the slightest sound, but heard none. The house smelled of cigars and bourbon, just as it had the first time she'd been here. Her stomach tumbled like an Olympic gymnast.

Z's hand on her nape settled the momentary tailspin. He gave her a little squeeze, and then ducked around her to take the lead. His gun and gaze scanned the room one side to the other. On silent feet he whispered down the long corridor, dodging statues and high-brow paintings of foxes running for their lives while men on overbred horses followed their baying hounds. My, how the tables turned.

At the doorway to the study, Z stalled. He pulled a telescoping mirror from his pocket and positioned it at the bottom corner of the door. One nod told Greer her dad was inside and alone. She scoured the corridor, foyer, and the tip of the stairs visible from their position. All clear. She kept her heartbeat in check and prepared to face her father.

"Stockton, put your Walther on the desk, draw the curtains, step to the front of the desk, and hike your pant legs," Z hollered.

"I have to give it to you. No one has had the gall to stand up to my brother, not even me."

"I don't need your respect, but you need immediate compliance to survive."

"Hah, survive? You think any of us are going to survive this? He won't let me live more than a week. A tragic crash will befall me or a heart attack, perhaps."

His words pricked her hardened heart. Had her father become a victim in this as much as she? Z pinned her with a quelling look before snapping his head back to the mirror. Maybe she'd stiffened or whimpered, but he'd known instantaneously that she'd softened. She scanned the perimeter and refocused her attention.

"Those will end you quickly," Z warned.

"But you won't?" her dad called. "Not to worry. I'd like to set the record straight before I go. If anyone can thwart my brother, I suppose it's you, Wraith. That's what they call you isn't it? They can't find out your real name. They can't tie you to an organization. So, they call you the bringer of death and destruction."

"How sweet. Get those pant legs higher and hold them there. Any sudden movement and you'll regret it."

Z dropped his left hand in a flat palm, commanding her to stay put. A part of her sighed a long note of relief. The other part howled at her own weakness. He shoved the mirror into his pocket and stepped around the corner with his Glock high and tight.

"I ask, you answer. That's how this goes—or it doesn't."

"You're bigger than I expected," her dad said.

"Why did you have your daughter abducted?"

Even though she'd voiced this thought earlier, the statement jerked her up by the collar, constricting the flow of air to her lungs.

"You waste your first question on my daughter. Intriguing. Whoa, now." His voice rose an octave. "Yes. Yes, all right. I tried to protect her, but she held delicate family secrets, ones I hid as long as I could. Only, she wasn't the only one who knew the hideous truth. When one of those involved has a sudden crisis of conscious you can't plan for it. You deal with the storm and its aftermath."

"What made Greeson grow a conscience?"

Greer's stomach settled atop her pelvis. She drew breath through her open mouth and blinked back stinging tears.

"He was married two years ago and two months ago welcomed a daughter into the world. Children give you a whole new perspective on the world. He told my brother, and of course, the mess needed containment. He's tossed his hat in for another term, you see."

"You sided with Grieves over your daughter by keeping it a secret fourteen years ago. Why?" Z veritably roared the question. Greer jumped at the sound, forced another scan of her perimeter, and waited for the answer.

"It was either deal with my daughter's battered emotional state and keep her as far away from Greeson as possible or deal with her funeral. I chose the one I could handle best."

Had he really cowed her in order to save her life?

"What happened to make you believe her life was in jeopardy?"

"It's not relevant. Wait!" her dad cried. "I have evidence in my suit pocket that proves my brother stole funds from the American people and funneled it into US Elite to use as his own personal military. He controls their every move, where they go, who they conquer." Silence followed. "Oh God, no. You don't need that."

Greer couldn't hold still any longer. She leaned her right eye to the edge of the frame and peeked inside the room. Z slowly screwed a black barreled silencer onto the end of his gun.

"Okay. Okay." Her dad flailed his hands about. "Grieves killed my wife when my daughter, his niece, was an infant."

She straightened, and then sagged against the wall. Why?

"Why?" Z snarled.

"It was all a horrible accident. My Rachel picked up the phone to dial her mother, but Grieves and I were on the line. He started talking about that night, the night we never spoke of, the night that started this unbearable chain. You see, Grieves decided to run for the Senate, and he was afraid the woman would come forward. Money bought her silence for so long, but he wanted a more permanent solution. He knew a guy, but he needed me to make contact. He couldn't dirty his hands."

Her dad sighed. "Neither of us knew Rachel had heard the conversation, but when she left me the next day, took Greer to her mother's, and told me she was never coming back, I knew." A sob broke and she was surprised to find it wasn't her own, but her dad's. "I guess he had my house bugged. To this day I don't know how he knew, but he found her at a rest area halfway to her mother's house nursing Greer. He snapped my wife's neck and left Greer for dead."

A tear slipped down her cheek.

"That night, when Rachel didn't show at her mother's, she called me concerned. My wife told her she was coming to show off her baby. Grieves said it was the only reason he spared my wife's family. He told me where to find my wife and daughter, fully expecting them to both be dead, but the car had been running. The heater kept her warm until it ran out of gas, but it was long enough."

The sound of a grown man's weeps funneled out into the hallway and cloaked her in sorrow.

"I was so enraged. I was going to tell, to hell with what happened to me as long as Grieves went down too, but then I looked at my daughter's rosy little cheeks and I knew he'd kill her and Rachel's entire family before we even went to trial. I knew I had to protect my daughter by whatever means necessary."

"Who was the woman?" Z asked.

"A co-ed he'd raped at our alma mater. Her name was Anita Price, and I had her killed."

"You said you were ready to tell, to hell with what happened to you. What was your part in her rape?"

"I gave her a line of cocaine and was so high myself, that when Grieves...when he started in on her I watched the whole thing and cheered him on."

Greer was so numb the words hit her like individual fists, but the blows only echoed in the distance.

"What about the Stas?"

"To vanquish my demons I tried bargaining with the devil. I corrupted politicians, bought favors, and eliminated anyone who got in their way. In turn, they protected me and my daughter until Grieves became the president. He one-upped me, and before I knew it, turned the tide. Suddenly the place where I'd maneuvered my daughter to keep her safe was enemy territory and there was nothing I could do."

"Nothing?" Z snorted.

"You don't realize it yet, but we're all dead. You can't go against my brother and win."

"You're wrong." Greer surprised herself by stepping around the corner with her head held high. "Your brother can't go up against us and win because, no matter the cost, we won't give up until he's stopped."

Z's focus remained on her dad, but his shoulders stiffened.

"I hope you're right, Greer." Her father looked as though he'd aged ten years since he'd hurried from the HELO across the lawn.

"Tell me, Dad, what did you plan to do if I showed up alone?"

"I'd planned to have them ferry you out of the country, but once I saw them I second guessed the idea. You alone with six armed men seemed as dangerous as handing you over to Grieves."

"I've spent the last six years of my life surrounded by armed men."

"We need to move," Z announced. "If they weren't loyal to you, they've probably contacted your brother by now."

"They were loyal to the check. I promised to pay them the full amount to leave." The man she shared DNA with, but little else, gulped a breath. "I really do have evidence. It's on a flash drive in my top coat pocket."

Z lifted two fingers and pointed to the breast pocket. "Use two fingers, reach slowly, show it to me front and back, and then toss it to Greer."

As ordered, he moved with extreme caution. When Z nodded at the small silver device, her father threw it in a low arch. Z snagged it out of the air and shoved it in the cargo pocket of his pants. "I didn't think you'd explode your own daughter. Me," he shrugged, "you probably wouldn't have any qualms about incinerating. If this is a tracer, I'll have it disabled before we leave the grounds."

Her dad shook his finger at Z as though speaking to a child. "It's not a bomb and it's not equipped with a tracking chip. It's probably the only thing that's kept me alive all these years."

"Does your brother know you have it?" Z asked.

"No, but he knows it's possible, and that's been enough." He wiped beads of sweat from his forehead.

"That, and your shared skeletons." She couldn't keep the accusation from her voice.

"And that." His head hung in a downcast nod.

The muscles in Z's shoulders rolled.

Greer looked at the man who'd protected her life and at the same time neglected to nurture it. The love and loyalty she'd lived by all her years, through trial and terror, faded under the harsh light of reality. She wanted to tell her dad to come with them, that they'd get through this together, but her mouth refused to form the words.

Z shifted toward the door, but stopped. His shoulders rolled. The barrel of his gun lowered ever so slightly. "Senator, you breathe a hint of this to the president, US Elite, Stas, anyone, and you'll beg me to take you to prison." He tugged down the collar of his shirt until the top of his gnarled skin appeared. "I'll make the shit the Stas did to me look like pre-school finger painting."

He took another step toward the door. His left hand wrapped around Greer's forearm and tugged. "It's time to go."

She met her father's tear soaked eyes. "If there's a way to make this right, we'll find it."

When he blinked a fresh wave of lament wet his cheek. "I didn't do a very good job being a father or a man, but you loved me through all my faults. You are the best daughter. I didn't deserve you, but I do love you."

Again her mouth hardened, making a response futile. Even if she could speak, she didn't know what to say. Anger, betrayal, and disappointment clouded her conscience.

"Let's move," Z ordered.

Greer tipped her head to her father, and then followed Z from the room. They hustled down the long hallway.

The crack of an exploding bullet split the cultured air.

Their weapons snapped toward the sound, ready for battle. Z used his chest and thrust her backward until her shoulder blades hit the wall. A statue shielded her from the other side and blocked her aim. Seconds passed. The thud of metal hitting hardwood forced bile into Greer's nose. Tears clouded her vision.

"He..." A sob filled in the gap. The gap she couldn't cross. Her father loved himself too much to... He would never take his own life.

"I have to check. Stay here," Z barked close to her ear.

A quake started in her knees, working its way up her thighs. Greer sagged to the side. Only an arm on the statue stopped her complete collapse. The rolls of white wig of the head and shoulder statue dug into her arm. She sucked choppy breaths through her open mouth. Too soon for the outcome to be anything other than suicide, Z hooked her arm around his shoulders, snugged her to him, and walked her down the hallway.

"Did he..." Another shiver rocked her to the marrow.

"Yes."

The soles of her shoes shuffled along the oriental carpet of the master bedroom and squeaked across the bathroom tile. At the window he grabbed the sides of her face. "Sixty yards and we're clear. I need you on point, Britton."

Her name on his lips shook away the fog. There was nothing to be done about her dad now. Training took hold. She checked the horizon, climbed through the window, and dropped to the ground. Seconds later Z followed. They hit their stride, running full tilt toward the new car.

Chapter Eighteen

"You work for the CIA." Several nearly translucent fly-aways flitted about Greer's brows. She smacked them from her face and glared at him.

He tried his damnedest not to grin. The anger in her voice and red in her cheeks beat the hell out of her shocked, chalky silence of the last three hours. "Why on earth would you think that? I have a British accent, in case you've forgotten."

"I haven't forgotten," Greer said, using an atrocious British accent. Her palm struck the large metal door to the ten-by-seven steel and concrete-reinforced vault in the basement of a small cabin in the middle of the forest off Highway 28. "I'd think that," she added sans the Brit emphasis, "because you have skills only someone trained outside the boundaries of the law would possess. Because you have safe houses, guns, and cars stashed across the entire country it seems." Each reason earned another smack on the wall. "Because no one knows who you work for or who the hell you are. And last, but absolutely not least, because I've known you for nearly eight months—the last of those rather intimately—and I still don't know your name." Her wild hands turned to fists, and she shook them in his direction.

"Call me Zeke."

Her jaw grazed the floor for a full eight count before she snapped it up. “What? Call you Zeke or is that your actual name?” Again her hands flailed about.

“My name is Zachariah Slaughter. Most people, who know who I am,” he qualified, “call me Zeke.” He rubbed at the scar on his chest, weighted his words, and then forged ahead. In for a penny, in for a pound. “My sister calls me Z. So, really you’ve been calling me by the truest name I’ve ever possessed.”

Since they’d left the house of horrors she’d drawn inside herself, only answering direct questions with one word responses. The outburst proved she wasn’t conquered. He dragged his knuckles down her cheek and wished she’d soften enough to walk into his arms. Her arms petrified by her side. She stepped away from his touch, turned, and ran up the steps. The act knocked his heart against his spine. It also shored his resolve.

He followed her up the steps, through the trap door that blended into the floor boards and required a special tool to pry open. To keep either of them from falling through to their death, he stopped long enough to close the hatch and kick the rolled rug into place with his heel.

Greer clipped along in a tight circle, her arms knotted across her chest. All the rose tint he’d coaxed into her cheeks before the mission, and the bit he’d seen return, drained onto the hardwood floor like the blood from the hole in her father’s head. More than anything in the world, Zeke hated the bonds of helplessness. He hadn’t a clue how to help her through the tirade of emotion she refused to set free.

“Talk to me,” he prodded.

She whirled around as though only now noticing his presence. "How are we going to go after the president of the United States, with or without all this evidence? Evidence is destroyed. People disappear with this kind of stuff."

They'd just secured the loaded drive in a vault even Houdini couldn't escape, but he had a hunch her frantic ramblings had little to do with vanishing evidence.

"I wondered why your father blamed you for the assault. Most parents deny it ever happened. He didn't deny your assault took place because he knew the bastard had done it. Like father like son. The man deserved a bullet for that alone." Zeke reeled himself in, tried to anyway. It took Herculean effort. "He was your father, Greer."

Her gaze dropped. He stepped in front of her, bracketed her face in his hands, pulled her chin up, and waited. Those blue orbs slid from one side to the other refusing to rise. "Talk to me," he begged.

"It sucks being locked out, doesn't it?" she snapped.

Yeah, it hurt in a way he'd not experienced—and he'd experienced the full spectrum of pain the world had to offer, emotional and physical.

"Worse than any torture the Stas dreamed up, and they were damn creative. I'm sorry for putting you through it for so long. I took an oath to keep these secrets and I will not jeopardize your safety with them." She met his gaze and then pinched her eyes shut. A small stream leaked out their corners. "Talk to me," he prodded.

"He was my father, and I'm glad I don't ever have to see his face again." Her lids opened, her sad gaze centering his. "I'm mad at myself for feeling that way. I'm sad for what should have been, but he made horrible decision on top of horrible decision.

Then he lacked the guts to face them. He wasn't a good person, but I'll miss the potential he had to change, what could have been. I hate him for that, and then I hate myself."

"It's not your fault."

She dropped his gaze.

Zeke released her face, grabbed her hand, and pressed it against his beating heart as she had what seemed a lifetime ago, but in reality was only days past. "Until this very moment, I never understood that it wasn't my fault. It's not your fault, Greer. Don't waste your life thinking it is."

Her head crashed into his chest. He wrapped her in his arms, and dropped to his knees to better hold her. She felt smaller and more fragile in his arms than she had when she'd been drugged out of her mind. But he hadn't cared for her then like he...like he... No. He didn't. He couldn't love. Sobs wracked her body. Tears soaked through his shirt. He pulled her legs into his lap and held her fast against his chest. God, how he cherished her.

The sun fell past the tree tops and still he held tight. He would hold her as long as she'd let him. Her tears dwindled. She stayed in his embrace.

"What wasn't your fault?"

When the dam shoring his darkest secret broke it gave way under Greer's simple touch. The words flowed like they'd never been locked away. "My father beat me every day of my life. Every day I saw him, anyway. Some nights he drank himself into a stupor and couldn't make it home. Those were the only good nights. He hit my mother, my sister. My mother stayed through it all."

Greer's arm banded around his torso, encouraging the surrender.

"My sister, Khani, got us out when I was twelve. I was just a kid, but I never forgave myself for not protecting her."

Soft, wet lips grazed his cheek, and then his lips. He let her comfort seep into the depths of his soul, because after she heard the entire story she might never kiss him this way again. Maybe she sensed something in his demeanor. She sealed a desperate kiss on his mouth, and then eased back in his arms.

"I let the disappointment destroy me, corrupt me."

"You're not corrupt, you're hurt." Her head shook, caressing his fingers with her silky hair.

"I killed my father."

Zeke blurted the words, tired of her misplaced worship. The moment they slipped from his lips dread knotted his intestines, but the boulder he'd shouldered for so many years rolled onto the floor. The buoyancy lifting him contradicted the hitch in his breath as he waited for Greer to shrink away, to eye him like the murderer he was, to flee.

After an eternity, she pushed off his chest. He let her go. On her knees in front of him, she spread her arms wide, corded them around his neck, and crashed into him with a ferocity that left him gasping.

"Why would you hug me after I told you that?"

She kissed his temple. "Why would you think I'd do anything else?"

"Because I'm a murderer."

Her fingers knotted into the strands of hair behind his ears. "The world doesn't mourn women and child beaters, but you have for a long time. I can feel it pouring off you in waves. A murderer would have no remorse. You do."

He'd never talked about that night, though he relived it every day. He'd killed men in battle, but never anyone he hated. He'd hated his father. He still did.

"Tell me about it," she coaxed without breaking her hold or her intent gaze.

He thought to deny her, but with the earnestness of her wide, pleading blue eyes the words tumbled out. "I went into the Royal Marines for the steady meals and a place to sleep. Turned out, I was a good soldier. The Commandos recruited me. I traveled for missions, killed men in the cover of night with my bare hands, trained harder than most military forces, and I still woke with nightmares. A grown warrior clutching his sheets like a scared kid was no warrior at all. I decided to face the past before it ruined me.

"On leave, I tracked my father to a dive bar in a seedy part of London. I didn't plan to kill him. The son of a bitch didn't even recognize me. When I told him who I was he asked for money. I told him to fuck himself six ways to Sunday."

Greer smoothed her hand over his cheek.

"He did what he'd done so many times before. He pulled off his belt. Coming out of the last loop, the leather snapped like it did in all those dreams. In all those memories. He said, 'Talk to your old man that way, just like your whoring sister, and you get the buckle.' His boots stomped, splashing swill off the asphalt. He lunged. A part of me shrank inside myself like I had so many times before. The other part reacted.

"Just one punch. It connected to the center of his sternum. The crunch of his ribs echoed in the alley. He hit the piss-soaked pavement and never made another sound. I walked away. I left everything behind, my marines, my country, my sister, everything I'd thought I stood for without a word."

Chapter Nineteen

The people designed to love them above all others had failed so miserably at the task that they fostered children who locked out the world. And yet, they both just breeched massive barriers. She'd known something haunted Z. It always lurked in the edges of his gun-powder eyes. He'd killed his father. She only regretted the fact because she couldn't snuff out the man's life, and because guilt stalked Z for so long.

When she first met this stalwart man she'd been lost in a deep and winding hate crush. His distant bearing and stinging regard earned her abhorrence. At the same time the brutal perfection of his body and the mystery in his eyes towed her under. Slowly, painfully, his true nature revealed itself one steadfast act at a time.

Now, he bared his soul.

Greer had thought herself incapable of love until she realized, if she could, she'd take away all Z's pain and add it to the shattered pieces of her own heart. Foolishly, she'd thought love a healing potion for all her problems. In truth, it compounded them. She loved a man she had no future with. She loved a man who would leave her when all the answers were revealed. She loved a man unwilling to love her in return.

And there it was all the same. Love. A gut-rending, traitorous emotion.

The veneer flecked off, leaving them both exposed.

Z sat on his heels. His narrow gaze awaited her reaction. From the set of his jaw, he still expected her to push him away.

Each segment of her broken heart beat in a frenzied race. It stole the blood from her extremities, numbing her toes and fingertips. She released the hold on his hair and let her hands fall to the side, completely unsure of what to do or say. A confession of her own chanced his retreat. Pushing him away would save her future sorrow.

She moved on instinct only Z coaxed from her, bending at the waist and pressing her lips to his. He held himself in invisible restraints with his hands fisted at his sides. Her mouth glided over the hard line. Simple kisses marked his skin with the barest hint of moisture.

The rigidity challenged Greer to tempt a reaction. One hot edge at a time she covered his lips with her tongue. His breathing doubled, fanning against her face, but it wasn't enough. She dropped her hands to the hem of her shirt, peeled it off, and then reached for his.

Z's wide hands encircled her wrists, squeezed, and yanked them wide. "You have to stop. I can't—"

"You already said you can't fuck me and you can't make love to me." She gnashed at his lips and rubbed her face against his prickly scruff. His hold stopped pushing her away and slackened a little. The leeway allowed her to rub the very tips of her lace covered nipples across his chest in shameless taunting. "How about something in between those two?"

"Greer." He said her name like a man dangling off the ledge of a building.

"I know you want me." A stupid tear slipped down her cheek. "I'm not conceited, Z. But I'm not blind, deaf, or void of any other sensory perception either." Her lips slid down the side of his neck and found his violent pulse. "Your heart is beating as fast as mine, your breathing is as rough."

"You're hurt. You want something to take that away for a while."

"You're scared and pulling back."

"You're not mine to have." The sharp tone echoed in her ears.

Greer jerked her hands toward his thumbs and broke his hold with bruising effort. She stood over him, not backing away one inch. Her hands flew to her pants. While she unfastened them she toed off the boots she'd loosened in the car. He didn't move, except to track the progress of her hands. The hook at the back of the bra unfastened with a flick of her wrists. She stepped out of every stitch of clothing and kicked and tossed them to the side. The damp cabin air cooled her skin, sending a parade of goosebumps marching across her body.

"I am mine to give." She knelt in front of him and kept her hands at her side. "I'm yours to deny."

The muscles in his neck strained against his tanned skin. His mouth puckered, and then frowned. Greer braced herself for his rejection. She'd taken so many of them over the past several days. This one though, trumped all the others.

"I can't deny you or myself, not anymore."

He lunged forward, attacking like a wild animal. His chest collided with her breasts. The force knocked the breath from her lungs. Unforgiving lips plundered her parted ones. Harsh breaths siphoned into her mouth, kick-starting her own pants. One arm encircled her ribs. Fingers sank into the meat of her bottom. He yanked her against his hips.

Greer cinched her legs around his abdomen. The stinging cold of his matte black belt buckle abraded her clitoris. She bucked. His unmoving hand on her ass redirected her escape into a grinding roll of the hips. The large flat of metal licked her slick flesh like an icy tongue. A gasp gurgled in her throat. Z devoured it along with her mouth.

She clawed at his shirt, grabbing handfuls from his back and working it to the tops of his shoulders. The heat of his bare abs connected with her lean belly. Discord between cold on her clit and hot on her middle sparked an explosion of kaleidoscope colors behind her eyes, forcing them closed.

His mouth broke away and nipped a trail down her neck. The same time his teeth sank into her sensitive skin of her trap, he spread her cheeks wide and slipped a hand between her taut globes.

"Z." Her moans reverberated off the low cabin ceiling and uncovered windows.

The rough tips of his fingers teased her puckered rosette. Using the fistfuls of his shirt, she arched into his hand and brushed her breasts against his pecs. He didn't invade her body, but if he'd tried she would have let him. That surprised her, given the past.

Zeke Slaughter was nothing like her past. He was nothing like anything she'd dared to dream.

He released his hold on her back and his teeth slipped off her shoulder. She didn't move, locked around his body. His hand snagged the top collar of his T-shirt. Greer helped tear the thing from his head and arm. Z shoved it to the side, dangling off his occupied arm. The palm of his calloused hand smoothed up her abs to the swell of her breasts. His thumb taunted her nipples in turn while his other hand explored her slick folds. He smeared her arousal from front to back in maddening strokes.

Her hands latched around his nape. Their gazes met in a kinetic storm of lust and emotion—emotion on her part at least.

That was okay.

Greer lied to herself. She didn't believe it though.

Z rose to his knees, hefted her higher on his hips, and used the finger that had tormented her breasts to release his buckle and shoved his pants down his legs. He wrestled the elastic of his boxer briefs over his swollen cock. The full length of it smacked against her fevered bottom. She met the touch with carnality, shifting in his hold, seeking his wide crown with her aching flesh. When the silk head glided across her clit to the opening of her eager channel he lifted her cheeks with one hand.

"No you don't."

Shock dropped her jaw. "You're not going to —"

"I'm going to when I'm good and ready."

"You're not ready?" She scoffed.

He bombarded her with a savage kiss. "I've been ready since you strutted onto my training field. You're not ready."

"I am." Need pulsed through her veins like an illicit drug. It prodded her heart beat and dampened her skin. "Z, I'm ready for you."

"Tell me what took you away from me."

"What?"

Striations flexed and rolled in his chest. "One second you were with me, so in sync it hurt, and next your fiery eyes cooled."

"No." She used her body to protest, undulating against him.

"Don't lie to me, Greer. I know sorrow when I see it."

"Not sorrow."

"Then what?"

She clamped her lips together and glared in challenge.

A hint of a smile kindled in his eyes. He reached between them, fisted his length, and stroked twice. Hefty beads of pre-cum formed at his pretty pink slit. Z pressed the wide head at the base of her clit and dragged it over the live wire of her sex, caressing all the way to the back. She sank into his touch. The grip on her cheeks held firm, barring her hips from the promised ecstasy.

Greer whimpered. He only reversed his stroke. She grabbed a handful of his hair and pulled him forward into a merciless kiss. Of the two he was more heartless. On the next rub, he levered her down until the barest of an inch spread her lips wide.

"Yes. Oh, Z. I'm with you. I'm so ready." Her insides wept for his intrusion and still he held back.

"If it wasn't sorrow, then what?" His hoarse voice gritted through clenched teeth. He started to pull out.

"Regret," she moaned.

His forehead dropped to her shoulder.

"Not how you think." She yanked his head with serious effort. Sorrow clouded his gaze. Another piece of her heart broke away. What more did she have to lose?

Greer melted her gaze to his and swallowed her fear. "I love you, Z."

Everything suspended for a heap of seconds. She watched his face for a reaction, but found none. No horror. No shock. No reciprocation. Only unfettered desire.

She pushed herself onto his throbbing cock at the same time his hands locked around her hips and he scored her onto his length. Z's roar muffled inside her mouth fusing with her cry. He filled her to the point of pain. Tears welled in her eyes. His arms grabbed at her back and shoulders, pulling her closer. Pain marbled with pleasure. His hips receded, and then plowed forward once more.

He unfastened the clasp of her feet, adjusted her legs lower on his hips. His grip levered her up, and then drove her down to meet his thrusts. She tugged him ever closer. Her hips rolled in time with his demands. Sweat slicked their bodies. The air around them charged. Pressure rose inside.

Her pants filled the air, fusing with his low rasps that stumbled toward the tattered edge of growls. The harder he pushed the shorter her breaths became. Tension coiled the tips of her fingers and curled her toes. Z lowered his head, clasped his teeth onto her lower lip, and popped the tender flesh through the unforgiving points. He jerked her hips back and drove the head of his dick into a place she never knew existed.

Once. Twice. Three times.

The ache she wrestled with ballooned to a fine point, and then disintegrated. She clung to Z's shoulder to keep from flying apart with it. Shrapnel ricocheted through her insides, pinging and thrilling everything it touched. No words formed on her lips. Only shattered moans declared her rapture.

Z tightened his already crushing hold, sealing her torso to his hard front. His hand tangled in her hair. A firm tug exposed her neck. Stuttered breath and molten kisses caressed her as his hips jacked frantically. The width inside her swelled. He barked a hearty string of curses, mixed with, “so tight, so beautiful.” Spasms rocked her body from inside. Spurts of liquid heat filled her.

When the cursing stopped he stood with her in his arms, toed off his boots, and shook off his pants and briefs. She buried her face against his neck, unready to face him. The prospect of being pushed away burned more acutely than the first thrusts of his girth. Not that she could hold her boneless neck up if she wanted to. His heavy steps told her he’d expended an ample amount of energy as well.

Old floorboards creaked under their combined weight. He moved through the kitchen and living area down a short hallway to the first door. Every step shifted his still pulsing cock, stroking her to maddening need. Like she hadn’t just taken her fill. They entered a stuffy bedroom. Z shuffled between the wall and the queen sized bed. He jerked back the hideous rose and white checked quilt.

Her back hit the sheet. His body followed, covering her front. A pinch gathered at the center of her scalp. Z used her hair to pull her face from his safe scent. He leaned over her, the hard ridges of his body visible for the first time since they’d come together. Droplets of sweat collected in the grooves of his abdomen. Veins bulged along his forearm scant inches from her gaze.

“You can’t hide from me. So, don’t try.”

Totally at his mercy, Greer stared into the torrent.

She waited for a lecture or his denial of her feelings.

He moved his hips slowly, almost imperceptibly, pressing his hard length in an inch, and then almost leaving her body. His free hand braced on her hip, while the V of his flexed and contracted with his steady seduction.

Greer's legs splayed wide, allowing him better access. Distended, red lips clasped his shaft. Each slow stroke brought him both deeper, and then farther from her core. His tempo never sped. The tattoo on his oblique danced with the tension of his abdomen.

Her hips jerked, trying to rev things, but his hands held her in place. "What are you doing?" she panted.

"I fucked you." His voice rasped with the barely hinged barbs of lust. "Now, I'm trying to make love to you."

The hold on her hair loosened. His rough palm abraded her cheek. His thumb rubbed across her lower lip. She turned into his touch and his eyes closed for the briefest of seconds. He urged her through pleasure to the untenable precipice of orgasm with the tenderness of his love making.

She covered both his hands with hers, and then pressed her lips to his palm. Her breath cascaded over his skin with choppy exhales. Their gazes tangled. The tension in his jaw broke.

Z grabbed both her hands. He spread them wide, holding her palm to palm. His heart covered hers. He thrust hard and deep, binding them like forged metal. They came together, losing themselves in each other's souls.

Chapter Twenty

Fractured sunlight poured in through the window as the sun found its way to the horizon. How in the hell had a street kid from London found his way into the arms of a woman who loved him? She'd said it only once and he believed her. She was pure and fierce and good. Well, not quite so pure now.

Greer's head lay against his chest. Gentle breaths escaped from her slightly open mouth, blowing a damp clump of blonde hair sandwiched between them. Long lashes rested on her cheeks. Her arm and leg crossed his body not just draped, but clinging to him even in sleep, holding him close...as though she knew.

A lump formed in Zeke's throat. He kissed the top of her head for the hundredth time. Terror, stark and daunting, reached inside his chest and played table tennis with his heart.

He didn't sleep around, but when he enjoyed the company of a woman he always used protection. Without fail. It had been within arm's reach two hours ago when he'd known they'd both reached the boundaries of their control. He'd made the conscious decision not to protect her. Now...he hated himself for it. Yet, at the same time, the vision of Greer cuddling a dark haired, fat cheeked, blue eyed babe to her breast—their baby—brought the biggest dopey grin to his face.

Never had he wanted a partner. The thought of kids had not once grazed his scalp, but with Greer he wanted it all.

Cue the terror.

Zeke was many things. A family man didn't hit the list, not even a thousand feet down. His chest cramped at the ugly realization.

He hugged Greer to his chest one more time, placed a kiss on her corn-silk hair, and then pried her limbs from his body. After standing and cursing himself once more, he covered her with the blanket. When she snuggled in and her breathing evened he moved back to the living area.

In the corner of the kitchen he found the hollow board with a few quick taps. It slipped up without a sound. In the shallow hole a white handkerchief lay wrapped in a neat rectangle just the way he'd left it when setting up this place nearly two years ago. Zeke plucked the cloth from the hole and unwound it. He stared at the small black cell phone for a long minute. His gaze lifted to the closed bedroom door.

No turning back now.

A series of buttons activated the device and dialed the only programmed number. Into the silent line he said, "Sierra. Hotel. Romeo. Oscar. Uniform. Delta. Two. Zero. One. One."

After a series of beeps an operator answered. "Voice confirmation complete. Lieutenant Slaughter, how may I direct your call?"

"OIA, Commander Hawk."

Forty seconds passed. Not unusual for the number of safeguards in place. Salma Hawk, the director of Oversight and Internal Affairs—the clandestine division of the most covert operations group in the world—always liked to throw in a few added stockades before answering. They needed those fail-safes today. Zeke's jaw twitched.

A hard feminine voice cut onto the line. “If you try and die on me again, I’ll kill you myself and save the worry.”

“Aw. You’re getting soft in your old age.”

The woman who’d recruited him into the secret division of the Base Branch, who’d saved him from himself when he’d taken off into the dark after killing his father, chuckled. “Five years doing what I do and, hell yeah, I’m feeling old age.”

“You’re the oldest thirty-three-year-old I know, and I’m about to make you feel seventy.”

“I’ve never known you to fail a mission. Finally missed your man, huh?”

“Not quite.”

“So you found the source?”

“Yeah, but you’re not going to like it.”

Chapter Twenty-one

The *thump, thump, thump* of a propeller jerked Greer from a deep sleep. Bright, temporarily blinding morning light spilled in through the unshaded windows. Twice during the night, he'd woken her. The desperation she remembered in his ardent thrusts drove a spear of dread straight to her heart. Her arms patted the bed in search of Z.

Her fingers found only cold covers. Greer shot from the bed and ran naked through the small maze. Sticky evidence of their lovemaking clung to her thighs. They hadn't used protection. She hadn't protected herself against Z, not her heart or her body. No way would she regret the cognizant decisions.

Not even as hollowness filled the four walls that hours ago had teemed with action and emotion. The house was empty. Suddenly, so was Greer.

She tossed back the rug and searched frantically for the tool to open the hatch. A stack of her clothes, a knife, two pistols, and a rifle lay in neat order on the table where Z's bag had been. He was gone.

Again the whir of a HELO's blade drew her attention. She grabbed Z's rumpled T-shirt from the floor and threw herself at the front door. Headed toward the far clearing on the rim of an oak forest,

Z stalked the distance, his wide frame covered in a vest and full tactical gear. Greer wrenched the handle, yanked the door open, and screamed his name.

Maybe it was his uncanny senses that turned his head. Maybe it was the utter despair in her voice. Maybe he just happened to look above the cabin, searching out the arriving bird. Uncaring of the reason, she seized the opportunity to snare his attention; Greer used the T-shirt as a flag. While her arm arched wide, her heart tried desperately to break free from her chest. She let the balled weight of the shirt swing through the air while she rushed down the steps and the crest of the long sloping hill.

He pivoted and broke into a dead sprint before the soles of her feet hit the harsh mixture of dirt, rock, and grass. The craggy ground bit into her heels, but she didn't stop. If anything, she sped with the increasing whop of blades.

They covered the uneven thirty yards in a flash, meeting at the first line of trees separating the yard from the pasture. Sadness, confusion, and rage clogged her throat. Just as well. Z pulled her against his chest so quickly it forced the little bit of air left in her lungs out. He whirled with her in his arms and shoved her back against the coarse bark of a large oak. His grip encircled her wrists and he pulled her arms from around his middle. Before her eyes, he seemed to grow a foot taller and wider.

A Blackhawk filled to the open hatch with weapons and soldiers screamed overhead. Z held her still, hiding her from view.

When the Hawk passed them Z's gruffness molted. His damp forehead met hers. "What the fuck, Greer." He panted the words. She didn't so much hear as see them on his pale lips.

"What's going on?" she hollered.

"I have to go."

"I can see that." Her arms thrashed, but his grip contained the gesture. "Why are you leaving me here? I can help."

His jaw screwed tight.

"We're back to that? After…everything…"

Hard lips stole the words out of her mouth. His kiss was sorrowful and oh so sweet. And over too quickly.

"You're not coming back." She choked the words so softly he may not have heard them.

"Listen to me, Greer. You have to stay here, stay hidden. When it's safe a car will come for you."

His hands slipped from her wrists. When she tried to reach for him a tempest glare stayed her. He turned, snaked through the line of trees to the edge of the clearing, and then broke the tree line.

The tendons in her legs turned to rubber. Greer gripped the tree to keep from crashing to the ground. She turned slowly, trying to stay hidden as he'd asked and trying not to fall. Too late. Like a fool she'd fallen in love with Zeke Slaughter, international man of mystery.

Z ran toward the Blackhawk. When he neared, the soldiers parted for a woman with a long, slicked-back pony tail and more military decor than Greer had ever seen. She extended a sturdy hand to Z. He used it to leap into the belly. The moment his feet hit metal the landing skids lifted. He never looked back.

Chapter Twenty-two

For so long he'd straddled the fence between good and evil. Sitting in the midst of eight Base Branch operatives he'd never met Zeke felt like a pimple on a rhino's ass. The feeling didn't have long to root. Hawk shoved a thick stack of maps, city grids, and schematics at his belly. He flipped through the highlighted routes they'd planned during the night, checking alternate courses, and then ranking the order of probability. They had a tight window, but if anyone could do it, Hawk and her team could.

"Checks clean." He returned the laminated papers.

"Did you have any doubts?" His superior snatched them back and winked.

"Only about two a second," he hollered in the wind tunnel created by the two open doors and a change of direction.

"You had to make a splash on reentry, didn't you?" Salma Hawk peeled the rank patch off her shoulder and stuck it to the fabric covered wall.

"If there was another way..."

"But there's not." She shrugged. "Let's see if I can earn my keep." She gave the team captain a hand signal; Hawk had called him Prosper over the phone. Prosper in turn signaled the men's legs inside, and then closed the doors. Her fist balled and rapped twice on the ceiling. The men turned in a short burst of movement. Hawk looked over her shoulder. “Welcome home.”

“Good to be back.”

Hawk nodded, and then addressed each of her men with a measuring gaze.

“You’ve all been with me a while, but none longer and more entrenched in the filth of our jobs than Lieutenant Slaughter.” Hawk hiked a finger in his direction. Ten pairs of eyes landed on him with the weight of a freight train. He stared back, unmoving, but his insides crawled, reminding him why he worked under a shroud.

“Each of you were handpicked to protect this organization and the balance it works tirelessly to maintain. I’ve trained you. I’ve pushed you as far as you could go, and then demanded you steel yourself, gore the ground, and push harder. Today, I’ll take you to the limit of even my own mettle, and I ask you to stand with me as I dig in and do the unthinkable for the greater good.”

The men jarred fists against each other's backs. Oorah’s and hoorah’s punctuated their anticipation.

“I like your enthusiasm, but let me finish, and then see how anxious you are to follow me.” Hawk’s shoulders straightened a degree more. The men leaned forward, their gazes intent on their leader.

“Thanks to Lieutenant Slaughter’s undercover efforts, we know the location of the Stas's US strongholds and that US Elite is in violation of over a dozen policies. Base Branch regular teams one through five are moving into position for a simultaneous strike on both. Our target is the president of the United States.”

To their credit none of the agents gasped. They each gripped their pre-battle calm, if not a little tighter than necessary.

"I have verified proof that Grieves Stockton, the President of the United States has used US Elite forces for his own profit, to forge alliances not sanctioned by the citizens of this great country and in stark opposition to its ideals, to murder, and intimidate. The evidence and the crimes are overwhelming. Something must be done today, and we will do it."

Hawk pointed to the hatch. "If anyone on this plane can't move against the commander in chief... speak now and I'll drop you on our way. I might give you a parachute. I might not."

A smile threatened Zeke's stony demeanor.

She gave them ten whole seconds to dive. No one moved. "Trust comes into play here, but trust me when I say this man is one of the worst terrorists our soil has ever seen. I have the backing of the heads of military, but the FBI, CIA, and the legislative bodies of this great country had been kept out of the loop for security purposes. If the mission fails we will be viewed as terrorists ourselves and be dealt with accordingly."

Prosper eyed each of the men, let his gaze rest on Zeke for a long second, and then turned to Hawk. "Ma'am, I didn't vote for him anyway. Let's impeach his ass."

Chapter Twenty-three

"Hope he's not too attached." Greer tossed a piece of the BMW's steering column onto the gravel next to the Philips head screwdriver—the only tool, besides a palm sized Swiss Army knockoff, she'd found after ripping the cabin apart in search of the key for the damn car. Turned out Germans used triple square fasteners.

He couldn't be that attached. He'd left the doors unlocked. Smashing a window might have done her nerves some good. She braced one palm on the door, the other on the roof, and rammed the toe of her boot into the stubborn plastic. A crack allied her irritation...a little. Another blow rewarded her with a hint of bound wires ranging the colors of the rainbow. Hot-wiring an old Jeep in the sands of the Helmand River Valley in Afghanistan couldn't be any harder than this sleek car on a quiet plot of home soil, could it?

One way to know.

The plastic bit into her fingertips. Her teeth gritted and muscles bunched. He'd left a brisk note in the pile of clothes.

"Stay put, someone you don't know will eventually be by to pick you up," she told the sporty sedan. "Like I'm a package to be delivered or a... car." The plastic broke free under her strain and indignation. "Sorry to break it to you, pretty, but he's not attached. Not at all."

Hot tears slid down her face. If he was going to leave, why relent and finally screw her? Where the hell was he going anyway? And if she ever got this fancy thing with all its fail-safes started, where the hell would she go? Her dad was dead. She didn't have an apartment. No real friends to speak of. The only family she had left were the very ones who'd taken everything from her.

An idea lit like a spark on a drought ridden savannah. Z couldn't get close to the president. She could.

Greer kicked through the blur of emotion. She kicked with renewed purpose. The large chunk gave way, revealing fuses, bound cables, and her ticket to retribution. Small rocks and pebbled dirt dug into her knees. Damn the man, but he hadn't left her a clean pair of pants. Only a single pair of too-short khaki shorts, a new clingy tee—into which she'd managed to sweat three dark green lines—socks, and lacy panties.

"He doesn't need a bra. So, why leave me a clean one?"

She tugged at the stiff material around her middle with one hand and yanked out a tightly banded mass of wires. When the adjustments did little to relieve her discomfort her fingers fished inside the front pocket for the knife. The dull blade nicked the cinched zip-ties more than actually cut it.

"Only twenty more to go."

The crunch of tires at the end of the winding drive pricked her attention on number six. They couldn't be in the clear yet. It hadn't been more than an hour and a half since Z left. She hadn't wasted that long weeping in a huddled ball before ripping the cabin to shreds, finding nothing, and showering while she'd formulated her plan. Time moved faster when seduced by joy. It moved slower when hounded by sorrow. When devastated...it stopped altogether.

There wasn't a clock in the cabin. The car's digital readout only displayed with a freaking key. Her sun positioning method of time keeping wasn't all that accurate. So, maybe it had been longer than she realized.

Time or not, Greer closed the knife, stuffed it into her pocket, tossed the pile she'd made onto the floorboard, and slammed the door shut. As casually as she could muster, she propped herself against the car. She gulped and prepared to do some fancy talking. No way was she going with whomever he'd sent to be shuttled to another hidden locale and wait for who knew what.

A heavily tinted town car wound its way to a stop mere feet from the car she intended to drive off this country road. The door opened and a wall of a man hoisted himself from the seat. His wavy mass of white hair nipped the set of her jaw.

"Hello, Ms. Britton." Four meaty fingers hitched the front of his belt. He closed the door so hard the car shimmied.

The first wave of apprehension snuck up Greer's shoulder blades.

White teeth, too white to be natural, peeked from behind a wide smile. "I hoped I'd catch you here."

Had Z told him to hurry because she might try to leave?

He rounded the hood and ambled toward her. Despite his slow pace and the deep lines and hair color showing his age, Greer gained a sense that this man had been lethal in his day, and likely could be still.

"Who are you?"

"Forgive me for not introducing myself. I feel like I already know you." He stopped roughly four feet away. "I'm Xavier."

No last name. No reference tags. "Just Xavier?"

"Forgive me again." He extended his left hand. "Xavier Grisha Filipov, senior."

Greer's gaze sought the man's right hand, even as she reached for the one he offered. A gasp wedged inside her throat. Uneven, discolored tissue covered the knuckles where Xavier's first three fingers should have been. Her gaze flew to the incomplete hand clutching hers. Something had taken his pinkie. A gnarled scar ran up the top of his hand and the bottom too. The raised line pressed against her fingers. She caught herself gawking like a fool.

"I'm sorry. I didn't mean to stare."

He shook her hand and released it with an easy smile. "Do not be. I am not ashamed of my appearance."

The phrasing he used set up another red flag. She'd thought she heard a suppressed accent. His name shrieked Russian. He canted his head as though waiting for her to speak

"You shouldn't be," she stammered.

But no, his blue gaze roamed her legs. His smile turned crooked. "I worked with explosives for many, many years. Even the most careful man can make a mistake." The smile dipped past sane. "I venture we all have battle scars. Some of us wear them on the outside, others only on the inside."

Chapter Twenty-four

Four heavily tinted, even more heavily armored, SUVs rolled slowly through the gates of a private airfield just outside the Clifton Park city limits. After the last car cleared the fence the lead car's front end gripped the pavement, stopping abruptly. The two in the middle jerked to a halt, leaving several feet in between. Car four never hit its brakes. The last car's grill crunched into the third and kept pushing. Black billowed from the screaming tires as it closed the gaps. The lead car reversed, pushing from the other end, compacting the president's caravan.

Man, it helped to have a Base Branch Operative or two rooted in the security forces of heads of countries.

"I told you to trust me," Hawk yelled. She gripped the black rope hooked to the ceiling of the HELO and lowered her bottom out the door, bringing her to his level.

"I can't believe it. How long have they been there?" Zeke's palms itched to release and repel. Not yet. They still needed the men they'd dropped at the adjacent air base to follow through before they got blown out of the sky.

"Long enough that one of them signed the vehicles' security check this morning." Pride glinted in her dark eyes.

"Don't make it too easy for me. You know I like a challenge."

"The car's communications are down. As well as the agents' inside. Not their guns though. And that damn thing is still armor plated and independently ventilated. We have to break the seal."

Zeke patted the hydraulic spreader attached to his belt. "I plan to."

Four jungle-green Humvees breached the tree line on either side of the caravan and barreled toward it. Their tires spit dirt behind them. One gained air off a low hill.

"Non-lethal force unless absolutely necessary. We don't know who's corrupt and who's just doing their job," Hawk reminded through the comms.

They closed the short distance to the line of SUVs in seconds. Zeke's fingers ached to draw a bead on the cars below with his AR, while he waited for the broad fronts of the military-grade vehicles to barricade the caravan doors. This was the sticky part. The part where people could die. If the agents inside the SUVs decided to exit with any of the high caliber rifles stowed under the seats or in the back, they'd have no choice but to strike or risk being eliminated themselves.

Instead of striking, the Secret Service followed protocol. They bastioned the president inside the vehicle. The drivers revved the engines and maneuvered their wheels in an effort to gain their freedom. Surrounded on all sides, they had nowhere to go, but they'd never give up.

"Now." Zeke loosened his grip. He shoved off the landing bar. Gravity sucked him toward the earth.

Hawk followed. The wind whipped her dark ponytail as she fast-roped out of the HELO.

The top of the third SUV—the one that housed the president—came hard and fast. Impact jarred his hips into his spinal column. Every old battle scar smarted, forcing a groan from Zeke's lips. Maybe he should have squeezed the rope a little. Adrenaline and rage wouldn't let him back off. Not one bit.

He cleared the rope and dropped to his knees. The metal vibrated from the hum of the engines and all the opposing forces being inflicted upon it. Hawk whispered onto the second SUV's roof. The tip of the spreader jammed into the tiny crack between the rear passenger door and roof. He pressed his shoulder into the machine.

"Clear," Hawk said into the comms.

Zeke nodded and switched on the device. Metal groaned and shrieked. The outer edge of the frame slowly bloomed.

A gunshot sang above the roar of a thousand horses.

Then another.

To the left the Humvee's windshield pocked with two circular spiderwebs. Brass slugs stuck in the layers of bullet resistant glass. The collected calm of battle settled over Zeke. He drew left-handed, ready to annihilate the pistol tip protruding from the barely opened window.

Hawk's charging form stalled him. Her knees slid across the slick black top. Both hands simultaneously unlatched gas grenades from her vest and launched them through the crack on either side of the weapon.

The boom dully echoed.

Zeke paid it no attention. His gaze already turned back to the spreader's end, waiting for the bullet that awaited him the moment he breached the door. He shifted the spreader, firmed his grip, and peeled again.

Why the hell couldn't someone in the car crack a window and try to shoot him? It would make things easier...well, unless he took a bullet.

"You have a quarter-inch yet?" Hawk's shoulder bumped his. She peered down, but stayed far enough back to keep her head out of the line of fire.

"Barely." He gritted. "This shit is stout."

"Great. Hold what you got." She rummaged through a vest pocket. Her first-aid pouch smacked the roof.

"I'm not shot yet." Zeke kept the device running to cover their conversation. Not that the chaps would hear them through the tiny hole and the roar of blood in their heads.

"Maybe this way you won't be."

She yanked the small medical tubing from the pack and cut off a one-foot segment. The rest of the pack went scattering. "I need this." Hawk jerked a gas grenade from his vest, but kept the pin engaged. She unsheathed her knife and lifted it into the air.

"I like shot better than blown up." Zeke winced.

A tiny pop and hiss followed.

Zeke exhaled long and heavily as Hawk stuffed one end of the tube into the hole she'd made in the end of the canister.

"Hold that." She handed him the pinched end of the tubing, reached for another grenade on his vest, and then repeated the maneuver.

"And people call me crazy." Zeke kicked toward the back of the car just to keep them guessing.

"You are. You'd rather chance the bullets."

Hawk pinched the end of the newest tube. She guided it toward the tiny gap and motioned him to do the same. They jammed the plastic ends just inside the opening. On cue they released their hold. The stunning explosion had been the winning ticket on the second car, but this slow leak...

"You know they have rebreathers." Zeke reminded as they siphoned the gas into the SUV.

"I'm hoping they won't all get to them."

Zeke waited as long as his nerves could take it. Coughs and wheezing gasps seeped out through the tiny hole in the door. He rammed the spreader into the breach and worked the metal.

It keened one long moan and gave under the stress, fanning wide. The bulletproof glass crunched and crumbled one fragment at a time.

The wavering end of a pistol extended toward him. An easy bend of the wrist and the agent relinquished his weapon. Gas poured from the rift. He unhooked the hydraulic machine. It clattered to the roof.

Zeke snaked a hand into the fumes and unlocked the door. A biting grip seized his arm. He didn't wait for a slice of pain. His large palm snatched a handful of meaty flesh and heaved. The body thrashed about. The hold on Zeke's arm released. He didn't.

"What happened to 'wait for my signal'?" Hawk asked.

"Blokes inside didn't get the memo." Zeke hoisted the face of a secret service agent through the hole and sank his other fist into the man's jaw.

"One down." Hawk signaled the Humvee in front of them back. The Base Branch agents moved the truck, and then exited with their weapons drawn, tracking end to end on the SUV. Zeke released the man and bailed from the roof. He motioned the lead agent to the door.

Hawk stood over them, an avenging angel ready to strike the damned. When she gave the nod the agent muscled the door wide. The unconscious man collapsed to the ground. The second Base Branch agent pulled the body back and patted him for weapons.

Zeke reached blind, but kept his vitals covered. His fingers grazed hair. He latched tight and pulled.

The president of the United States grabbed at the rebreather in his mouth with one hand and at the top of his head with the other. Zeke released him. His chest met the earth with a solid thud. The apparatus flew from his mouth. Loud coughs wracked his torso.

Grieves Stockton—the ruler of the free world, the piece of sewer scum—scrambled onto his hands and knees.

"No getting away, Stockton." Zeke planted a boot on his keister and helped him to the ground. "Arms wide, palms on the ground, if you want to live. Personally, I hope you're stupid enough to run or fight back."

The man's arms stretched on either side of his sprawled form. His fingers stretched wide.

"A damn shame." Zeke wrenched his arm high, slapped cuffs on him, rolled him over, and patted him down.

The cool composed face of the president boiled over with white hot rage. "My brother always was the weak link, even when we were kids." Spittle flew from his puckered mouth.

Behind Zeke, the other agents cleared the vehicles one at a time, spreading the Secret Service agents onto the ground, cuffing them, and then loading them into the backs of the Humvees. The two still conscious found the bliss of oblivion in short order.

"I was really hoping he'd run." Hawk sidled up to Zeke and *tsked*. "Oh well, this will be fun too. Grieves Stockton, you're under arrest. You have the right to remain silent. Anything you say can and will be used against you in the court of law. You have the—"

Stockton's unbalanced laugh kicked up the dirt near his face. "Alliances are a funny thing."

"Hilarious." She sneered.

"I scared my brother into cooperating. I wonder if I could scare you into it." His stark blue gaze centered Zeke's.

"He's not a pussy." Hawk sat on the man's ankles and smacked cuffs around them. She looked up at Zeke. "Should I gag him too?"

"Not yet." Stockton shook his head. "If I can't scare you, maybe I can negotiate."

Zeke bent at the waist, grabbed a handful of the president's collar, and levered him close. "You can't negotiate your way out of this. Just be glad she's transporting you. If you were with me, they might find your body. A piece or two anyway. Your lungs maybe. Enough to declare you deceased."

A smile quirked the man's fat lips. "So, Lieutenant Slaughter, would you like to negotiate a truce for my niece or is she as expendable to you as she is to me?"

Before thought or consequence settled, Zeke's fist found his Glock. He sealed the barrel against the bastard's head.

"Where is Greer?" Hawk asked the question just over Zeke's shoulder, but made no other move to stop him.

His finger longed to ease back the trigger, to let the arterial spray coat his face, to watch the destroyer of so many lives lose his own. Hawk's calm question suspended him on that jagged edge.

"She's right where you left her. The condition you find her in though…that depends on the outcome here." Sweat dripped off Stockton's brow. His voice wavered.

"You don't wager with a wraith," Hawk whispered. "If you want to live, spill it."

Zeke's finger slid to the base of the trigger guard.

"I wagered an alliance with an old friend of yours. His bereft father, actually. So how about that deal?"

"Filipov." Zeke roared and emptied his clip in a halo above the man's head.

Chapter Twenty-five

"I venture we all have battle scars. Some of us wear them on the outside, others only on the inside."

"Yes, we do," Greer agreed.

An electric current of rage ran on a closed circuit in the man's light gaze, gaining amperage with each pass.

She took a step backward, but tried to distract from it. "Is Zeke okay?"

"Zeke Slaughter?"

Every receptor in Greer's body pinged. "Yes."

"He won't be. Not when he finds the woman he loves trussed up and ready to explode like a firecracker on the Fourth of July."

Xavier stepped forward.

Greer countered the move with a retreating step. Her heel landed unevenly on the wheel of the BMW. "Who are you?"

"You haven't heard of me, but maybe you have heard of my son. Your precious Zeke killed him. Zeke and his sister, Khani."

He lunged. His mangled hand grabbed her throat in a flash and clamped the breath from her esophagus.

Greer wheezed her response, but it was lost in the man's punishing grip.

"What was that? I couldn't hear you." His laugh echoed from far away.

She refused to struggle. Even old and disabled, the man outweighed her by 150 pounds or more. Her brain needed oxygen to function, but it needed to function to get oxygen.

Greer slipped her fingers into her front pocket.

"All right, I'll let you have your say. You're not the cunt I want to kill anyway." His grip eased ever so slightly.

Though she tried to inhale calmly, her body wracked and hacked with abandon. It was all she could do to keep her hand inside her pocket. Xavier's grip on her neck actually helped keep her balanced.

"We don't have all day." His gaze dropped to her breasts. "Actually, we have quite a few hours."

Air wheezed into her lungs. She held it there and gathered her courage. "Your son deserved it."

The second his hand clamped, Greer opened the small blade. She rammed it into Xavier's exposed tricep and shoved with all her might.

One hand flew to his arm. His grip faltered.

Greer struck his wrist high and hard. His hold broke. She turned and used the side view mirror to propel herself.

Her gaze centered on the door. If she could just get to her gun...

Loose gravel slipped beneath her boots, pitching her forward.

A bulldozer rammed her from behind. Jagged pebbles and rock stabbed into her palms and knees. Unforgiving hands crawled up her bare skin. He flipped her with what seemed like barely controlled rage. Hot breath hit her face.

"I'm going to fuck you and make him watch."

Greer knew he meant it. She fought the urge to flail and kick.

"You might like it."

She jerked her free knee high, catching the protruding knife.

His scream lit the valley. A mangled fist arched high in the sky. His weight pinned her arms. She braced for the blow.

Chapter Twenty-six

"If I don't slow down and your line gets tangled in the carabiner, I'll drag your ass through the trees until we have to cut you loose. I'm not letting your reckless hide take us down," the Blackhawk pilot explained through the HELO's communication system.

"I'm not planning to use the clip." Zeke yanked the hatch wide until it clicked into place.

"Are you planning to fall to your death?" The flight crewman nearest him, Eton, peered out to the tops of the dense forest.

"No. But I plan on killing someone shortly."

"Hope you get the chance." Eton double checked the clip on the ceiling of the helicopter.

"It'll only take me two minutes more to land this bird," the pilot said.

"I don't have two minutes, and if I did, I don't know what kind of traps this son of a bitch has set."

Eton took the headphones Zeke offered him and followed him to the door. The wind from the propellers bent the tops of the pines and oaks under its hailing force.

"Good luck, man."

Zeke needed all the luck he could get, and then some. He couldn't seem to tap the breaks.

He'd ignored Hawk's requests to think it through, plan it out, or even wait until some of her agents could accompany him. Once again he hoped it wasn't to his detriment…or Greer's.

Both feet dangled in the breeze. His hands clenched the rope. Zeke waited for the calm to come, but his heart assaulted his sternum with unyielding beats. The cabin entered his field of vision. An ache clamped his chest and at the same time threatened to rip it wide open.

"Go," Eton barked.

He'd already launched off the platform into nothingness. The man's order faded into the whir of wind and the cacophony of his heartbeat.

Rope whizzed through Zeke's hands, sheering off layers of callouses. He didn't hold tighter. If anything he loosened his grip, descending like a bomb. The small house grew bigger and bigger, until Zeke thought he might run across the roof or at least crash through it. He held tight for a spit second, and then dropped. Free-fall ushered him to the ground. Without the cumbersome spreader and AK, he tucked into a ball and rolled to a stop twenty feet from the front door.

Zeke ran headlong for it, looking for trip wires and mines the best he could, aware he might be incinerated by a blast before he noticed the trigger.

Xavier wouldn't take him out now. He'd want Khani first. The logic wasn't foolproof, but it was all he had.

He barreled through the front door with his Glock drawn.

Wood splintered and skid across the floor. A tiny shard bumped into Greer's big toe. Blood smeared the top of her feet and the ropes binding her ankles to the kitchen chair. It dotted her widespread porcelain legs. Taut knots laced her naked torso and barred her arms behind her back.

Dry, dirt-outlined tear tracks streaked her cheeks. But not a hint of moisture clouded her wide gaze as it bounced from him to Filipov senior and back again.

An all too familiar necklace graced the long column of Greer's quivering neck. A rusty green grenade hung at the end by its pin and four fat fingers gripped the wide oval so completely it nearly disappeared in the scared flesh.

Filipov's son had worn one around his neck like a badge of courage. The thing had swung back and forth in front of Zeke's nose while Grisha Junior exercised his futile rage on Zeke's ribs. He remembered the crunch of the ice under the man's boots. He remembered the numb shivers that wracked his body as the Alaskan chill seeped through his knees and took hold in his blood. He remembered the deafening explosion that rocked the cabin Grisha and his sister had been inside. He remembered the chaotic fear of thinking her dead.

Zeke held Greer's gaze.

Something inside him broke away. It soothed his long held guilt. It shattered the last pieces of his reserve. It revealed a future he never knew he wanted.

Now that he'd seen it, he'd be dead before he'd let anyone take it away.

"I knew you would save her." The rust in the old man's voice matched the relic of a weapon in his heavy fist.

Since he'd walked inside, Zeke actually looked at the man who threatened his future. Chalk white lips matched the color of his thick hair. He'd never met the man, but his mug shots showed a ruddy complexion that now drained into puddles onto the oak floor. Blood coated the bottom left portion of his shirt and dripped in a steady beat onto his soaked khakis.

Despite his leak, a sinister sneer contorted the man's lined face. "It was almost too easy to trap you. A little tracker in the skin and here we are." His dazed blue eyes drifted to a bleeding hole in Greer's forearm, and then to a pill-sized tracker on the ground beside her.

"I thought you might save Derrick too. I turned him while he worked at the warehouse." Xavier shrugged. A grimace revealed the effort it cost him. "People say I'd never hurt someone I love. That's a lie." He hissed. "It's about finding their price. Everyone has a price, even you, Slaughter."

Xavier swayed, and then shuffled to the side.

Zeke's cross-bow strung muscles tensed impossibly farther.

The man regained his footing. "Don't worry. I have to hang on yet. You see, I don't want to hurt Greer. I want you and your sister. I'm willing to make a trade." His mostly nub hand caressed the side of Greer's face, and then down over her collar bone.

"Stop." Zeke warned.

"There's one way to make me. I'll trade your lover for your sister."

Chapter Twenty-seven

Greer's head shook before the vile words ever left Xavier's mouth. She'd known she was the bait from the moment she realized the man hadn't come to her rescue. Khani, Z's sister, was the only person he had in this world. The only one he loved. She loved him enough not to make him choose between them. She loved him enough to sacrifice everything.

It wasn't like Xavier would actually let her leave anyway. If Khani showed up, Greer would get a bullet in the head, a knife in the gut, or fracture into a thousand pieces with the rest of them. This wouldn't turn out. Not for any of them.

Xavier was as good as dead anyway. When she'd come to—stripped and tied to the chair—he'd sat across from her, holding pressure to his arterial nick. The injury was a blessing and a curse. He hadn't had the strength to rape her or even touch her overly much. At the same token, what little will he had siphoned off him like rain water.

The moment he finally dropped, she'd go too. Z could save himself, as long as he didn't come any farther into the cabin.

Panic bubbled up. The ropes bit into her flesh. Still she jerked and twisted her wrists and ankles. The last two hours of fighting hadn't helped, but she'd be dead before she stopped.

"Greer." Zeke's voice called across the room. The utterly calm tone warmed her from the inside out.

Her gaze found his. Xavier jerked her head to the side, but his mangled hand didn't have the force necessary to turn her away from Z's quiet grey eyes. Truly, the collected serenity in his usually tumultuous gaze stole her breath.

"Awe. Isn't that sweet. The lamb fell in love with the wolf." Xavier shoved her head. A jarring *thunk* danced in her skull.

Again she didn't look away from Z. If this was the end, she wanted to see him.

Her defiance incited the old man. His two fingers twined in her hair and yanked. Greer dug in, even as her scalp stung and roots gave way. She trained her gaze on Z.

The lips that had brought her rage, fulfillment, and love quirked into a wide smile. Hers dropped into a wide gape. *Trust me*, Z mouthed.

"Yes, she did and she does." Greer smiled.

"What a pity." Xavier sneered. "He doesn't love you. He can't love you."

"Yes, he does," Z barked.

A lone tear dropped off Greer's eyelash.

Xavier jerked and turned to Z with a loose jaw and drawn brow.

Sparks spit from the barrel of Z's Glock. The gun coiled and kicked another bullet, and then another.

They landed in a tight spread on Xavier's chest.

Before Greer could rejoice in the declaration of Z's love or the death of the man who'd tormented her, he lurched away.

The thin chain tightened around her neck. "Run!"

Z ran. His legs already stretched wide and contracted with speed reserved for four legged animals and olympians. Only he ran in the wrong direction.

Each stride gobbled the distance between them. Each breadth brought him closer to danger.

Xavier's knees hit the floor. He collapsed face first onto the cold wood. The pin snapped from the grenade.

"No." Greer reached to catch the live explosive. Her arms didn't move.

A cold prick slapped her chest. The empty pin of wire weighted her more than the grenade.

When the thick metal crashed to the floor Greer flinched, tearing at her raw skin.

Z slid on his knees. He caught the grenade on a bounce. One arm lifted Xavier's shoulder. The other stuffed the explosive under the corpse.

It wouldn't be enough.

The muscles in Z's exposed neck and arms knitted. He lunged. Her chin met his chest with a hard knock. The icy floor disappeared beneath her toes. Z was up and running. Two strides and he slowed.

No. Farther. They were too close.

The cold intensified at her back. A bright white wall hit her right shoulder. Not a wall. A refrigerator. Could Z fit behind the shield with her in this chair?

Detonation ceased her thoughts.

Chapter Twenty-eight

The buzzing whined wide and then honed to a sharp point. Zeke kicked the refrigerator door off his back. Jagged stars shimmied in his periphery. He shook them away, managing to replace them with a lancing headache. His vision blurred. A few blinks brought the screen of dust, curtaining the cabin into focus, and his sweet Greer.

Blood trickled from her nose. Long, matted lashes rested soundly on her bruised cheek. Her head lolled back, pointing her chin toward the ceiling. Her lips parted in the slow signature breathing of the unconscious. But she was breathing.

Zeke peeled himself from around her, straightened the chair to all fours, and heaved off his knees. The refrigerator door hung lopsided with its broken top hinge, giving him a straight line view to the mangled remnants of Xavier Grisha Filipov, senior.

When his gaze wandered over Greer's naked, bound form he wanted to kill the man all over again. He yanked the knife from the small of his back. The ropes were so tight he wouldn't chance wedging the blade between them and her skin. He sliced at the fibers from underneath the chair.

She'd thrashed against the bindings so hard it gouged her tender flesh. Zeke's stomach churned.

His hands shook. His hands never shook. He tightened his grip on the blade and freed her ankles, torso, arms, and wrists. She slumped forward. The suppleness of her body pillowed against his chest.

"I shouldn't have left you." The whispered words blew whisps of her hair. He sheathed his knife and breathed her into his soul.

The *whop, whop* of helicopter blades vibrated the cabin. It sounded far away in his abused eardrum, but it wasn't.

Through the busted out window Zeke watched the Base Branch HELO descend on the uneven gravel drive. He cradled Greer against his chest, covered as much of her as he could with his arms, and bolted for the Blackhawk.

To the men's credit—or his half-hinged scowl—they didn't gawk at the naked woman—at his naked woman. He sprinted across the lawn and carried her into the belly of the war plane. The moment his feet met metal they lifted off.

Eton averted his black eyes and busied his hands, lowering the stretcher from the wall. The other member of the flight crew shoved headphones onto his ears, opened a wool blanket, and secured it around them with an upturned chin.

"What's her condition?" The pilot's voice crackled over the air waves.

His fucking lips moved like brittle clay. "Solid pulse and respiration. Unconscious. The nearest hospital."

"We're ten minutes out, but it's civilian. Closest military hospital is twenty-three minutes away."

"Civ—" A small, cold hand on his days' old scruff cut him off.

"I don't need to go to the hospital." Greer offered him a smile too brilliant for their environment.

His cheeks knotted into the goofiest grin. "You look like you've been through battle."

"I have been," she agreed.

"Why do you look so damn happy about it?" He gently lowered his forehead to hers.

"I won." She shifted his chin down. Her lips molded to his.

"Sir?" Eton knelt next to the cot with his box of first aid supplies opened by his knees. The other crewman, Bradfield, hooked an IV to the low metal peg and unkinked the length of tubing.

Greer's hand dropped from his face to the front of his shirt. She bunched the collar in her fist and yanked him down for a wearing kiss. "Don't put me on the stretcher. I'm fine right here. Just a few cuts and bruises. No big deal."

"Kiss me all you want. You're still going to the hospital."

"Ruthless." She grinned against his lips.

Zeke shook his head to the men. "Thank you."

They snickered while they pulled down seats and reclined into them. One of them said, "Whipped."

He braced his back against the cockpit wall, spread his legs wide, and nestled Greer onto his lap, not caring one damn bit what they thought.

"Where to?" the pilot asked.

"Take us to Basement Underground," Zeke said.

"Sir, I'm ordered to deny your request. We have a civilian on board," the pilot countered.

"She's not a civilian. She's a marine, the woman who dethroned Stockton, and I'll keep her occupied on approach. Clear it with Hawk and take us to the Underground."

"Yes, sir."

"How exactly are you going to occupy me?" Greer's blue gaze rolled toward the men across from them. "We do have company."

"I'm going to bandage your wrists and ankles." He kissed the end of her nose.

"That doesn't sound like fun." Her lips plumped into a pout.

"I'll make it up to you."

"Oh yeah?" A hint of sadness crept into her bright gaze. It slid to his neck, and then drifted out the dull cargo window.

Zeke pulled the headphones from his ears. "Greer?"

"Filipov's dead?"

"Yes." Lord, he sounded like a mythical forest creature.

"The Stas?"

"Being dismantled."

"What about US Elite?"

"The same."

She nodded. "My uncle?"

"Is discovering the joys of captivity and intensive interrogation."

"Torture?"

He shrugged.

"What about Raisa?"

Finally, he could impart some good news. "Someone's being sent to pick her up."

"Someone?" Her brows and red cheeks widened.

"Someone trusted with several countries' security secrets. I think he can deal with an orphaned Russian girl."

Greer blew two swollen cheeks' worth of air through her lips and squinted.

"That doesn't look good," he groaned.

"It's complicated."

"How complicated?"

"I know you can keep a secret." While she stalled his stomach sank. He narrowed his gaze. "Okay." She held up a hand and leaned in conspiratorially. "She's Roman Everly's daughter."

"Jesus." His head smacked the cockpit. When he regained his wind and looked at Greer he saw the sadness clouding her eyes. "She'll be protected. Don't worry about that."

"I trust you." Her gaze danced off again. "Then it's over."

"You don't look happy about that."

"It was the only thing holding us together." She said it so quietly he almost didn't hear.

He buried his hands in her hair and tilted her face.

The blanket shifted. She hauled it up to her chin, but refused to meet his gaze. "I won't make things hard."

"Since when?"

Her gaze snapped to his. "That's why you want me to go to the hospital. You could slip out and know I'd be taken care of. It's fine. For the best, really."

"Greer?"

She looked at him, her lips pinched between her teeth.

"I work for a clandestine sector of the special operation force for the United Nations. They recruited me after I dropped off the grid, after my father. I haven't had a place to call home in almost five years. Every week brought a new mission. They kept me busy, kept me moving, disconnected. I liked it."

Her gaze slid away.

"Greer?"

"What?" She snarled at him and probably the tears tracking down the side of her face.

"I liked it until I made a connection...with you." His lips grazed her mouth, her wet cheeks, her forehead. "I love you."

She grabbed his hands, covered them, and pressed them against her face. Her eyes closed. Fresh tears leaked out from her lids.

"The mission wasn't the only thing holding us together. We were both held prisoner by our pasts. You set me free, Greer."

"We set each other free."

"I'm so used to being caged. I don't think I can handle life without a little bondage." Her lids flew wide. One brow kicked high. He smiled and pressed on through the thunder of his heartbeat. "I might like a ball and chain, if you're the one with the key."

Greer buried her face in his shirt. Sobs shook her shoulders. The guys murmured across the way.

Way to bomb. It wasn't the reaction he'd hoped for

"Talk to me," he begged. "What do you think?"

"I think you're crazy." Her breath steamed his chest.

"I'm serious." He sat her in his lap and pulled the blanket high around her shoulders. "After we get you checked out, make sure everything is in order to annihilate your uncle, and handle the arrangements for your father—"

"My grandparents will disown me as soon as they talk to my uncle."

“They won’t talk to him. Not for a long time.”

“We weren’t close before, but now, I don't have any family.”

“Pay attention, Greer. I want you to be my family. Marry me.”

“I can’t marry you just because I don’t have a family or a house or a job.”

“I don’t want you to marry me for any of those reasons.” He pulled her close. “Tell me what you told me last night.”

“I love you,” she whispered.

“Did you mean it?”

“With my whole heart.”

“Marry me. We’ll go to London. I need to tell my sister about what I did to our father, and I want her to meet you. We’ll figure it out from there.” He tugged her closer. “Be my future, Greer.”

“Z?”

“Cor blimey, woman, what?”

“Did you really think I’d let you ditch me? If that bastard, Xavier, hadn’t shown up, I’d have had that BMW shoved right up your keister, right after I dealt with my uncle.”

“I took the keys.” He winked.

“I hot-wired it.”

“No shite?”

“Almost.”

She rubbed the smirk off his face and pulled his mouth to hers. “You’re my future. Why wouldn’t I be yours?”

“Not going to give me a straight answer, are you?”

“Ask me again.”

“I asked you twice already.”

“Three times,” Eton shouted.

"No." Her head shook, pulling her wet hair from the blanket. "He demanded I marry him. He didn't ask."

The men groaned in unison.

Zeke sighed, and then placed his hand over Greer's bare heart. "Greer Britton, angel I never deserved, will you marry me?"

"Yes, Zeke Slaughter, I'll marry you."

FOR ALL TO SEE
A BUREAU NOVEL

Pristine waters and purified evil.

Two by two, dark-haired beauties vanish only to reappear as hanging, plundered corpses. The Virgin Islands boast diamond-white beaches, lush green mountains, a rich cultural heritage—and a brutal killer.

Three years on the "Field-Dresser" case and Special Agent Nathan Brewer is days away from catching the bastard—if he can convince a certain brunette to trust him. Only the woman is more likely to take a casual stroll on the surface of the sun.

After fleeing her troubles in the United States for the quiet life of a school teacher on the island of Tortola, Madelyn Garrett never imagined she'd be fixated upon by pure evil.

In a fight for her life—with a dwindling number of friends—she must rely on her cunning and Nathan's skills for survival.

PAINTED WALLS
A BUREAU NOVEL

Deadly daddy-issues.

The Blood-Red Killer, America's most notorious serial killer, tucked Supervisory Special Agent Ava Shepherd into bed every night with a bedtime story and a kiss on the cheek.

Thirty years after his apprehension, Ava—still running from his memory—becomes the prime suspect for a murder eerily similar to the ones her father committed all those years ago. Shattered by the accusation, Ava reluctantly accepts former flame Special Agent Kenneth Hunt's assistance in clearing her name.

Kenneth is on the mend, and though their fling is ancient history, the bruises Ava left on his heart throb in her presence. He'll help her, but she'll have to play by his rules.

When the body count and undeniable heat rise, Ava must face the demons of her past and present—or be consumed by them.

Megan Mitcham was born and raised among the live oaks and shrimp boats of the Mississippi Gulf Coast, where her enormous family still calls home. She attended college at the University of Southern Mississippi where she received a bachelor's degree in curriculum, instruction, and special education. For several years Megan worked as a teacher in Mississippi. She married and moved to South Carolina and began working for an international non-profit organization as an instructor and co-director.

In 2009 Megan fell in love with books. Until then, books had been a source for research or the topic of tests. But one day she read *Mercy* by Julie Garwood. And oh, Mercy, she was hooked!

Megan lives in Southern Arkansas where she pens heart pounding romantic thriller novels and window-steaming erotic romance. For information on releases and giveaways subscribe at meganmitcham.com!

Facebook: @MeganMMMitcham
Twitter: MeganMitchamAuthor
Pinterest: MeganMitcham5
Website: www.meganmitcham.com

FOR INFORMATION ON NEW RELEASES & GIVEAWAYS, SIGN UP FOR MEGAN'S NEWSLETTER AT WWW.MEGANMITCHAM.COM.

www.ingramcontent.com/pod-product-compliance
Lightning Source LLC
Chambersburg PA
CBHW071137170626
46809CB00002B/658

* 9 7 8 1 9 4 1 8 9 9 1 8 2 *